The Ninth of the Month Murders

by

Michael Davies

The Ninth of the Month Murders

Acknowledgements

This book was written in collaboration with Greg Dickson who generated many of the ideas, plot-lines and   twists and turns. The brain-storming sessions were stimulating, exhausting and rewarding.

Sincere thanks to Robin Sheppard who conducted an intensive edit, hunted out the spelling errors, the technical gaps and the mistakes in time sequences and legal issues.

Note: the character of Jack Savage and the members of the New South Wales Police Homicide Department appeared in a previous book, *"Ready, Steady, Kill!"*

Other Works by Michael Davies

The Nightmares of God
The Janus Conspiracy
Accounts of a Killing
A Friendly Killing
Dreamkill
Ready, Steady, KILL!
Helix Dreams
Helix – The Second Renaissance
Helix - Ascension

For the Young Adults (12-18)
The Many Worlds of Mickie Dalton
The Many Galaxies of Mickie Dalton
The Many Universes of Mickie Dalton
The Strange World of Mark and Anna

For the 8-12 age group
The Julie Malloy Gang and the Smugglers
The Quest for the Locket
The Secret of Yuri Kirilenko
The United Nations and the Extra-Terrestrial
The Secret of Charlotte's Cello
The Star of the Yshan Kings
The War of the Yshan Empire
The Star of the New Yshan Empire
The Saga of the Yshan Kings
The Red Fog of Time
The Mysterious Recorder and The Door to Elsewhere
Prisoners of the Picture
A Step Back in Time
What Can't be Seen Can Exist
How I Spent My Evening

For the Little Ones (3-5)
Mary's World
Bethany's World
Quinn's Adventures in Australia

And in non-fiction
The Business School Approach to Writing Your Novel

Chapter 1 - The Ninth of March, 2022

The silent figure dressed in full protective clothing that she had bought from the hardware store two weeks ago, stood motionless in the shadow of the large bush by the back fence of the house. The Moon was behind some dense clouds and the figure was almost invisible. Carefully, she operated the controls of the almost silent drone, flying it all around the house at below roof level, but nothing triggered any security lights. A previous exploration had found there was no dog in the house, the only resident was the elderly man who took a regular stroll around the back garden each evening.

Satisfied she had a clear ground for operations, she brought the drone back and switched it off, laying it down at her feet. Backing off a metre, she took a run at the fence, used her gloved right hand on a post and vaulted over into the garden. The thick covers over her shoes made movement a little clumsy but she was fit and strong and managed it easily. She took cover again in the shadow of a bush by the fence and waited.

Fifteen minutes later, the back door of the house opened, shedding a white light over the garden as a man came out. He began a leisurely stroll round the perimeter of the grounds, occasionally stopping to pull a weed from the lawn.

In the shadows, the woman slowly extracted the large box-cutter from one pocket and eased out the blade. She waited, holding her breath as the man approached, feeling her heart beating faster and as he passed, she moved out behind him, seized his hair and pulled him back, his head facing up, throat exposed. One slash was all that was needed, she saw blood gush like a fountain, covering her right hand and arm...

Chapter 2 – The Tenth of March, 2022

"Probably some time last night, maybe between ten o'clock and two this morning. But it was a hot night, so it could have been earlier."

"Cause of death, as if I have to ask?" Detective Sergeant Melanie Carter was clearly in distress at the sight of the body by the Medical Examiner's knees and struggling not to show it.

"As you say, pretty bloody obvious, no pun intended," said Doctor Mortimer, the police medical examiner. "A clean, single slice across the carotid artery with an exceptionally sharp blade. He'd have died within seconds. You can see just how much blood there is on the grass."

"So perhaps a surgical scalpel?"

"Perhaps, but a well-sharpened kitchen knife or a box-cutter would have been just as effective. It looks like the killer grabbed the victim by the hair from behind, judging by the signs of a few hairs pulled out by the roots and the cut went from left to right, so almost certainly you're looking for a right-handed killer, which is no use at all to you."

"There's not a hell of a lot that is of use to us, doc," said Carter. "He's the owner of the house, judging by his driver's licence, so nothing suspicious about him being in his back garden, the back door is open from when he came out for whatever reason, the weapon has vanished, of course."

"If your team are through," said the doctor, "I'll get him back to the lab for a better look. I'll call you when I've finished cutting him up."

"That's fine, doc. I'll talk to the examiners."

Carter moved away to the back deck of the house as the three crime scene investigators did the same, starting to peel off their protective suits and shoe coverings.

"Not a goddammed thing, Sarge," said a young constable. "The ground is hard, so no footprints, there's some flattened grass where the killing took place but there's no way any footprint will show there, either. There's a slight indentation from a couple of feet when the attacker pulled back on the victim, but there's no definable shape of a shoe. It's almost as if the killer was wearing the same sort of gear we're wearing."

"There's another similar dent in the ground by the back fence," said another of the team, a woman in her thirties. "So it's possible that the perpetrator jumped the fence or vaulted over it, which suggests a fairly athletic sort, but there's no sign of any material or hand grip on the fence. There's a similar dent on the other side where the perp landed on his or her way back. Again, if what Joe is saying is right, he or she could be wearing full protective gear, including shoe covers, gloves and a hood."

"This is well planned," said Carter. "Okay, get your reports on my desk as soon as possible, I'll call the office and get uniforms to start house to house inquiries."

"I hate to be negative, Sarge," said the other woman. "But the nearest houses are at least a hundred metres away. This is an old stock route, all little twenty-five acre hobby farm type homes, the houses are well back from the road, even if the perp did drive down it, which I doubt, seeing those dents by the back fence."

"You're probably right," said Carter. "But we have to go by the book. I'll have people examine the track for tyre traces also. But dammit, I have no idea how we can identify a killer from what we have here."

They fell silent as two men arrived with a stretcher, loaded the body onto it and carried it out to the waiting van at the front.

Chapter 3 – The Fourth of October, 2021

The Spring garden party of the Writers' Group was going well.

"I'd call it a most successful year," said Carl Hitchcox. "We produced that great book of paintings and associated short stories as a collaborative project and we've all written some great short stories. It sure inspired me to start work on a sci-fi novel, something I've always wanted to do."

"Absolutely agree," said several other voices from the group sitting around on the lawn.

"So what about another collaborative project?" asked Caroline Collins. "I'm working on my Regency period novel and these joint projects really keep me inspired. Nona, any ideas?"

"Well, seeing as how you lot have just elected me to the chair of this brilliant group..." Nona was interrupted by a round of chuckles from the dozen people sitting around the garden with drinks in hand. "... I'd like to suggest we do a joint mystery-thriller novel."

A short silence hovered over the group.

"How would that work?" asked Jean Worrall. "What, we each write a chapter?"

"Exactly that," said Nona with a smile. "We could each write a story of committing a murder and then at the end, we assemble all the chapters and publish the book."

"That's got possibilities," said the man sitting further away from anybody else and who had not joined in much of the conversations. Allen Miller's slight American accent was still detectible after ten years of living in Australia and although he regularly produced well-received short stories in the monthly meetings of the group, he had not established any real connections with anyone. "I've written mostly political thriller stuff, it would be a good experience to try my hand at a murder story."

"I like it," said Ollie, the youngest in the gathering, a man in his twenties, powerfully built, the muscular arms under his tee-shirt indicating a regular body-builder.

"It would certainly suit you, Ollie," said Nona. "All your stories so far have shown some violence in them and I know a few of the ladies here have been a bit disturbed by them. It would be a development in a new direction for you."

She looked around the garden. "Is that okay with all of you? We try and get one chapter from each of us, we read it at the meetings starting in January and we try and get it finished by the end of the year and we publish it."

"Hey, what about a title!" said Gabrielle, the slender blonde sitting with Ollie in one corner. Dressed in tight white jeans and a yellow tee-shirt, she had attracted the attentions of all the men in the group for some years and consequently caused some irritation in the other women, but her stories were always gripping, usually involving some theme of sexual violence.

"Well, today is the ninth," said Nona. "How about all the murders are committed on the ninth of the month and we call the book, *'The Ninth of the Month Murders.'*"

A laugh ran around the group with various sounds of agreement.

"I do like that," said Tanya, a young woman of such slender build that she looked as if she could break into pieces if struck by anything solid.

"Sounds popular," said Nona. "All agreed? Our new project is to write a murder mystery with one murder a month, written by each of us in turn and we aim to publish it by the end of next year? All in favour?"

All hands were raised.

Chapter 4 – The Seventh of November, 2021

"Tanya! Ollie! I'm so glad you came. Come in and I'll pour coffee and lay out some goodies."

"How could we refuse when the Writers' group Chairwoman invites us?" Tanya smiled and followed Nona into the living room with Ollie Simpson behind her.

The young man looked a little overawed in the presence of Nona Markham but this was nothing unusual. By far the youngest member of the writers' group, he often looked a little uncomfortable during meetings. But Nona had a charismatic presence that enabled her to get her ideas accepted with ease and it was no surprise when she was elected Chairwoman of the group after only a few months of membership.

Coffee poured, a plate of small fruit pies in the middle of the coffee table and the three ensconced in the armchairs, Nona laughed lightly.

"Don't look too shy, people, I just wanted to review the thought we had at the garden meeting last month about our next project."

"But why us, Nona?" Tanya looked uncertain. "We're the youngest in the group. Wouldn't some of the more experienced members be a better source?"

"That's exactly why I invited you. This is going to be a rather difficult topic for a book and murder mysteries might not be your thing. Ollie, I know you have some violent scenes in your stories, but nobody has ever been killed. Are either of you worried about this project?"

Ollie finished his pie, wiped his fingers and looked down at his coffee.

"Actually, no," he said. "I think it's pretty exciting really. I've often thought about what it would be like to kill somebody and this is a safe way to think about it."

"My thoughts, too," said Tanya. "It's really rather thrilling. We lead such ordinary lives and I can't help thinking like Ollie, what would it feel like to kill somebody?"

"And what if you do it in such a way that you knew nobody would ever find out?" said Ollie. "Just think how it would feel, seeing the police go past your house, or talking to people who knew the person you'd killed and feeling all safe inside."

"And there would always be just that little current of fear that somehow you had made some slip and eventually the cops would find out you'd done it and were coming for you." Tanya's eyes were wide open with excitement, her coffee and pie were forgotten and she was looking into some far distance.

"I remember when I was in the army, a guy in my unit got killed," said Ollie. "We were on a night exercise and he got run down when he stepped in front of a Land Rover. I was surprised I didn't feel bad about it, I was just fascinated looking at him."

"I didn't know you were in the army," said Tanya, returning from her distant imaginings.

"Only a couple of years after leaving school. My dad said it would toughen me up and I suppose it did, but I didn't really like it."

"Is that why you left?"

Ollie looked down at his lap.

"Not really," he mumbled. "Things just didn't work out."

"Tanya, do you think about that as well?"

"Actually, yes, I do. I spend all day behind the counter at the pharmacy, counting out pills and labelling packets for prescriptions. Everybody I see is old and silly and sometimes I think it would be fun to get rid of them."

Nona laughed and poured herself a refill of coffee from the jug on the table.

"Would you like to hear a secret?" she said, sitting back.

"Ooh, that sounds mysterious," said Tanya.

"You're right. It is exciting to know you've killed somebody and nobody will ever find out, the body is buried, the police think it's suicide or natural causes and you still meet people who knew the person you'd killed and you don't say a word."

"Nona! My god, Nona, are you saying...?

"Yes, I am," said Nona. "It was my mother."

* * *

Ninth of October, 2016

"Nona! Nona! Get me my tea."

"For God's sake, Mother, I'm trying to work. Can't it wait?"

"No it can't. I want my tea now. And what work are you talking about? Another of your silly novels? You know they're rubbish, nobody will ever read them even if they did get published and that's not going to happen."

Nona took a deep breath and counted to ten in her head.

"Yes Mother," she said and went to the kitchen. Even as she prepared the sandwiches of roast pork and salad, her mother was still going strong.

"You've been working on that stupid hobby of yours for years and nothing has ever come of it. If your father was alive, he'd have told you to give it up and concentrate on your job. Why do you think you never get promoted? Because your mind is always on those stupid stories, that's why. Anyway, you're too stupid to get promoted, never mind write a good book. It's just as well I got crippled in that accident that killed your father, the only thing you're good for is looking after me now and you're pretty useless at that, too. I should get a proper nurse but that costs money but at least she'd be able to help me more. Where's my tea?"

"Coming, Mother," said Nona, struggling to keep her voice calm. She carried the tray to her mother's bedroom and placed it on the side table.

"About time," snapped her mother. "You should have had that here half an hour ago. Can't you do anything right, you stupid girl?"

Nona stared down at the old woman in the bed.

"You know what, you miserable old bitch, there's one thing I could do properly."

"You what? What did you call me? How dare you speak to me that way."

"I called you a miserable old bitch and that's understating it. And you want to know what I could do well?"

The woman stared at her daughter in shock, unable to speak.

"I could kill you, you old cow. I'm sick to death of your constant whining and screaming, your insults and total ingratitude. My career has suffered because all my time is taken up looking after you and your persistent attention seeking."

The old woman began breathing hard, a shadow of fear growing in her eyes. Nona turned to the lounge and picked up a cushion. In one movement she turned to her mother and rammed the cushion over her face, pushing hard and pressing the old woman against her pillow. The struggle lasted only a minute before the woman went still but Nona kept up the pressure for a few more moments before the frail old body seemed to subside like a leaky balloon.

Nona removed the cover and looked down. The old woman's eyes were wide open and she seemed to be staring at her.

"Goodbye, you foul old bitch," said Nona. "I think I'll just leave you there for a while."

She realised her heart was beating fast and her main sensation was excitement. "You know what, Nona," she muttered aloud. "You really enjoyed doing that. And by Christ, the old bitch deserved it. I think I'll go and watch some television."

Seventh of November, 2021

"Good God, Nona," exclaimed Tanya. Her hands were in front of her mouth, she was leaning forward in her seat, eyes open in astonishment. "What did you do then?"

Ollie was also looking astonished and excited, his hands clasped tightly together, staring at Nona.

"What I did," said Nona, "was nothing for the rest of the evening and night. I slept well and the following morning, I prepared Mother's usual breakfast tray and took it to her room. That's when I called her doctor. He came round an hour later, didn't seem surprised, told me what I already knew that her health was very bad since the accident that had killed my father, her heart was weak and this seemed quite normal. No need for a postmortem, he signed the death certificate, so I called the undertaker and they took care of everything. No complications. The only other thing I did was take the cushion away and burn it in the company's incinerator."

"Ho-lee shit," said Ollie. "That's incredible. And there's never been a single question about it?"

"Not a one. She was cremated a couple of weeks later, I got the million bucks in her estate, I kept the house and all in all, I did very well out of it."

"Quite amazing," said Ollie. "I can't help thinking I wish I could do the same, kill somebody and not leave a trace."

"I've studied the whole business," said Nona. "I know exactly how to do it. Have another coffee and I'll tell you how."

Chapter 5 – The Fourteenth of January, 2022

"Alright people, the Fourteenth of January meeting of the writer's group, the first of the New Year is now in session." Nona rang her ornate china bell and waited while the writers took their seats and arranged their papers. "Phones off everybody, let's get started."

She looked to her left. "Caroline, will you read the minutes of the last meeting?"

Caroline Collins opened her document folder, extracted the sheet and began to read.

"We ended the last year's season with a party at the Chairwoman's house in November and a good time was had by all."

A small round of applause and sounds of approval ran around the table.

"The group unanimously agreed to a joint project, to write a murder mystery thriller in which each of us would write one story of a murder being committed in such a way that it could be seen by the police and medical personas as death by accident or natural causes. Those murders that would be obvious would be so well hidden that no clues would be left for the investigators. The Chairwoman, Nona Markham said that she would give us a workshop at the first meeting of the year on how such a cover-up could be achieved. The party broke up at five pm and everybody left to prepare for the Christmas festivities."

"Thank you, Caroline. Can I have a motion to approve the minutes and a seconder? Excellent, thank you Ollie and Tanya."

Nona looked around the room. Everybody seemed cheerful and relaxed.

"I'm going to beg your indulgence by changing the program a little," she said. "We can do the workshop later, but what I would like to do first is read you a short story I wrote over the last few days about a murder I heard about. It's unusual in the manner of the killing, so is everybody okay with this?"

As usual, there was no objection to her request. Nona had always known she had a powerful personality that made people follow her, even become influenced by her when she wanted. In this writers' group, that power seemed even greater than usual and she had enjoyed exercising it in the year she had been chairwoman. She opened the folder before her and began reading.

Ninth of January, 2022

The woman stood silently at the back door of the house that was one of only six along the country road. She had left her car a kilometre away, driven a few metres into the forestry reserve and well out of sight now that darkness had fallen. On getting out of the car, she had donned the protective coveralls that she had bought in a packet of six from the Bunnings hardware store a few days ago, slipped on the shoe covers and gloves purchased at the same time and pulled up the hood over her head. The mask was in her pocket and she would cover her mouth with that later.

She quietly moved onto the deck at the back door and tapped on the door. There was no reaction and she repeated the tap, a little louder. This time, she heard movement and the shuffling of an old, tired woman approaching the door. The kitchen light was switched on.

"Who is it?" the woman's voice called out.

"It's the nurse, Mrs Henderson, Lorna. I just found I left something behind this morning and I'll need it before I see you tomorrow."

"Oh you silly woman, Lorna. Just a moment, I'll open the door."

There was the sound of a lock being undone, a handle turned and the door opened inward. A small, fragile woman appeared. She stared briefly at the figure in the suit and shock appeared on her face. "You're not..." she began but the intruder pushed her forcefully into the house, grabbed her by the shoulders and steered her into the lounge, forcing her hard to sit down and stood over her.

The old woman couldn't speak. Her wide eyes showed her fear.

The assailant took a small cube of chocolate from one pocket and put it to the old woman's lips.

"Eat it," she ordered.

The older woman tried to resist, turning her face away, but the assailant forced her head back, held her nose until she was forced to open her mouth and the chocolate was pushed in, her jaws clamped down by the gloved hands.

The scene was immobile for the next few moments until it was clear that the chocolate had been eaten.

"Now we're going to sit here for a while, Mrs Henderson. You're not going to try and stand up, you'll say nothing until I let you. Understood?"

The terrified old woman could only nod. Her face was white.

Nothing more was said for twenty minutes. Then suddenly the old woman was gripped by a violent spasm that shook her whole body, she gasped in pain and vomited all over her front. The assailant said nothing but watched her carefully. The spasms got worse, the victim vomited once more and then collapsed sideways.

The killer stood up, walked out and left the house by the back door. She retraced her steps to the car, backed out of the trees and drove home. There, she carefully removed the shoe covers, the protective coveralls and the gloves, put them in a garbage bag for disposal the following morning and went to bed, feeling satisfied with the work of the evening.

Fourteenth of January, 2022

A brief round of applause broke out as Nona put her papers away.

"What was the poison?" asked Gabrielle.

"It's called the Rosary Seed," said Nona. "I found out about it doing some research."

"Nona, that was a great story," said Jean. "But isn't it taken from the police report I heard on the local radio a few days ago? It said that Judy Henderson had been found dead in her house on Littleton road by the visiting nurse. The police said initially it was thought to be a heart attack but now they think she was poisoned by an intruder."

Nona smiled.

"The police are quite right. Mrs Henderson was poisoned by a Rosary Seed the night before she was found. I know. I did it."

Chapter 6 – Nona Markham

April, 1985

"Go on, I dare you." Nona stared hard into the eyes of the little girl sitting across from the lunch table just outside the side entrance of the school. Nona had taken the chair in front of the child, having watched her for a few days and decided that she was a likely subject.

"No, I can't," the other girl replied.

"Yes you can. All you have to do is walk into her office, take that clock and walk out again."

"But that's stealing. I can't do that."

Nona maintained her stare and leaned forward, even nearer the girl's face. Slowly, she saw the child's eyes become unfocused, even a little glassy. This was something Nona had discovered in recent weeks, she could somehow influence people to do what she wanted.

"She's at lunch right now," Nona said and nodded over at the staff table where the school secretary was sitting with the teachers. "And she never locks the office, you know that. Go on, do it now."

Looking forlorn, the other girl stood up and walked into the building. The principal's office and the vice-principal's offices were the first doors and the little girl stopped at the first. Watching her, Nona could see how she swayed on her feet in indecision, then walked in, picked up the small antique clock and walked out again.

"Fiona Green! What do you think you're doing?" The door to the vice-principal's office opened and the woman standing there looked at the little girl with astonishment.

Fiona stood motionless, looking deep in shock, staring at the clock as if she had no idea how it got there.

Hearing the voices, the Principal entered the building.

"Put it right back, Fiona," said the Principal and waited while Fiona replaced the clock on the desk. "Now, just why did you do that?" The Principal's tone had become more gentle as if understanding that something was not right with the girl.

"Nona told me to do it, Miss."

"And do you always do what Nona tells you?"

Fiona burst into tears. "I couldn't help it, Miss."

"I understand. Fiona, I'm not going to do anything about this now, but please, don't even talk to Nona again. I know how she can somehow influence people and I don't want you getting into trouble for her. So dry your eyes and get back to your class, alright?"

"Yes Miss," Fiona said and walked out of the room.

The Principal went back to the dining area and saw Nona sitting on her own. This was not unusual. The girl had few friends in the school and those that did associate with her seemed to do so more in a mistress-servant relationship. The Principal found her deeply disturbing. She went to the doorway and pointed at Nona.

"Nona Markham, come with me," she said and watched as Nona stood up and walked into her office. She sat down behind her desk, leaving Nona standing before her, not looking at all worried.

"Did you tell Fiona Green to steal the clock?"

"Yes Miss."

"Why?"

"Just for fun."

"Just for fun? Telling children to steal things is fun for you?"

"Yes Miss."

The Principal stood up. "I know you seem capable of influencing other children here, Nona. But here's your first and last warning. If I hear you do anything of this sort again, I will have you expelled from the school. It means that when you get to High School next year, you will always be under observation and that will not be easy for you. Do I make myself clear?"

Nona's eyes dropped. "Yes Miss."

"Good. Now go and join your class."

Nona turned and left, a smile breaking out as she reached the corridor.

* * *

February, 1987

"I gave you that name for specific reasons," said her mother.

"I don't understand," said Nona. She rarely had conversations with her mother and it was a surprise when she had suddenly spoken at the normally silent dining table. Her father was away, as was common, as a judge on the local court, he was often away at regional assizes. He didn't speak much to his daughter, either.

"You need to look it up," said her mother. "But you will understand when you do. You are a goddess, you have the power of life and death over ordinary mortals, even the gods themselves and they are frightened of you and your sisters."

"Sisters? Mother, I don't have a sister."

"You do, but they are goddesses, also. One day, you will meet them and you will understand."

"But life and death? Does that mean I get to kill people?"

"Not directly. But you and your sisters will choose when people die. You must be very careful how you use those powers."

Nona looked carefully at her mother. Her eyes were wide and she seemed to be staring into some distance, her face alive with excitement, possibly ecstasy. Nona found the conversation disturbing but also fascinating. What the hell was this daft old woman babbling about?

Nona searched the library shelves and found a section on Greek Mythology. She read it with interest.

"Nona was one of the Parcae, the three personifications of destiny in Roman mythology (the Moirai in Greek mythology and in Germanic mythology, the Norns), and the Roman goddess of pregnancy. The Roman equivalent of the Greek Clotho, she spun the thread of life from her distaff onto her spindle. Nona, whose name means "ninth", was called upon by pregnant women in their ninth month when the child was due to be born.

"She, Decima and Morta together controlled the metaphorical thread of life."

"So that's what my name means," she said to herself. "How the hell did my mother know that? But now I understand. I really am a goddess. That's why I can make people do what I tell them. And I can control their lives, I can end them when I want. This is wonderful."

* * *

March, 1987

Nona looked deep into the eyes of Suzie Benson, her classmate. They weren't friends, Nona didn't have friends at school, but she knew that a number of the girls followed her around and talked to her in a somewhat submissive manner. She enjoyed the effect she had on them. At fifteen, she was beginning to sense something powerful inside herself and the discovery of the meaning of her name had expanded that sense of power like a rosebud opening under the sun.

"Have you heard about Sarah Morris?" she asked.

"No, what about Sarah Morris?" asked Suzie. A small frown appeared on her face.

"She's not a virgin," said Nona.

"How the hell do you know that?" Suzie looked annoyed and Nona knew that the two girls were friends.

"I talked to a kid at the boys' school. He said he'd had her a few months ago, several times."

Nona began to feel the power growing. Suzie's face had lost the irritation and she was now listening intently, her eyes fixed on Nona's.

"Are you sure?"

"Absolutely. And he's not the only one. He said she obviously enjoyed it and he wasn't the first. Several of the blokes have had her, she seems to like it a lot."

The other girl was silent for a moment and Nona could feel her absorbing the information.

"That's terrible," said Suzie eventually.

"It sure is. She's a real slut."

Nona repeated the conversation with three other girls over the next two days and saw them all go from disbelief that a popular girl at the school could do such a thing to acceptance of the fact.

Nona sat back and waited.

* * *

The Courier, April, 1987

A tragedy occurred this week when Sarah Morris, aged fifteen, a student at the High School was found dead at her home. The police report says she had slit her wrists and killed herself. Our investigations revealed that Sarah had become increasingly distressed as unpleasant rumours had begun circulating about her. The school refused to comment, but two of the girls from Sarah's class said that they had heard that Sarah was sexually liberated. They were unable to say where that rumour had originated.

Nona read the article with a warm glow of satisfaction. She had decided that Sarah Morris should end her life and it had happened. She really was a goddess, she was certain now.

She cut the report out of the newspaper and filed it away in a scrap book.

July, 1987

Nona had the house to herself for a few days. Her father was away acting as a judge in a local court in Bathurst and her mother was visiting her sister in Melbourne. Nona enjoyed these days of solitude. She would try on her mother's clothes, search through her father's desk which he never kept locked and peer at his clothing, especially his underwear.

The parents had left the previous evening and she had three whole days to herself. She decided to try her father's wardrobe first. There was little of interest in the suits and shirts and she had seen his army uniform with the badges of a Captain hanging before in a suit bag, smelling of mothballs.

Several sweaters were neatly folded in one drawer and then she saw something new. She took it out and unfolded it to reveal a fibrous coverall that could be used for protection when painting or dealing with anything that could stain clothes. It reminded her of the cop shows she liked to watch, especially those that showed mangled corpses. Her particular favourites were British police detective shows like "The Bill" and others where pathologists examined the bodies of unexplained death victims.

One thing that had always irritated her about those shows was that the cops never seemed to wear anything to stop themselves messing up the crime scene. She thought it should be obvious that several cops walking around would ruin footprints or any small blood stains.

The idea exploded in her mind like fireworks on New Year's Eve. She went to the kitchen and pulled out rubber gloves used for dishwashing, and in the lounge she knew there was a packet of face masks left over from when her father had developed pneumonia a couple of years ago and had coughed badly for two weeks. Gathering all the items, she left them on the dining table and decided to wait till dusk.

Being winter, it grew dark by early evening. At six, Nona gathered the items and left. It was a thirty minute walk to the woods with just a few homes along the way. Most of them housed elderly retirees and

Nona knew that some of these occasionally took a short walk before or after dinner.

She reached the woods, slipped on the protective suit and the overshoes, pulled the hood over her head and donned the face mask, leaving it hanging down by her neck until needed.

And she could hardly believe her luck! An old lady appeared, walking along the path from one side of the wood, heading back to her house which Nona had passed just a while before. Maybe she had been visiting somebody, but Nona knew the Gods were smiling on her plan. This old lady's time had come for Nona to wind it up. Slipping the mask over her mouth and nose, pulling on the rubber gloves, she eased her way out from behind the bushes, moved up behind the old woman and grabbed her throat.

It took almost no time and no effort. Nona was astonished at how easy it was. Within moments, the old woman lay dead at Nona's feet. Nona left, walked back towards the houses.

Dark had fallen by the time she got home and had taken off all the protective clothing. She lit the wood stove and bit by bit, pushed the coveralls, shoe covers and mask into the fire and when satisfied there was nothing left but ash, used the rubber gloves to wash up a few plates to make sure she washed the surface with soap and water. She wasn't going to make the simple mistakes that crooks made in the cop shows.

Feeling exhilarated, she filled a glass with scotch from her father's cupboard and watched television until ten before going to bed and sleeping soundly.

* * *

The police came knocking the next day. She had expected that from all the British cop shows she had watched when the cops did their door-to-door inquiries. When a young constable called, she found no difficulty in saying simply that she had seen nothing at all, having watched television all evening. The officer left, clearly suspecting nothing.

"I am Nona, the Goddess of life and death," she said after closing the door. She felt wonderful.

Chapter 7 – The Tenth of January, 2022

"I called you in because there are some big questions here," said Doctor Mortimer, the Medical Examiner.

"How so?" asked Detective Sergeant Melanie Carter. "I thought this was just a simple natural causes event. Judy Henderson had been suffering from a heart condition and high blood pressure for years, according to her GP."

"All true," said Doctor Mortimer. His youthful, unlined face showed some excitement. "She was sixty-eight and as you said, not in the best of physical health. Her regular nurse visitor thought that it was a simple heart attack, one had been brewing for a while, so she called her GP. But when he saw the vomit which is not normal, he called me and that's where you come in."

"But you agree with him, it's not natural causes?"

"I'm quite sure it was not. That's why you're here."

"Doctor, you think it was a murder? What's caused this change?"

The doctor looked a little smug and settled down in the seat behind his desk as if about to tutor a student. "Ever hear of the Rosary Seed?"

"I haven't. What is it?"

"It's a beautiful little seed, usually bright red with a tiny black dot. It's very hard, so much so that you can drill through it and it's often made as a decorative necklace and it's also popular as a rosary bead, hence the name. They were labelled *Abrus precatorius* and they are very, very lethal. They contain a toxin called Abrin which is a close relative of Ricin."

"Christ, Doc, is this what you found in her body?"

"Eventually. Before I started the post mortem I saw nothing suspicious enough to cause comment, given her medical history of some heart problems. But I still felt curious, because she'd been vomiting badly before she died and when I cut into her, I found some gastro-intestinal bleeding, severe dehydration and some damage to her kidneys. Given her age and poor condition, this was not necessarily cause for concern, but I called for a toxicology screen and that's when I found tiny traces of this little seed. It had been ground up and swallowed. Finding traces of Abrin in her blood was much harder, but the lab worked at it and they did find some."

"How long would it take to kill somebody?"

"A healthy adult male, maybe three to four hours. But a frail old woman in this condition probably thirty to forty minutes."

"And how much would it take?"

"One little seed, that's all. Especially if ground up and delivered in a drink or a sandwich or something."

"Doc, where the hell would you get one of these?"

"It's a pretty invasive plant. I did some reading. It started in Asia but it has been found here in Australia, the US and Europe. I can't find any reference to known occurrences here, however. I did find something else that sort of confirms what we saw. The incredible toxicity of Abrin was occasionally used to secretly kill people in 19th century Bengal. The seeds were ground into a paste, shaped into a point known as a sui and left to harden in the sun. This was then mounted on a handle and stuck through the person's skin by a surreptitious slap to the cheek."

"That's nasty. I've never heard of that."

"Nor had I till I started reading this afternoon."

"And your estimate of time of death, Doc?"

"Some time between eight and midnight last night, the ninth."

"Okay, I'll talk to my boss. Can I get a copy of the PM and tox reports?"

Doctor Mortimer shifted a folder across his desk to her. "I knew you'd need it."

The detective put the papers away in her briefcase and left the mortuary.

* * *

"This is a bitch, sir," said Carter to Detective Inspector Russell Comley later that day. "There's absolutely no clues of any sort. Somebody has done a really good job of covering their tracks. They probably wore the same sort of protective clothing we use at crime scenes, there's not a witness within a hundred metres, it was dark, there's nothing at all."

"And it's getting worse, Melanie. As you know, the Homicide people in Paramatta usually take over these investigations, but they're still short-staffed after the pandemic thing of the last two years and I've been directed to help out the people in Canberra because they're swamped too. They've got six homicides and they're overloaded. I've called around the State, there's nobody available to come here and help. You're on your own."

"That's a bit scary, Sir."

"I've no doubt. You've been a detective for what, just two years, this is your second homicide?"

"Yes, Sir."

"You did damned well on that one and the other investigations you've been on. I have faith in you. Call me or come and talk to me when you need to, but stick with it. Maybe things will break soon."

"I hope so, Sir."

"Meanwhile, you need an office if you're taking the lead role. Take over the one we keep for visitors, because we won't be getting any for a while. Get Maintenance to put your name on the door."

"Thank you, Sir, that will help a lot."

Chapter 8 – Melanie Carter, 2000

Melanie was sick and tired of the whole thing.

"Mum, I wish everybody would just stop it! I'm fed up with all this 'Oh Melanie, how beautiful you are,' and 'I wish I looked like you Melanie,' all the time. Even Dad does it."

"I know dear. I try and tell him it's not doing you any good, but he can't help being so proud of you."

"Well, I wish he'd be proud of my school reports and not what I look like."

"I know he is, dear, but he's a man and you know what they're like."

Melanie finally laughed. "I'm not sure I want to find out! Mum, I'm ten years old, it's just too much. Everybody's always hanging around and staring at me."

"It's been said before, dear, beauty can be a curse. Let's make sure we try and minimise it a bit. Don't wear skirts as short as the other girls do, keep your hair short and when you fill out in the chest, we'll give you loose blouses made in thicker material. It may help a bit."

"I wish the other girls would understand, Mum."

"They can't help being jealous, Mel. The simple fact is that you're ridiculously beautiful, even at ten. God knows what you'll be like in another two or three years. But you're also top of the class in almost everything, so concentrate on that. High school, then University. Any idea what you might want to do after?"

"Not really. I thought maybe medicine."

"That would be good. Okay, go and set the table for dinner, Mel."

"Yes Mum."

* * *

2006

"Mum, I really hate this. I just wish I could dress like a girl instead of this half-man look."

"I know, dear, but this is what we decided to try. Loose jeans, loose tops, short hair, no make-up. It keeps some of the worst attention away."

"I know and it's necessary, but it's a real drag. Why can't I just be me?"

"Because as you've already found, being beautiful means nobody thinks you can also be intelligent. The world is a bit sick, sometimes."

"Does this mean I'll have to be like this all the time? What happens when I go to University and start a job? Do I always have to dress like an old peasant?"

"Not that bad, dear. But you'll need to be very selective about what you want to do? You've got two more years of school, what then?"

"I still think I want to do medicine."

"Well at least you could wear scrubs all the time! Nothing sexy about those!"

"Yeah Mum, you're right. But just once, I'd like to put on a tight dress, high heels, wear makeup and let my hair grow."

"I'm not sure the world will be able to handle that, dear. Though if you did become a model, you could do all those things."

"No Mum, I refuse to have a job that just involves being beautiful. I want to use my brains, not my boobs."

"I know you will, Mel."

* * *

2008

"University? Why on earth would you want to go to university? Nobody else in the family has ever done that."

"Dad, I want to do something useful. I've been offered places at every university I applied to."

"But why? Everybody has always assumed you'd be a model, I mean, look at you! I bet every modelling agency in Australia would sign you up tomorrow. And think of the money you could make."

"Dad, I've already had offers. I had three agencies come and see me at school this term alone, and yes, I could leave school and start making money right away."

"So why don't you? I bet you'd be the best-known model in the country within a year."

"Dad, I don't want a job that consists of being beautiful. Okay, that's nice and all that, but I do actually have a brain. I'd like to use it. Anyway, being beautiful doesn't last. At best, I'd have ten years and then what? Or what if I had an accident and couldn't be a model anymore? What else could I do?"

"I suppose so. So what will you study at university?"

"I wanted to do medicine, become a doctor. But I decided it would take too long. So I'm going to do psychology."

"Wow, that'll be something, eh? Maybe you could do some modelling on the side and help out with the fees?"

"Maybe, Dad."

*　*　*

'Dear Miss Carter:

The University of Sydney is pleased to confirm your place in our Psychology Department. Term starts on...'

Chapter 9 – the Eighth of February, 2022

Carl Hitchcox realised his hands were trembling and there was a deep sickness in his gut.

It had all been so exciting as he planned his assignment, found the tools to carry it out and gone through in his mind again and again how he would actually do it. But as the time neared, reality was seeping in and his resolve was melting away like butter under a hot sun.

He sensed her presence moments before his doorbell rang and he knew who it was. With a strange mixture of anticipation, fear and excitement, he opened the door.

"Nona! This is a surprise, do come in."

"Thank you, Carl."

A few moments later, they were sitting across from each other at a coffee table. Carl felt that he should have offered her something, but there was a force emanating from the woman that stopped offers of hospitality.

"I thought I should come and see you, Carl. Are you ready for your assignment tomorrow?"

He felt the sickness in his stomach and sensed her eyes boring into him. His hands were still shaking.

"Well…" His voice was a dry croak. He took a deep breath. "Nona, this seems such a terrible thing to do. Killing somebody, this is dreadful."

"It's a good thing I came," she said. She leaned forward over the coffee table. "Carl, look at me."

Unable to refuse, he leaned nearer and stared into her eyes. He felt them drilling down through his soul, touching senses, images and dreams he had never dared to explore before.

"Remember how we discussed this," she said. "Can you remember how exciting it would be, to be in such a powerful position that you can end a person's life. You'd be like a god, supreme, it's the greatest power you can have and the greatest satisfaction."

"But what if I get found out?" he muttered, feeling even to himself that his words were childish, cowardly. "I don't want to go to prison."

"Remember everything I have told you. Follow all the instructions I gave you and there will be not a single clue that the police will be able to find. You are quite safe, Carl."

He had no idea how long he stared into her eyes but he sensed the fear and doubts fading. It really would be god-like, he realised, to choose to end the life of another person, just because he wanted to. He would be supreme, he could laugh as he saw the police flailing around, trying to work out who had committed the murder, he could be among them, talk to cops in the town and they would never, ever realise that he was the man they were hunting. He felt the smile grow on his lips, began to look forward eagerly to the next day when he would be a god for a time.

"You are sure you have everything you need?" she asked.

"Yes, I've been collecting the bits and working out the location over a few days. It will work well, I'm sure."

"That's good, Carl. I know all of us are looking forward to hearing the story at our next meeting. You're the first one after me and I know you will do an amazing job."

She stood up and walked out, leaving him staring at the wall.

How amazing she was, he thought. *She has made it possible for me to be a god for a time, to laugh at the cops, to know that I am immune. What a wonderful gift she has given me. Tomorrow can't come quickly enough. How silly I was to be afraid of this.*

Chapter 10 - The Tenth of February, 2022

"God, what a mess."

The uniformed police officer stared at the wreckage of the car at the foot of the cliff. "That's a twenty metre drop onto rocks. No wonder there's not much left."

Doctor Mortimer stood up from his examination of the body behind the wheel.

"At least she died quickly. As you can see, the car landed on its right side, she was slammed against the door as it hit rock. She would have died instantly. Her neck broke, ribs were shattered, one went through her heart. We're going to have to tear this thing apart to get her out of it."

The patrol officer waved to the engineers waiting at the side and they moved in with the drills and equipment to pull the shattered bits of the little red Toyota away from the body. It took half an hour before the sad remains of the elderly woman could be loaded into the waiting ambulance. All the vehicles had arrived at the scene by a rough, unsealed track that had diverted from the main road some five kilometres away.

"Any ideas, Doc?" asked the officer.

"I'll have to get her on the slab, but it will be bloody difficult to find anything but broken bones and busted organs. If there's a trace of booze or drugs, the toxicology exam will show it. But my initial tests says she's been dead a few hours, probably between nine and midnight last night."

"It happened late last night? Could she just have fallen asleep?"

"That's possible. I'll call her GP and see what he thinks. I got her bag out and found her wallet. She's seventy-two, so it could be a case of a simple micro-sleep." He handed the driving licence to the officer. "Does that check with the registration?"

"It does."

"Okay, I'll have your report by late afternoon and a copy for the coroner. But from what we've seen, this is accidental death all the way."

"Thanks, Doc. Hell of a way to start the day, eh?"

"Damn right."

Chapter 11 – Alex Welland, October 2021

"Control to Two-Seven."

Constable Marie Hebert touched the button in the patrol car. "Two-Seven," she said.

"Two Seven, domestic at 12, Patterson Road. Screams heard."

"Two-Seven responding." Marie Hebert cancelled the call. "Pedal to the metal, young man," she said to the driver. "Could be serious."

Constable Alex Welland smiled. "I've always enjoyed this bit," he said. "Make some noise, will you?"

The siren cleared the way as Alex accelerated and it was only three minutes before they slammed to a halt at the address given. They ran up to the front door and Alex banged on the flaking paint on the wood. Inside, they could hear raised voices, a man and a woman, the latter almost screaming.

Alex banged on the door again.

"Police! Open up!" he shouted. The screaming didn't stop, but the door was opened slowly and a child looked through the small opening. Tears were rolling down his face and he looked terrified.

Marie knelt down in front of him.

"Hello, young man," she said. "Can we come in and help you?"

The little boy nodded and opened the door fully, letting the two officers enter. The noise got louder and there was a sudden crash of something heavy falling. They moved into the room where the disturbance was happening. A man stood there, his fists raised. On the floor in front of him, a woman lay, blood running from a cut over one ear.

"Oi!" shouted Alex and this attracted the man's attention. He turned and took a swing at the officer's head. Alex leaned back like a cricket batsman avoiding a bouncer, the fist swung past his chin and he grabbed it, continued the motion and brought the man crashing down on his face, one arm pinned behind his back.

"Naughty, naughty," said Alex and pulled the other arm back, snapping handcuffs on both wrists in a practiced motion.

Meanwhile, Marie had called up on her radio.

"Nicely done," she said to Alex. "Ambulance will be here any moment. I'll check on the kid."

She didn't have to look far, the boy was staring with wide eyes at the scene. Alex studied him, feeling intense sympathy as the sight of the terrified face, worn clothing and ugly shoes brought up painful memories of his own childhood. Something about the face nagged at him, but he couldn't identify what it was.

Before he could suggest it, Marie was back on the radio, speaking softly. She finished the call and nodded at Alex.

"Child Protection on its way, also," she said.

A few minutes later, an ambulance had arrived and taken the injured woman away. A young agent from Child Protection also arrived and the little boy reacted well to her gentleness and obvious caring. When she started to walk him out, the boy suddenly broke away and ran to Alex, hugging him round the knees. Alex felt his heart turn over and he bent down to touch the little boy's shoulder.

"What's your name?" he asked.

"Ben," was the muffled reply.

"Well, okay Ben, you go with this nice lady and she'll make sure you're well looked after. And I tell you what, I'll come and see you tomorrow and make sure you're alright and we can talk a bit."

The little boy smiled through his tears and turned back to the Child Protection officer and they walked out.

Alex hauled the handcuffed man to his feet and began walking him out to the patrol car. Ignoring the small crowd of onlookers, he guided the man into the back seat and got in alongside him as Marie took the wheel and drove them back to the station.

Paperwork completed, Alex went to his desk and began work on the computer. Something about that little boy... His shift ended about then and he knew he was free to work on the problem.

"Working late, Constable?"

He looked up and had to stop himself smiling. Detective Sergeant Melanie Carter stood in front of his desk. As always, it was a struggle not to study her from her feet, up through the obviously beautiful body only partially disguised by the loose-fitting trouser-suits she always wore, to the exquisite face framed by dark red hair, usually worn in a pony-tail. He concentrated on looking her in the eye.

"This domestic we attended this afternoon, Sergeant. A thug called Peter Welch. He's got form, assault, house-breaking, the usual thug stuff. He'll go down for a decent stretch for assaulting his partner. But it's the kid that worries me."

"What about the kid?"

"Something about the face, Sarge. I know I've seen it before."

"It should be the detectives doing this, but we're short-staffed, as you know. If you feel okay doing this in your own time, nobody's going to object."

"Thanks, Sarge." He tried not to watch her as she walked out of the room and failed badly. Once again, he wondered who the man in her life was and couldn't help envying him.

Two hours later, he found what had been nagging him.

"His name is Ben Bradshaw," Alex said, seated across the desk from Detective Inspector Russell Comley. Melanie Carter sat a few feet away, facing both of them.

"He was reported missing from his home in Narromine two years ago and not seen again and it remains an unsolved crime, though the boy was assumed to be dead. I looked up the files and although the boy is two years older, the face is much the same."

"What triggered the search?" asked Melanie.

"Mostly a hunch, Sarge. It was one of those cases circulated round the country soon after I was transferred here and I just remembered it."

"Excellent work, Constable," said Comley. "That will go on your record."

"But that's not all," said Alex. "I kept looking. The rest is even worse."

Comley leaned forward, his chin on his hands.

"Go on."

"I talked to Centrelink. Their records show that Welch and his common-law wife, Angela Harker have no children. But there's certainly one child living at that address."

"Interesting," said Melanie.

"I went to see young Ben this morning and we had a great talk. He said that sometimes, two more kids are brought there by other people in the street and those days are when there's a lot of work to be done, like cleaning the house, moving rubbish and stuff like that. When that happens, another adult watches over them and there's no chance to get away. And the same thing at other houses. Ben said he's often moved to another house and several kids are put to work."

"Oh my!" said Melanie. "Forced child labour."

"And nobody has ever noticed? Nobody thought they should be at school?" asked Comley.

"There's just four houses in the street," said Alex. "Those are the houses where the kids are kept. And it's not the sort of neighbourhood that has social gatherings. I bet if somebody asked them, nobody would admit to having seen anything suspicious."

"There are always some areas like that," said Comley. "We can never clean them all up."

"Sir, can we take this case?" asked Alex. "I'd want to see the documentation of every local child, check them out and I bet we can find some kidnap cases."

"Did Ben give you any indication of sexual abuse?" asked Comley.

"No, Sir, he didn't. But there were a few times when he hinted that may have been the case with some of the others. I really would like to work on this."

"So would I," said Comley. "But no, you can't, we can't spare you from patrol duties and this is specialised work. But I'll pass this upwards and somebody will be assigned. But I tell you what, this may result in breaking up a complete ring of these people as well as finding some missing children. This will be a major police success and your name will be on the record."

"Damn good work, Constable," said Melanie and smiled at him.

Alex took a deep breath. "Thank you, Sarge," he replied.

"Tell you what you can do as a reward," said Comley. "Call the parents in Narromine, give them the news and then you and Marie can take the kid home."

"That'll be great, Sir. I'll go and tell her right away. Our shift starts soon."

He stood up and walked out, an image of Melanie's smiling eyes firmly in his memory.

Chapter 12 – the Eleventh of February, 2022

"Good morning all," said Nona and rang her decorative china bell. "Take your seats, phones off, welcome to the February meeting of the writers' group."

She paused while the writers took their seats, finished their first cups of coffee and settled down.

"Caroline, would you read the minutes of the January meeting?"

Caroline opened her folder, took out the single sheet.

"This will be an extraordinary report," she said and waited for the low hum of laughter to fade. "Minutes of the meeting of the fourteenth of January, 2022. After welcoming the members to the new year session, Nona Markham changed the program. Instead of running a workshop on ways of hiding all possible clues when committing a murder, Nona read a short story of the murder of an old woman by an exotic poison known as 'Rosary Seed.'"

"But as one member pointed out, it appeared to echo a news report that an old lady of the name used in Nona's story had been found dead of a heart attack. Nona astonished us all by telling us that she had been the killer, and we spent the next hour listening to her description of how it felt, how she had prevented any clue to her presence at the scene and the exhilaration she felt at knowing the police had accepted the death as natural causes. All the members of the group admitted to having had fantasies of killing somebody and getting away with it. They all committed to keeping the secret of this death. Then Carl Hitchcox announced that he would like to try something and would present a short story at the February meeting. The group agreed to await his story and keep the details secret."

"Thank you, Caroline," said Nona. "Any objections to the minutes being adopted as read? No? Then done. Carl, we're all eager to hear your story."

Carl grinned cheerfully, took the printed sheet from his document holder and cleared his throat.

It had been a great day at the airfield, Jack Simmonds decided. The weather had been classic soaring conditions for eastern Australia and Jack had taken a couple of visitors to the field for short joyrides in the two-seat Janus sailplane while waiting for the day to warm up and the thermals to begin. The two young women had been thrilled by their flights in a glider and each had reacted in similar fashions with the take-off, the steep climb as the massive winch at the far end had hauled the two-seater plane into the sky at the end of the steel cable.

Being an instructor at a gliding club had some of the same joys of being a ski instructor at a ski resort, Jack believed. It had glamour, a talent that impressed almost everybody and the effect on young women was most satisfying. Many dates and exciting affairs had come from such days.

At eleven, pilots reported that thermal activities had started. Jack hauled his fifteen metre Standard Class Jantar from the side of the field to the flight line, put on his parachute, climbed in and for the third time that day, rode the steep climb to twelve hundred feet, released the cable and almost immediately found lift. Three hours later, he returned to the field after flying a short triangle of two hundred kilometres and climbing to over nine thousand feet on several occasions.

Yes, a great day he decided as he pulled the Jantar back to the hangar with his Land Cruiser and left it in its regular position against the south wall. Thanking the two young men who had helped, he walked around the plane for a final check and saw several lengths of winch launch steel cable in one corner. This was normal, cables occasionally broke during a launch and were quickly repaired, but several lengths were still left and were kept until there was enough to take for recycling. He took out a pair of industrial work gloves from the car, wrapped a length of some forty metres of cable and lifted it into the back of the Land Cruiser.

Driving home later, he looked for a spot for the plan he had in mind. About twenty kilometres from home he found it. The tree-lined road took a sharp bend round the edge of the mountain and there was a major drop of some twenty metres onto the rocks below. Warning notices on either side of the bend advised a slow speed and great care. Jack had always considered this stretch a seriously dangerous spot but the Council had never agreed to building a safety fence along the edge of the road.

Jack completed the drive home and spent a quiet evening planning the action.

At ten that night, he drove back to the spot he had identified. The road was lightly used but there were a few houses near the airfield and people did drive there from the town. Jack drove off the road, parked behind a tree and got out, lifted the cable and selected the tree as the first anchor point. He wrapped one end three or four times round the tree trunk at a height of about a metre then crossed the road to find the second anchor. He selected a tree about twenty metres further west on the road, returned to the cable and pulled the loose end to the second tree. When lifted, the cable would be at an angle across the road. Any vehicle approaching from the village and heading for the airfield and the houses nearby would strike the cable and be driven to the right and over the edge.

Jack sat down and waited.

Nearly an hour passed before he saw headlights approaching. He hauled the cable to a metre height and wrapped it round the tree, the weight of the steel leaving the stretch in the middle of the road about half a metre high.

The headlights got nearer and a small car approached driving at a moderate speed. Jack felt worried that it would be too slow, but the car hit the cable, was deflected sharply to the right and went *over the edge without any sign that the driver had tried to brake. Jack quickly unwrapped the cable from the tree, hauled it back across the road and unwrapped the other end, returned the pile to his car and drove off. He didn't bother looking over the edge, it was far too dark to see.*

Back home, he unloaded the cable into his garage. The following week, he would return it to the hangar when he could find himself alone by the structure.

Then he went back inside and poured himself a large scotch. He sat in his favourite armchair, finally letting his emotions emerge.

"Wow!" he called out aloud. "That was fantastic! Worked like a charm!" He let the reactions take over, feeling excitement, satisfaction at his planning and workmanship and looking forward to reading the news of the accident in the local papers. Next week's gliding might feel like an anti-climax, he thought.

Applause ran around the table.

"And we did read about it," said Gabrielle. "It was a little old lady. The cops say it was an accidental death, she might have fallen asleep at the wheel after visiting her daughter and grandkids in town. That was a great job and a fine story."

"Absolutely agree," said Nona. "So well done, that was the first episode in the book after mine. I'm sure we're all looking forward to the next one in March. Okay, time for coffee and biscuits."

Nona stayed in her seat as the group drifted out of the room after the gathering of writers. The meeting had been useful, like all the others as a way of reading the personalities in the group so she had not been bored by the short stories so far. She had been able to write a story for each meeting, based almost entirely on her experiences, smiling inside as she told the group about how she had made a little girl steal a clock from the school and later initiated the hounding of a teenager to her death. They had all approved of the stories, quite unaware that they were based on fact, not fiction.

She focused on the man who had attracted her attention from quite early on. He seemed unreadable, almost closed off behind his impassive face and she sensed great intelligence and quite probably a challenge to her skills. The American accent added intrigue. She wondered what made an American emigrate to Australia. Was there a dark story there?

"Got a moment?" she said as Allen Miller walked past her on the other side of the table.

He looked down at her, his face expressionless.

"Sure," he said. "What's up?"

"Nothing," she said and smiled, trying to stare into his eyes. "But I'm a writer, like all of us here and I like to understand other writers and learn from them. Would you mind if I just ask you a few questions?"

"No problem," he said and sat down across from her. "What can I tell you?"

Again, she tried to stare directly into his eyes but felt almost a wall protecting him. She realised that she had a challenge. Bringing this man under her control would not be easy.

"I can't place the accent exactly," she said. "American North-east?"

"Pretty good," he said. "Baltimore."

"And what brings you to Australia?"

"New horizons. And have you been to Baltimore in winter?"

She laughed. Maybe there was a tiny brick or two crumbling in his defence.

"You've read us some interesting crime stories," she said. "But you don't have a murder in them."

"Killing people is silly," he said. "You can achieve everything you want without physically killing somebody."

"Physically? Is there any other way of killing a person?"

"Damn right there is. Nona, I think I know what you're doing here. I've met people like you before. Am I right that you are working towards having us kill people as part of a group story?"

She sat back, shock making her whole body feel like iced water had been poured on her.

"Allen!" she said, her voice hoarse. "How could you possibly think that?"

"In my line of work, I've learned to read people," he said. "You're an open book. You're what the shrinks call a Dominant. You can make other people do what you want, and I bet you reckon the ultimate achievement will be to make us do some murders. Those stories you read us, I know all the suckers here thought they were fiction, but every line in your body gave you away to me. You really did make that little girls steal the clock, didn't you? And you really did make the girls at school hound some poor kid to death because you spread the line that she was a slut. Am I right?"

Nona's throat was dry. She knew she could never get this man under her control. She picked up her coffee mug and sipped the cold remnants of the coffee break two hours before.

"Well, don't worry," said Miller. "I won't tell anyone and I'll play your game, too. It will be interesting to see if you can make this ordinary bunch of people commit murder. And then I'll show you the most efficient and the cleanest way to kill somebody."

He stood up. "Have a nice day," he said and walked out of the room.

It took Nona twenty minutes before she could regain control of herself and follow him.

That night, she couldn't sleep. Occasional catnaps were all that she managed and they were small nightmares of the impervious face of Allen Miller looking at her with contempt.

"You're a failure," his voice said with the trace of American accent. "I know you. You can't control me."

Again and again, she woke up at that moment, feeling cold shivers and a sick feeling of fear in her gut. This was the first ever block to her powers as a goddess and she felt terrified of what it could mean.

Chapter 13 - The Eleventh of March, 2022

"Gabrielle, your turn," said Nona, the Chairwoman. "We're all looking forward to hearing your story of a murder."

Looking nervous, Gabrielle opened up her folder and extracted the printed pages. Clearing her throat, she began to read...

Ninth of March, 2022

The silent figure dressed in full protective clothing that she had bought two weeks ago stood motionless in the shadow of the large bush by the back fence of the house...

Eleventh of March, 2022

"Gabrielle, that was wonderful!" exclaimed Nona and a round of applause ran around the table. "Great descriptive writing, it had me holding my breath."

"I agree," said the American, Allen Miller. "That had me holding my breath also. Well done."

"And good details," added Bella. "I like the way you remember to jump back over the fence, collect the drone and the control box and then walk back along the river bank to the road."

"But what about the box cutter and the protective clothing?" asked Bella's husband, Mitchell. "What about those?"

"Ah, yes," said Gabrielle. "I forgot to mention those. I knew they'd be critical clues in a murder, so I threw the box cutter into the river when I got back to the car, then stripped off the coveralls and shoe covers being very careful to avoid any blood getting on my hands or clothing, put them in a garbage bag I'd brought with me and sealed it. When I got home, I lit the wood stove and put everything in there, making sure there was nothing left."

"Wouldn't somebody notice your chimney smoking?" asked Jean. "It was one of the hottest nights of the year. Who would have a fire going?"

"I waited till two," said Gabrielle, slightly irritated. "Nobody in my road would be up at that hour."

"Excellent," said Nona. "This will make a great chapter for the book. Okay, other group matters..."

When all the others had left, Nona checked her notes. Next month's episode was Paul's. She had no doubts that Paul would do the job professionally and rapidly, leaving no trace. But although she had drawn him into her plans fairly easily, she realised people could change when faced with the job of killing somebody unknown to them.

She decided she would pay a visit to Paul a day or two before the ninth of the following month and reinforce his conditioning.

Chapter 14 – The Ninth of April, 2022

"Thank god for wetsuits," muttered Paul to the freezing air over the lake. He dipped a hand into water and felt the iciness. Maybe this was not the best way to get his chapter of the book written, there were a hundred more comfortable ways. But he was committed now.

He slipped the oxygen tank over his shoulders and strapped it securely to his back, folded up the hood over his head, fitted the air mask over his mouth and checked the fit of his gloves. Finally, he slid the goggles down from his forehead and over his eyes.

Only about fifty metres away, the barely seen shadow of the only other boat on the water didn't move. He did not seem to have noticed as Paul gently rowed his little boat out from the small beach and anchored the short distance away.

Paul shifted to sit on the edge of the boat, put his feet in the water and quietly lowered himself into the lake. He kept his head above water for a few seconds, checking on the direction of the shadowy fisherman then let himself sink below the surface and began swimming towards the other boat. Estimating about half the distance, he stopped, lifted his head and checked his progress.

Great, he thought to himself and resumed the underwater journey. Finally, seeing the underside of the boat, he stopped, sank a little lower in the freezing water so as not to be seen and gently moved out in the direction of the fishing rod held by the other man.

This part was difficult. Not wanting to cause the fisherman to strike and haul the rod up, Paul gently moved cautiously in the area where the line might have sunk and eventually found it. Lifting the end, he swam slowly back to the boat until he was under the water just below where the fisherman was sitting. Wrapping the line around his hand, he gave it a small tug. Reacting as fisherman have reacted for centuries, the man in the boat struck upwards, jerking Paul's hand sharply. Paul stayed under the surface, giving the line several small tugs as if a fish was struggling to escape. He watched as the distorted shape of the man appeared over the side, trying to see what he had caught, and Paul launched himself upward, seizing the man by his jacket and pulling him over the side and down into the water.

The man struggled, but swallowed water and choked. Paul held him down, fighting the support of the man's life jacket but after a few moments, the man's struggles stopped and he went limp. Paul undid the fastenings of the life jacket and threw it into the boat, let go of the corpse and swam back to his own boat, now more clearly seen in the first light of dawn. He climbed aboard, removed his flippers and rowed himself back to the small beach. He walked a couple of metres to where he had left his clothing, removed the wet suit and the scuba gear, packed them away with the flippers into the capacious canvas bag in which he had kept his clothes and then walked the kilometre to the bushy area where he had left his car. A few moments later he was driving home. He hadn't seen another car or a person ever since he had driven there at four in the morning.

"Good heavens, Paul," said Gabrielle. "So that was just this morning?"

"Bloody early, bloody cold," said Paul.

"It was already on the radio," said Bella. "I heard it on the nine o'clock news, the cops must have been alerted almost immediately."

"That's great," said Carl. "Do you actually have that expertise with scuba diving?"

"I sure do," said Paul. "I've been diving since I was a kid. I started at school in Queensland, did some on the Reef and later I spent a month diving in the Red Sea. I've swum with sharks and Manta Rays, it's just great."

"It's certainly an original way of killing somebody," said Nona. "I particularly like the way you tugged on the line a few times to get him to look over the side of the boat."

"I thought about it a lot," said Paul. "I decided that if that didn't work, I'd swim back under the boat, climb in on the other side and then take him into the water, but that would have increased the risk of being seen, if it was getting light. Anyway, he fell for it."

"That was clever thinking about removing his life-jacket," said Tanya. "But I wonder, if the cops check the boat, would they get suspicious about seeing the jacket all wet? How could that have happened, if he wasn't wearing it?"

"I checked the forecast," said Paul. "It was for bright sun all day, so I reckoned that by the time somebody saw the body and the cops took the boat into shore, the jacket would have dried up."

"And it seems like it worked," said Bella. "The report on the radio said that it was an accidental drowning and they commented on the fact that the dead man wasn't wearing his life jacket."

"But what about the boat you used?" said Ollie. "Where did that come from? Was it yours?"

"Good lord, no," replied Paul. "I'd been scouting round the shore in my own boat for a few days and I saw this one parked on the lawn in some rich bastard's waterside mansion. It was obviously the little one he used to get out to his yacht when he had it moored in the lake during the summer. You couldn't see the house from where the boat was parked, so the night before, I took my boat there and towed the little one to that small beach I'd found."

"That was really good," said Nona. "I'm so impressed by all of you and the clever, original ways you have found to create your stories. Now let's have our coffee break."

Chapter 15 – The Ninth of May, 2022

The old man walked carefully up to the prescriptions counter at the pharmacy. The young girl behind the counter smiled at him. He was a regular visitor.

"Hello Mr Fielding," she said. "Do you need to refill a prescription?"

The old man shook his head. He looked more weary than usual and the shuffling steps he had taken to the counter were less certain than the girl remembered.

"No," he said. "I need to return these. Maggie won't be needing them anymore."

The girl looked at him in surprise. "Mr Fielding, you don't mean...?"

"Yes, Maggie died last week."

"Oh, Mr Fielding, I'm so sorry."

"We were expecting it for some time, as you know and she was in a lot of pain, which is why she needed these. To be honest, I think it was for the best. She was eighty-six and we'd had a good life."

He handed over the packet he'd been holding since he entered the pharmacy. "I'd only just got these, so it's nearly full."

The girl took the packet and checked inside. There was a standard cardboard box with the pharmacy's label on one side giving the patient's name and dosage instruction. It was Endone, a powerful pain killer, the pills individually sealed in a blister pack. She slipped it into the pocket of her white lab coat.

"Alright Mr Fielding, I'll look after these. And may I say again, how sorry I am about your wife. We all knew her here. Can I call a taxi to take you home?"

He shook his head. "Already got one waiting outside." He turned, gave a small wave and left, not before the girl saw the small tear in one eye.

Tanya left the drugs in her pocket and at the end of the day, took them home. She had an idea for fulfilling a dream she'd had for years.

Soon after ten that evening, donned the coveralls, shoe covers, hood and mask and knocked on the back door of the Fielding house. She waited a few moments and then saw the light go on and heard the shuffling steps of the old man approaching.

"Who's there?" called out the weak voice.

"It's Tanya from the pharmacy, Mr Fielding," she replied. "I have something for you."

"Alright, alright, but what on earth are you doing at this time?"

A key was turned, a latch was undone and the door opened. Mr Fielding looked up at the taller girl in confusion.

"Tanya? Why are you here? And why are you dressed like that?"

She pushed the door open and seized the man by his shoulders, turning him round and steering him to his living room. She forced him to sit on the lounge and then straddled his knees, keeping him helpless. She knew he was ninety years old, very frail and he could not move her. She reached into one pocket of the protective coveralls, extracted a small bottle filled with water and into which she had dropped twelve of the Endone tablets. She opened the bottle and forced the top into his mouth, holding his nose so that he had no option but to let the contents drain into his throat. He stared in horror at her as he gagged and swallowed, but he didn't have the strength to move and all he could do was try and hit her shoulders with his weak, fragile arms.

Tanya felt excitement run through her body, a sense of fulfilment and achievement as she watched the impotent efforts of the old man. After twenty minutes, his struggles stopped and his eyes began to close. She stood up, went to his cabinet and found several bottles of liquor. She knew there would be some because Fielding had often told her how much he and Maggie enjoyed a nip of brandy in the evening after dinner. She selected a bottle of Napoleon cognac, opened it and returned to the figure on the couch. He was breathing lightly. She pulled his mouth open again and poured a considerable amount of the brandy into his throat. She left the bottle open and put it on the side table next to the lounge. She walked to the kitchen, found a brandy snifter, brought it back and poured more of the liquor into it, placing it next to the bottle.

Then she sat next to the old man and waited. It took an hour but she realised his breathing was fading. When it stopped, she got up, walked out at the back door, closing it behind her and walked the kilometre to where she had left her car, stripped off the protective coveralls, shoe covers, gloves, mask and hood that she had worn to commit the killing, stuffed them in a garbage bag and drove home.

* * *

Thirteenth of May, 2022

Tanya put down the paper and smiled at the round of applause from the writers' group.

"A lot like the way Nona killed the other old lady," said Gabrielle.

Tanya nodded. "I took a lot of guidance from that," she agreed. "I could have asked Nona for another of those Rosary seeds, but I wanted it to be a bit different and when he came to the shop and gave me that box of Endone, I realised I had a good way of doing it. Anyway, the old bastard was so old and frail, it was a mercy to put him out of his misery. He'd been getting lots of pills for blood pressure, cholesterol and acid reflux, so I knew he was a mess already."

"And this was done four days ago?" asked Nona.

"On the ninth, as we agreed," said Tanya with a proud smile.

"Has anything appeared in the local press?" asked Jean.

"I haven't seen anything," said Bella and several heads shook in agreement.

"Not worth reporting," said Carl Hitchcox. "If they did a post mortem, they'll almost certainly put it down to suicide as he'd just lost his wife of many decades."

"Probably," said Nona.

Eleventh of May, 2022

"Suicide," said Doctor Mortimer to Melanie Carter across the desk from him. "There was enough Endone and brandy inside him to kill a horse and the bottle was still open next to him. The poor old bastard had lost his wife only a week ago, they'd been married for over sixty years, very happily according to his family. It's quite common for a spouse to commit suicide in such circumstances."

"How sad." Melanie looked down at her notes. "And yet in some ways, a lovely story. How lucky can one be to have such a happy marriage for so many years that life is not worth living when it ends?"

"I suppose so," said Doctor Mortimer. "I've put it down for the ninth, as the nurse who visited every day found him the following morning. I'll have your report and one for the Coroner in about an hour."

"Thank you, Doc," said Melanie and got up to leave.

Chapter 16 – Nona Markham

June, 1996

"Sure you could," said Nona to the young man next to her at the bar.

"No, not my style at all. I don't attack people for no cause. That's for idiots."

"Hell, we've all got some violence inside us. Go on, I dare you, when we go outside, you just king hit the first man you see."

She turned her gaze full on the young man and saw the first hint of uncertainty in his eyes.

"No, I really won't," he said.

"Chicken," she said.

"Not at all, just common sense."

"You couldn't do it, even if you tried." She watched as the uncertainty grew in him, the glazed eye look that she had seen many times grow stronger.

"Yes, I bloody could."

"No you bloody couldn't. Go on, prove it."

His face strangely immobile, he got off his bar stool and walked out into the street. She followed a little way behind. He stood on the pavement, looking left and right and when an elderly couple walked by him, he swung his fist straight into the man's face. The older man fell backwards, banging his head on the concrete as the woman screamed. Several people watched in horror and three men ran up and grabbed the attacker, wrestling him to the ground. Others drew out their mobile phones and spoke urgently into them.

Nona walked back into the pub, smiling. *I don't know how I do this,* she thought to herself, *but it seems very useful.*

* * *

Twenty-Sixth of February, 2021

Nona sat in her car and watched the woman push her cart to the small Mazda hatch-back in the shopping centre parking lot, unload her shopping and return the cart to the stack. This was the third day she had observed the woman after finding herself behind her in the check-out line and heard her interactions with the cashier. She had sensed just how easy the woman could be manipulated. She had no idea how she knew that, but she knew she was a goddess and could influence her chosen subject easily. The time to make her move was fast approaching.

"You like that brand of milk also, I see?"

Tanya looked up at the woman standing next to her in the checkout line. "Yes, I do, it has a flavour that's different from the rest."

"And the family likes it too?"

"I live alone, just me to worry about."

Nona smiled. "Me too. So what do you do with your time?"

"Oh, there's plenty to keep me busy. I joined a writers' group last year and we're always setting new assignments for ourselves. I've always wanted to write a book and this seemed the best way to get started."

"Me too! What a coincidence! My name's Nona Markham. What sort of book do you want to write?"

"I'm Tanya Roberts." She looked down at her feet. "I suppose it's far too boring, but I'd like to write a historical romance story."

"Nothing to be ashamed about that. I'm working on a murder mystery."

"Ooh, that's exciting. But why don't you come to our writers' group? We meet at the library on the second Friday of the month."

"Sounds like a great idea. It would push me down the track a bit."

The cashier began checking Tanya's purchases while Nona studied her carefully. She sensed the possibilities of influencing the rather simple mind before her. The writers' group sounded like a perfect opportunity to begin fulfilling her own fantasy.

"See you at the library some time then," said Tanya as she collected her receipt and bags.

"Count on it," Nona said as the cashier began checking her own purchases. She waved as Tanya walked out to her car.

Twelfth of March, 2021

Nona was in line at the door when the library opened at 10:00am that Friday. She picked a chair near the window but with a clear view up the aisle to the meeting room where the writers' group met. She watched the people entering, her almost psychic sixth-sense reading their characters.

She saw Tanya Roberts walk in and Nona turned away on the slight chance that she might recognise her from the brief meeting, but Tanya was talking to a young man and didn't look round. Nona thought the young man might be a suitable candidate for her plans as well.

Then she saw what she felt was the perfect target. The woman looked in her fifties, slightly careworn, possibly a tired housewife with little in life but dreams of writing a successful novel, almost certainly a romance and lifting herself out of life's daily drudgery.

Nona counted eleven people entering the room, six women including Tanya and the new target, five men, all middle-aged or older except for the young man who had walked in with Tanya. Apart from her target, she also noted the tall, slender blonde with the tightly curled hair. There was something about the way she stayed isolated as the group walked in, not greeting any of the others, not even seeming to notice them.

"Very self-absorbed bitch," she muttered to herself. "Could be worth attention as well."

The door to the meeting room closed, Nona put down the book she had been pretending to read and left.

A few minutes before one, she returned to her seat and picked a book out of the shelves. She watched as the door opened and the writers strolled out. Again she noted the blonde walking alone, not even noticing the others and Nona sensed the slight disdain the other women had for her. But her interest now was in the new target, walking out and talking with a thin, dark, balding man dressed in black jeans and a red sweater. Nona got up and followed the crowd at a safe distance. Taking the chance that they would have parked in the parking lot attached to the shopping mall next to the library, she had done the same. Still watching the two, she got into her own car and watched them. Several of the group walked to their vehicles, the target and the red-sweater-clad man waved amicably and the woman climbed into a Toyota Corolla.

Nona followed her, trying to leave a couple of cars between them and eventually saw her pull into the driveway of a small house. Nona stopped fifty metres away, waited until the target was safely inside the house, noted the address and the car's licence plate and drove home.

She spent the next three days sitting for long periods in the street of the target's house, but eventually she saw her leaving and without surprise, followed her back to the same parking lot from which they had left. The woman pulled out a shopping bag and entered the supermarket. Nona decided that the same technique she had used to meet Tanya would work again and soon found herself in the check-out line behind her new target. The opening gambit worked just as well as it had the last time and within a few minutes she was chatting to Jean.

"Fancy a coffee?" asked Nona. "If you're not doing anything, that is?"

Jean Worrall smiled with pleasure.

"That would be lovely," she said. "I don't have many social events like this these days."

Walking back into the mall, taking seats in a coffee shop and placing their orders, they sat in a companionable manner.

"Why not many social events?" asked Nona.

"Too busy," said Jean. "I run a little cleaning business, I've got five people and they take some time to watch over, but that's just business, no real friendships."

"No family then?"

"Two girls, but they're both adults living in Melbourne, I don't see them much. I've tried to give them a good childhood, but my own was pretty crappy, so I didn't do too good a job of it."

"What was the problem, if you don't mind me asking?"

"Abusive mother, remote father. You know how it is, girls need a mother to guide them and a father to provide some strength and a role model."

"You really do have my sympathies. I had much the same. And your husband?"

Jean pulled a face. "There was, when the kids were young, but he walked out on us."

"Another younger woman, eh?"

"Another woman I could have dealt with. No, another man."

"Oh how horrible. And you had never suspected?"

"Not a sign."

"So what do you do to wind down from business?"

"I'm a writer," said Jean, a smile breaking out.

"Oh! Me too! What do you write?"

"I've written a couple of romantic thrillers, but they weren't too good, so I'm working on another one now."

"I think we all experience that, it takes a couple of first goes to learn the trade. So are you in a writers' group of any sort?"

"I am, you ought to come along. We meet just over there in the library, second Friday of the month."

Nona was certain of it now. This woman would be easy to influence, she obviously needed a strong figure to guide her.

Ninth of April, 2021

"Good morning! I'm Nona Markham."

Faces around the long table in the library meeting room turned to the doorway where Nona stood. Smiles broke out.

"Nona, I'm glad you made it here," said one familiar face.

"Hi, Tanya. I couldn't not join a writers' group once I'd heard you have one in town." Nona took an empty seat and looked around the room.

"I met Nona in the supermarket," said Tanya. "She said she was writing a murder-mystery, so I told her about us and said I hoped she'd come along."

"Hey, that's where I met her too," said Jean. "Obviously we both had an effect."

"Glad you did," said a tall, slim, blonde woman. "I'm Gabrielle Greenwood, I'm writing a number of short stories for a collection."

"And I'm Carl Hitchcox, I write murder mysteries as well, but I'm working on a science fiction novel now." The thin, dark, almost bald man standing by the hot water system across the room waved at her. He was dressed in a red sweater and black jeans. Nona remembered that he was dressed the same way when she saw him walking into the meeting room the previous month.

"And I'm Mitch Langer, I'm the chairman of the group." The elderly man with grey hair, sunburned complexion and bright blue eyes offered a muscular hand with a number of brown spots on it. Nona placed him immediately as a farmer and smiled at him, sensing a character that she could work on when the time was right.

One by one, the group of eleven men and women introduced themselves as Nona studied them, feeling a welling up of excitement as she sensed the characteristics that she had experienced in the past when she could have influence.

"Tell us about your current project," said a sixties-woman at the head of the table. "I'm Caroline Collins, I'm the group secretary and I write Regency-period romances."

"It's a complex one," said Nona. "I've been intrigued for a long time by serial killers who always use the same MO, the modus operandi to kill people, and I wonder why they do. So I'm researching this first, trying to work out how somebody could kill several people but use a different MO each time and how the police would tackle the problem.”

“Interesting idea,” said a military-looking man in his fifties. He was balding though his hair was dark brown, displayed a neat moustache and was the only man in the room to have a jacket and tie. “I’m Allen Miller. I like writing about corporate crime.”

The other man in the group, a fit-looking sixties type smiled, but said nothing.

“Nona, welcome to the group,” broke in Caroline. “We have some short stories to hear from people and then Allen is scheduled to give us a workshop on computer crime which we are all looking forward to.”

“Lovely,” said Nona and sat back feeling cheerful. This was exactly what she had hoped to find.

Chapter 17 – The Eleventh of June, 2022

"I've never seen a human body cooked like a Christmas turkey before."

Doctor Mortimer, the medical examiner looked down at the body laid out on the bench in the sauna and gently prodded the shoulder. The skin was red over the entire nude corpse and the doctor's fingers left a small shallow indentation in the skin.

"Any estimate of time of death?" Melanie Carter looked uncomfortably hot under the protective coveralls. Sweat ran down her face, leaving a trace of mascara under her eyes and running into the top of the mask over her mouth. The heat had faded considerably in the sauna but the air was still damp.

"Impossible to say," replied the doctor. "Standard measurements for loss of body temperature are obviously out of the question here. When I get him on the slab, maybe I'll be able to measure dehydration rates, but I doubt I can tell you within a couple of days."

"I'll talk to the witness," said Melanie, looking relieved at finding an excuse to walk out of the heat and humidity. "The cleaning lady found him, but I'm not sure what help she'll be."

* * *

"From the degree of dehydration and the contents of his stomach, the best estimate I can give you is that he died from heat exhaustion about twenty hours before," said Mortimer. He and Melanie sat in his office.

"So that's some time on the ninth," said Melanie making an entry in her notebook. "Any sign of a medical condition that could have caused this?"

"Minor only. He'd had a stent inserted some time ago. I called his GP and he told me it had happened four years ago. There was no heart condition of note, but he was about fifteen kilos overweight, had some cholesterol issues, so he wasn't the ideal candidate to be taking saunas alone."

"What about booze?"

"His doctor said that Jensen drank regularly, but not to excess. I found just the tiniest trace of alcohol in his system, but he was so dehydrated it was no indication of how much he might have drunk before entering the sauna."

"So you'll report accidental death?"

The doctor nodded. "I can't see an alternative."

Melanie Carter stood up. "Thanks, Doc. I'll wait for your report."

"No problems. You'll get it by the end of the day."

Chapter 18 – the Tenth of June, 2022

"Alright people, the June meeting of the writer's group is now in session." Nona rang her ornate china bell and waited while the writers took their seats and arranged their papers. "Phones off everybody, let's get started."

She looked to her left. "Caroline, will you read the minutes of the last meeting?"

Caroline Collins opened her document folder, extracted the sheet and began to read.

"The meeting of the thirteenth of May began at 10:00am. The minutes of the April meeting were read and approved. There were no apologies from any members, all were present. Tanya read her story of the poisoning of an old man with a powerful narcotic and how the crime scene was left totally without clues because of the use of full protective clothing, shoe covers, gloves and mask. Coffee was taken at 11:00am followed by more discussion about the group project to produce the book. Jean Worrall announced that she would be ready to read her story at the June meeting. The meeting ended at 12:15."

"Thank you, Caroline," said Nona. "Can I have a motion to accept the minutes as read?"

Mitchell and Bella Langer shot up their hands and Caroline noted the motion and the seconding.

"Great," said Nona. "Jean, are you ready? Can we hear from you?"

Jean nodded, took out her printed story and began reading.

Ninth of June, 2022

The cleaning lady quietly opened the back door with her key, held it open for a few moments while listening and then entered, leaving the door ajar. Softly, she walked through the kitchen, along the corridor and checked the lounge. Mr Jensen was not to be seen but this was exactly as she expected. It was fifteen minutes after eight in the morning and he always took his sauna at this time.

She moved out of the lounge to the sauna next to the bedroom and saw that it was switched on, the light was on inside. She didn't look through the small window in the thick, insulated door, she knew where Jensen was.

She took the two wedges from her handbag and softly pushed them against the bottom of the door until satisfied that it was firmly jammed closed. Making sure she didn't stand up in front of the window, she moved to the heat control. It was on high, but not at the maximum. She turned the dial fully to the right and walked back to the kitchen and into the outside. She gently closed the door and locked it. She had a two kilometre walk to the main road and her bicycle where she had left it hidden among the trees, but she was fit and healthy and the walk was no problem.

Tenth of June, 2022

"But, oh my goodness, this one is still in progress," said Nona.

"Yes, it is," said Jean.

"That's clever," said Gabrielle, her immaculate blonde hair reflecting the lights from the ceiling. "No need to worry about any signs of your being there, you're always there every week anyway. So how will this end, have you written the rest of the story?"

"Oh yes," said Jean and looked down at the pages again. "I wrote it just before coming here. This took place just a little while ago."

Tenth of June, 2022

At seven in the morning, the cleaning lady let herself in at the back door as usual and checked out the house. The heat was still on high in the sauna and the wedges under the door looked undisturbed. She looked through the little window, couldn't see Jensen but she knew where he would be.

She removed the wedges, turned the heat off and opened the door. Sure enough, Jensen was lying at the foot of the door where he had desperately tried to push it open before collapsing from heat exhaustion. But after a full day in the blistering heat, she was certain he'd be dead. She knew about the stent in his artery, the fifteen kilo excess weight and the high alcohol consumption.

She went back to the lounge room, took the paper overshoes from her handbag, put them on, waited half an hour for the heat to die down then entered the sauna, stepping over the body and bent down over him.

He was certainly dead. This would now be the hardest part of the assignment, but she managed to haul Jensen up under his arms and lay him out on the bench. She went back to her cleaning materials and equipment, took off the shoe covers and folded them at the bottom of her bucket, placing some towels over them. She undid the vacuum cleaner, opened the cover that allowed the removal of the contents, slid the wedges inside and closed the device.

Then she went to the telephone.

When the police arrived, she was sitting in an armchair, hiding her face in her hands, looking in deep shock. She stayed immobile while the Medical Examiner and a young female detective examined the sauna and the body, struggling to control the worries that they might suspect foul play, but also relishing the excitement that ran through her.

Eventually the detective came and introduced herself.

"Hello Jean," said the detective, taking a companion armchair across from her. "My name is Detective Sergeant Melanie Carter. I'm sorry, but I do have to ask you some questions, will that be okay?"

The cleaning lady nodded. She gripped the mug of tea firmly, trying not to look frightened.

"Thank you," said Carter and took a small notebook and a pen from her jacket pocket. "Now, you're Jean Worrall and you clean Mr Jensen's house once a week, is that right?"

"Yes, I come in every Friday morning, usually about nine."

The detective looked at her watch. "Today is the tenth, so this is normal for you?"

The cleaning lady nodded and sipped her tea.

"So tell me what happened?"

"I came in as usual, just before eight, I have a key. Mr Jensen is a real stickler for routine, so I expected to find him in the sauna so I could put the crockery from his breakfast into the dish washer while I started on his bathroom. But there was no crockery in the kitchen."

"That's not normal?"

"No, it's not. I know he takes a sauna every morning after breakfast, it's almost a ritual. So I looked through the little window in the door and that's when I saw him on the bench. One arm was drooped down touching the floor and that didn't look natural, so I turned off the heat and opened the door. He didn't move and I just knew he was dead. He must have been there since the day before. That's when I called you."

"You didn't touch him?"

The cleaning lady shook her head and pulled a face. "He looked horrible, his skin was all red, I just knew he was dead."

"It must have been a dreadful shock for you," said Carter. "I think you should go home now, come into

the police station tomorrow morning to give us a full statement. Will that be alright?"

The woman nodded, placed the mug on the coffee table and stood up. "I'll see you tomorrow," she said. She tried not to smile as she picked up her cleaning gear, the vacuum cleaner, got into her car and drove home.

Tenth of June, 2022

"And you think that's how it will work out tomorrow morning?" asked Caroline.

Jean nodded. "Almost certainly. The only worry was that they might examine the vacuum cleaner and my bucket, but it was almost certain that they'd assume accidental death. I got away with that quite well."

"And how are you feeling now?" Nona was smiling cheerfully.

"I must admit, there's a mixture of worry and excitement. I remember somebody once said that waiting to see if anyone suspects a murder and one day the cops will appear at your door was a real buzz and that's what I'm feeling right now."

"You'll let us all know tomorrow, after you've given your statement to the cops, won't you?" said Tanya.

"You can be sure of that," said Jean.

"Alright," said Tanya. "Before we break for coffee, who's next in the hot seat?"

"Er, that's me," said Caroline.

"Great," said Nona. "What's going to be your method?"

Caroline looked down at her hands. "I'm sorry," she said. "I've gone along with this so far, but I just can't do it. I can't kill somebody."

The room went silent.

"Alright Caroline," said Nona. "We do understand. Maybe you'll be able to do it later. So, who can step up and take Caroline's place?"

"I can do it," said Ollie. "I'll have a story for you for next month."

"Wonderful, Ollie," said Nona. "Let's have coffee."

The meeting broke up to pour coffee and eat some chocolate biscuits that Nona had provided. Caroline Collins walked out of the room.

Chapter 19 – Nona Markham

Fourteenth of May, 2021

"Mitch, Bella, do you have time for a coffee?"

The May meeting of the writers' group had just finished and Nona had manoeuvred herself next to the Langers. She was not surprised by the reaction. Bella almost glowed and Mitch smiled with obvious pleasure.

"That would be lovely," said Bella. "I was saying to Mitch only a few days ago that we'd like to have a chat with you. You seem such an interesting person."

Mitch nodded, the smile still obvious. "There's a coffee shop in the Mall," he said. "Why don't we meet there in ten minutes?"

"Sounds good," said Nona. She looked forward to working her goddess spells on these two. She knew it would be easy.

Nona looked deep into the eyes of Bella and Mitch and saw the familiar slight glazing over as both of them came under her spell. It had taken just twenty minutes.

"I've always thought that committing a murder would be an incredible thrill," said Bella. "Just the thought of snuffing out a life, knowing nobody could ever find out and then seeing the police going by, knowing they don't suspect you at all, gosh, what a buzz that must be."

"It's not difficult to hide the killing," said Nona. "Even the regular cop shows tell you how to do it. You see those crime scene investigators, they put on all the protective clothing, the gloves, the hood, the shoe covers, they don't mess up the scene at all. So if you wear all that stuff, you know perfectly well you won't be found out. And then you just make sure you thoroughly clean up anything you used. Have you ever watched a show called *'Silent Witness'*?"

"Ooh yes, we both love it," said Bella.

"Well, that shows you what the forensic pathologists look for, so all you have to do is make sure they don't find it," said Nona. She watched the faces in front of her, saw the building excitement and resolve and she knew she had them. "For example," she continued, "if you shoot somebody, you know they'll find the bullet, but if they never find the gun, they can't prove anything or identify anyone. Then you also wear the same protective clothing to make sure there's no gun residue on your skin or clothing and then you burn all the protective stuff. There'd be no way at all of being found out."

Over the next fifteen minutes, Nona gave explicit instructions on committing murders in several ways while leaving no clue at all. When they parted company, she was certain she had two willing servants of the Sister-Goddesses.

Eleventh of June, 2021

Paul Johnson finished putting his notebook and pens back in the briefcase he always used and looked up in surprise. The June meeting of the group had finished and he had exchanged a few words with Gabrielle about the short story she had read to the group. But as she left, Paul realised that Nona was still sitting at the end of the long table in the meeting room of the library.

"Paul, could we talk a little?" she asked.

He felt a small surge of anxiety and swallowed. He didn't talk much to anyone these days and the writers' group was his only social engagement.

"Sure," he said and stayed standing.

She smiled at him and gestured at a seat. Reluctantly, he sat down across the table from her.

"You don't talk much, Paul," she said.

He didn't reply.

"Is there anything I could do to help?" She was staring straight into his eyes and he couldn't look away. There was something in her that drew him like a magnet and it caused a twinge of sickness in his bowels. She reminded him of the officers at military training...

"Nobody can help," he said. "It's PTSD, I have it badly."

"And the writing helps?"

He nodded.

"What caused it? Do you mind me asking?"

He kept staring into her eyes, unable to look away even as the image of the face exploding just an arm's length away, the bullet leaving a wreck of blood and bone as it left the back of the man's head returned to his mind as it did so often.

"I can't," he said.

"It must have been terrible," she said.

Paul began to feel he could trust her, like he could trust an officer, she would keep him safe, never let him do anything harmful.

"It was," he said in a croak, feeling the trembles run up and down his body.

"And you want revenge," she said. Her voice was hypnotic, her face filled his universe.

"Yes."

"I can show you how to do it and never be found out."

"I need to know."

Twenty minutes later, Paul watched her leave the room. He sat a while longer, feeling well satisfied that now he could wipe out the pain, the memory of the blood and brains exploding in front of him. He trusted this woman.

9th July, 2021

"Carl, I liked the thing you read today."

Carl Hitchcox looked up in surprise. Nona hadn't said anything to him since she had joined the group beyond the usual morning greetings and he had felt intimidated by her.

"Well, thank you," he said.

"It was a chapter from your science-fiction novel, you said?"

"Yes, it was."

"But I remember the day I joined the group that you said you've written murder mystery novels?"

"That's true, but I wanted to try my hand at something different."

As they talked, Carl felt strangely disconnected from the world. All the others from the group had left the room and he was alone with Nona. He found he was looking into her eyes and they seemed huge. He couldn't really feel his hands and feet, the rest of him felt loose, not solid, almost as if he was made of powder and blowing away in a wind.

"When you were writing the murder mysteries, Carl, did you ever wonder what it would be like actually killing somebody?"

A small rush of excitement ran through him. He realised that he had thought of that at the time when he was writing.

"Actually, I did," he said. "I used to think how powerful it must feel to have somebody totally under your control, their lives depending only on your whim."

"How did the killers in your stories do it?"

Her eyes seemed to have grown even larger and Carl felt he was floating in a dream, remembering the scenes of violence he had created.

"One of them was a sniper, shooting somebody from a distance," he said. "My favourite was when the killer cut the brake cable in the victim's car, knowing she would have a winding hill road to go down with a ravine on one side."

"Not close up, with a knife or a handgun?"

"No, I found that quite horrible, all that blood and gore and a struggle. No, a long distance killing was best, like that last one, where the killer could see the effects of his work and watch while it happened."

"I bet I could show you how to do something like that and not leave a trace for the cops to find."

He found himself entranced by the idea. Somehow, the horrors of killing somebody faded under the rush of excitement that he might actually be able to do as he had dreamed, watch somebody die as the result of his work.

"Just think how much better your book would be if you had actually experienced something like that," Nona said.

"It would be so much more realistic," he murmured, almost lost in the fantasy.

"We'll talk further about it," she said and stood up.

Carl stayed where he was, still lost in a world of imagination, not noticing that she had left.

What an amazing woman, he thought. *I really must talk more to her about how to do something like this.*

Chapter 20 – The Fifteenth of June, 2022

Nona was having a seriously bad day. She could not drive from her mind the conversation she'd had many weeks ago with Allen Miller. The memory of being unable to influence another person and drag them into her world had been a recurring nightmare ever since. Many times, she had needed a sleeping pill to try for a night's sleep and that had usually left her dopy and sluggish the next day.

But she knew what she needed to lift her spirits.

Nona watched Gabrielle park her car in the space before the shopping mall and walk in through the sliding doors. She got out of her own car and followed the tall, slender blonde. She saw her walk into a watchmaker's shop and waited until she saw Gabrielle about to leave after a short discussion with the man behind the counter and handing her watch over, getting it back a few minutes later, presumably with a new battery. Nona timed her walk up to the shop and got it right.

"Gabrielle! How nice to see you."

"Nona! Same here. Do you shop here?"

"Nowhere else. Have you got time for a coffee? I'd love to talk with you outside of the writers' meetings."

"Sounds good, I'd like that too."

A few minutes later, coffees served in the regular café that Nona had used for other meetings, she smiled at Gabrielle.

"I do like the stories you've been reading," she said. "You certainly give men a hard time."

"They deserve it," said Gabrielle. "I've not met a man yet who didn't turn out to be a wanker."

"Bad experiences, eh?"

"Two terrible marriages and several miserable relationships. I gave up on men a long time ago."

"I can sympathise," said Nona. "I've had much the same. But the trouble is, we're still healthy women, so what do we do?"

"Can I tell you a secret?" said Gabrielle and leaned forward on the table. "I've made out with another woman a couple of times."

Nona felt a surge of satisfaction. She had been right in her impression of Gabrielle and she was on safe ground now. "Really?" she said. "How was it?"

"Well, to be honest, with the help of a couple of toys, it was pretty good. I got better orgasms than any man has ever given me, not that I got many that way."

Nona smiled. "I've done the same. I rather enjoyed it."

A moment of silence passed as they looked into each other's eyes.

"Let's go back to my place," whispered Nona. "I've got some toys at home that will make you scream."

Chapter 21 – Melanie Carter, the First of July, 2022

Melanie got to her apartment soon after nine that evening, feeling severely stressed. She recognised the mood, it hit her every few months. She was lonely, still struggling to be seen as an intelligent, competent woman in what was essentially a man's world. Promotion to Sergeant had been rapid and helpful in reducing some of the stress, but it was still severe. The extra responsibilities given to her as the leading crime investigation officer on the recent murders were exhilarating but added to the stress.

"Scott, my love, you were the only man in my life I've ever been able to trust," she said aloud as she poured a glass of gin and tonic and added a slice of lime. "Why did you have to leave me so soon?"

She finished the drink, poured another one and went to her computer. Twenty minutes later, she had booked her flight to Brisbane for the next morning and a hotel in the City. She made a light meal of baked salmon with a salad, drank a glass of wine with it and went to bed, feeling an old warmth and excitement building up in her. She had two days leave and she intended to use them as she had a few times in the past.

* * *

At eight that night in her hotel, she selected the short red dress, high-heeled shoes, stockings and a diamond necklace that her mother had given her as a graduation present. She let her hair down to its regular length, down to the nape of her neck.

She dressed and stared at herself in the mirror.

"You're an absolute knock-out Melanie," she said. "Tonight, sexy Melanie gets set free, Sergeant Carter gets locked away."

Twenty minutes later, she was in a cab, heading for the night life of Fortitude Valley.

She sensed the momentary silence as she walked into the room, well aware that every head turned in her direction.

She went to the bar and ordered a gin and tonic almost feeling the eyes studying her. She took a stool and waited. It didn't take long.

"On your own?" said the voice alongside her. She turned her head and studied him. Medium height, thirties, thinning hair, reasonable shape she thought.

But before she could reply, two other men had joined them, obviously friends and the conversation expanded.

For a while, she enjoyed the obvious competition for her attention while she studied the three men. Finally, she decided that the one called Derek had the best body and that was really all she was concerned with. She smiled at him, rubbed his arm and slid off the stool.

Ten minutes later, she and a totally astonished man were in a cab heading to his apartment in the West End. She followed him in, took his hand and said firmly, "Where's the bedroom?"

* * *

Six in the morning. She looked over at the sleeping man. He had performed well, she thought, kept her well engaged for a long time, showed imagination and energy and had satisfied her.

She slipped out of bed, quickly dressed and left the house, closing the door gently behind her. On her return to the hotel, she took a shower, changed to more casual clothing and ordered room service breakfast. She spent the day as a tourist, took the ferry to the zoo and strolled around the enclosures.

That night, she repeated the previous evening, this time going to a more upper-class club in the Valley. This evening, the man seemed older, possibly in his forties but displayed no lack of energy or commitment to satisfying her and she returned to her hotel soon after six, ignoring his sleepy protests.

That afternoon, she flew back to Canberra, found her car and drove home. She felt she could last another few months now.

Chapter 22 – The Eighth of July, 2022

Nona rang the bell and the writers' group members took their seats.

"Okay, phones off everybody! Welcome to the July meeting of our writers' group. Caroline is not here today and as you know, she appears to have pulled out of our arrangement. So we'll omit the reading of last month's minutes and go straight to our next story. Ollie, are you ready?"

Ollie extracted his sheets of paper and began reading.

Caroline screamed. "Ollie, what the hell are you doing?"

Ollie didn't reply, but swung the baseball bat hard. It smashed into the side of Caroline's head and she dropped to the ground emitting a single small sob.

"Whoa! Hang on, Ollie," said Allen. "You're going to kill Caroline?"

"You bet," said Ollie. "She's pulled out of our arrangement, she'd probably go to the police at any time. She has to be put out of action."

"But that was a month ago," said Jean. "If she was going to call the cops, we'd know about it by now."

"Sure," said Ollie. "But that's no guarantee that she won't at some time."

"Yes, but Caroline? She's one of us." Jean looked distressed.

"No, I agree with Ollie," said Carl. "She'd become a danger. It's poetic justice to knock her off. Do it tomorrow on the ninth and I think you have an excellent new chapter for the book."

"I'll go along with that," said Mitchell. "She has to go and this fits the program very well."

"I agree also," said Gabrielle. "But you know what? Has it occurred to anyone here that what we're doing is pretty ugly? I mean, we're killing people to create a book? Is this really rational?"

"Getting second thoughts also, Gabrielle?" said Mitchell. "Do we have to make you a victim as well?"

"Oh hell no," said Gabrielle. "I enjoyed my part in this and all the people we've knocked off were pretty useless specimens, old and frail and no further value to society, but I just wonder about us."

"Well don't," said Nona. "We're being creative, we're doing society a favour and the end book could be a real best seller and make us some serious money. Ollie, why don't you continue?"

Ollie nodded.

Ollie bent over the body. Caroline's face was covered in blood, one eye was hanging onto her cheek and several teeth were broken. She wasn't breathing at all.

"Ollie, you don't know your own strength," he said. "That was pretty good."

He walked back along the river path on which he had tracked Caroline, having watched her for a few nights and seen that she took this walk every evening. When he reached the road, he stripped off the protective coveralls, the shoe covers and the gloves, stuffed them into a garbage bag he had brought along with him. He stripped the baseball bat of the covering of cling-wrap that he had put on it the day before and stuffed that into the garbage bag as well before getting into his car and driving home. It was a cold night and he had lit the wood fire before leaving. The contents of the bag would be easily consumed.

"Why the cling wrap, Ollie?" asked Bella.

"Just in case anyone decides to look at my baseball bat," said Ollie. "I've watched all these cop shows and I thought that perhaps a small splinter might be left behind, or maybe the varnish on the bat could be identified somehow if a trace is left on Caroline's head."

"Clever," said Carl. "It's tiny things like that that can give somebody away. You watch these programs like *'Silent Witness'* and it seems even the tiniest clue can be the give-away."

"Well done, Ollie," said Nona. "Good luck tomorrow night. Let's have our coffee break."

* * *

Tenth of July, 2022

"It's our old favourite, Mr Blunt Instrument," said Doctor Mortimer, kneeling by the side of the woman's head. "A really savage blow, lots of damage."

"Any idea of what sort of blunt instrument?" asked Melanie. She was struggling to hide her distress at the appalling sight on the river bank. Two other uniformed officers were keeping people away from the scene. A police photographer was taking photographs of the horror and immediate surrounding areas.

"Pretty sure," said Mortimer. "I've seen a couple of similar sights in my time, I'd say this was a baseball bat. It's a pretty lethal weapon."

"And when?"

"It's been a cold night, but the best estimate I can give you is about eight to twelve hours."

"So sometime last night, the ninth?"

"Probably."

Something nagged at Melanie's thoughts at that, but she couldn't identify it. "You'll call me when you've finished the postmortem?"

"I always do, Sergeant."

"I know. It's happening a bit too often for my comfort. Can we move her now?"

The doctor nodded and stood up. Melanie waved at the two crime scene officers who had been carefully studying the area.

"Nothing Sarge," said one. "Same as the others, no footprints, not a single clue to be had. Somebody sure as hell knows how to cover up their tracks, probably wearing the same gear we've got on."

"Okay, check up back along the path, see if there's anything, especially at the road. The perp may have left a car there."

"Will do, Sarge, but this bloke knows how to hide, so it's probably unlikely we'll see anything."

"I know, but we do it by the book."

* * *

"Sergeant, this is Doctor Mortimer."

"Yes, Doc, what do you have for me?"

"Definitely a baseball bat. The measurement of the impression is exactly that of a full-sized baseball bat. The contents of the stomach were of an evening meal, a small lamb chop, some salad and a single potato, eaten ten hours before, so the first estimate was right, this occurred about ten last night."

"No other signs?"

"One tiny thing. I found some minute traces of very thin plastic film around the wound. It looks like the sort of stuff you wrap food in for storage, like cling wrap or something similar."

"That's unusual."

"But quite clever. It would have kept any possible splinter from breaking away and it would also have stopped any trace of varnish from the bat being left behind. I don't know if that varnish varies at all between bat makers, but it sure stopped any real identification of the weapon."

"Somebody's really worked hard at covering this up, Doc. He or she must have been wearing protective clothing, including shoe covers and gloves, just like we scene of crime officers were wearing. There was a hell of a lot of blood on the grass, there must have been quite a bit on the killer.”

“Almost certainly a he, Sergeant. That blow was horrendous. Even an average man would have been pushed to hit like that. I’d say a body-builder type or at least a professional athlete.”

“Thanks, Doc. You’ll send me the report?”

“It’s already on your computer, Sergeant.”

* * *

“This is insane, Sir. It’s the third killing this year, different MOs but all with the same characteristics, absolutely without a sign left behind.”

“You’re certain they all wore protective clothing?” Detective Inspector Russell Comley’s voice was loud in the phone speaker on Melanie’s desk.

“Yes sir, the whole lot, coveralls, shoe covers, gloves, everything. It’s not hard to get, you can buy the stuff at Bunnings any time.”

“But different methods. That almost sounds like a serial killer deliberately using a different method each time, but it’s most unusual.”

“Yes, I don’t know if there has ever been a serial killer who has used poison, a knife and then a baseball bat, but I’ll do some research. But I’m more inclined to think this is somehow coordinated.”

“You think it’s different people, all using their own methods but coordinating on hiding the clues?”

“It’s all I can think of for now, Sir.”

“I’m inclined to agree with you. Tell you what, contact the Homicide people in Parramatta, see if they can shine any light on this. Meanwhile, keep it up,

Melanie, don't let the bastards grind you down. We often find the perps through their errors."

"Thank you, Sir, I'll do as you say."

"Of course you will, it's a direct order."

The Inspector's voice held the trace of a laugh as the conversation ended.

Chapter 23 – Alex Welland, Tenth of July, 2022

"Would you please count up to ten, madam?"

Alex held the breathalyser by the elderly woman's mouth and she did as instructed. He looked at the gauge on the instrument and stood up.

"Thank you, madam, please carry on." He stepped away as the white Mercedes gently moved back into the traffic stream. He and his patrol car partner, Marie Hebert had drawn random breath test duties this morning with four other officers and the day had been slow. Nobody had shown any signs of alcohol on their breath in this, the first hour of the duty.

Two more vehicles were waved down to the roadside where they were waiting. A young man in a smart suit, driving a two-seat sports car coloured a brilliant red was clearly unworried by the test and greeted Alex cheerfully.

"Having a good day in paradise, officer?" he asked.

Alex had to grin in response to the question.

"A bit boring, to be honest," he said. "I don't suppose you've been boozing all night?"

"Not a chance," said the man and counted up to ten with the gadget by his mouth.

"Good man, you're clear," said Alex and waved him on.

A white Subaru Forester pulled up alongside him and the window was lowered. Almost immediately, Alex felt the tension in the vehicle. The driver looked to be in his mid-thirties, dressed in jeans and a red golf shirt. He had a thin build and the tattoos on both arms extended from the wrists to way past the short sleeves. It was the girl alongside him that drew Alex's attention. She looked in her mid-teens, dressed in a short black skirt and a white blouse and she seemed frightened.

Alex looked back at where Marie was standing by the roadside, ready to wave in the next car. She caught his eye and understood the message. She put down the sign she was carrying and moved to where she could observe the passengers, talking softly on her radio.

"Been drinking today, Sir?" asked Alex.

"No," replied the man, staring straight ahead, both hands gripping the steering wheel tightly.

"Would you please count up to ten," said Alex, placing the breathalyser by the man's mouth.

As he did, Alex saw Marie move closer to where she could see the girl more clearly and he saw that she was staring at the officer.

"Thank you, Sir," said Alex and leaned into the car, taking a deep breath. The smell was faint, but clear. He stood back, looked at Marie and she nodded to him. There was obviously something seriously wrong.

"Would you just move your car over there?" said Alex, pointing to a spot a few metres further along, immediately behind the second patrol car.

"Why, what's wrong?" asked the man, looking at Alex for the first time.

"Nothing, Sir," he replied. "Just a routine check for statistical purposes."

The man looked tense but did as he was asked.

Marie came up to Alex. "The licence plate says it's Colin Norton," she said. "He's got form. Bit of drug dealing, a bit of thuggery. The girl is frightened shitless, almost begging me for help, but daren't say a thing. He could be armed."

"His clothes smell of gunshot,' said Alex. "Something very nasty has happened. Is it his car?"

"Yes, and he lives down near Queanbeyan."

She was about to say more when his radio buzzed.

"Two-Seven, wrap up the RBT. Gunshot homicide reported, one fatality, address follows."

Marie and Alex stared at each other.

"Whoops," she said and waved the other officers over. "Guys, give us cover. That bloke in the car smells of gunshot, the girl is terrified, could be a hostage and there's a shooting reported."

"Well, shit eh?" said one of the officers.

Alex and Marie began walking slowly back to the Subaru, both of them keeping their right hands near their holsters.

Norton suddenly saw them coming, reached down and pulled up a revolver.

"Don't be silly, Colin," shouted Alex. "There are six of us, all armed. Put the gun down."

"Fuck off!" shouted Norton and fired the revolver.

Alex felt a breath of wind pass his cheek. He dropped to the ground, rolled the four or five metres to the car, rose to his feet and his pistol was pointed straight into Norton's eye. It had happened so fast that the gunman still had his hand extended pointing at where Alex had been standing.

"Don't even think about it," said Alex. "There are six guns pointed at you."

Norton's face was white. One of the other officers walked up from behind the car and took the revolver away. Marie went to the other side and opened the door, gently helping the girl out as she burst into a flood of tears.

"Christ, Alex," said the officer with the confiscated gun. "That was a bit silly."

"I know," said Alex and was sick on the ground.

"Better out than in," said the officer.

"Bloody oath," said Alex, breathing deeply.

"That shooting near Queanbeyan," said Marie as she climbed into the patrol car. "It's the same address as Colin Norton's."

"Okay," said Alex. He turned to his colleagues. "Call in the arrest, take this guy to the station and get him processed. And the other two, take care of this young lady, have the doctor check her out and look after her until we get back to talk to her."

A few moment later, he and Marie were on the highway, siren blaring.

* * *

"He can't be more than sixteen," said Marie, looking down at the body in the hallway of the dingy house. The boy lay on his side, blood from his mouth spread over the thin carpet. Three bullet holes were in his tee-shirt, ringed by blood.

"No exit wounds," said Marie. "The bullets are still in there."

"What's the betting that they match the revolver we got?" said Alex.

"Not taking that bet," said Marie. Neither of them moved far from where they were standing after entering the house through the front door that was open on their arrival. They had no protective clothing to stop them corrupting the crime scene and they had to wait for scene-of-crime investigators to arrive.

A few minutes later, four people entered, already wearing coveralls, hoods, masks and shoe covers, closely followed by Doctor Mortimer.

"Okay, Alex, leave it with us," said one. "Where's the gun?"

"Back at the station. One of the others took it in with the suspect."

"We'll tell you all about it when we can," said the medical examiner and Alex and Marie returned to their vehicle and drove back to the station.

"Cut and dried," said Detective Inspector Russell Comley later that day. "The dead kid was seventeen-year old Ken Richards, regular drug dealer. The girl in the car was Irene Hollings, his girlfriend. It looks like

Colin Norton was trying to take the drug turf for himself and killed Richards. There were four bullets missing from the revolver, the bullets in the kid's body are being tested now to see if they came from the gun, but it's pretty obvious. The girl said Norton had pulled her with him and said he'd kill her if she said anything."

"All pretty ugly," said Alex.

"She certainly was terrified," said Marie. "She had every reason to believe him."

"And there's an extra dimension to this, that you didn't see," said Comley. "After you'd gone, the scene-of-crime people checked the rest of the house and guess what? There were two teenage girls in the other bedrooms. Norton was running a small-scale brothel. We've got the girls safe and we're checking them out now."

"Shit, some people are just rotten," said Alex.

"Good call on the gunshot smell," said Comley. "But I have to say it, Alex, you were a bloody fool approaching him like that. That was against all standard procedures."

The two constables said nothing.

"Despite that, you and Marie handled that very well and it opened up some more dirt to clean out. So go and write up your report, I'll issue a commendation on you both."

"Thank you, Sir."

"So don't just sit there, you two. Shove off and write that report."

"We just left, Sir," said Alex and the two constables left the room, a wide grin on Alex's face, a copy of the one displayed by the Inspector.

* * *

Nona reviewed her notes. Next month's episode was by Allen Miller. Of all the people in the group, she had the most confidence that Miller would fulfill his commitment to the letter and would need no reinforcement. She also was uncomfortably aware that Miller was a completely closed book to her, she could not influence him at all. He frightened her.

Feeling relief, she decided not to visit him before the killing day, and she was intrigued by just what he would do.

* * *

Alex Welland knew there was something missing about the shooting episode. It nagged at him all day and he was quiet when Marie tried to get him to talk about the patrol they were on. But she had experienced these silent periods before and knew better than to try and break them.

"See you tomorrow," she said as they returned to the station and parked the patrol car for the evening shift to take over.

Alex nodded and walked into the station. He made a coffee in the canteen and sat and pondered the question. What had he missed? He got up and went to the white board that stood in the open office where the uniformed officers usually worked and began to lay out his thoughts. After twenty minutes of reviewing the events, it began to dawn on him.

The house where the shooting had occurred. Who owned that house? It was the address shown on Colin Norton's car registration. Did he rent the place or own it? Alex felt it unlikely that a drug dealer with a police record could have obtained a mortgage without a regular employment history and getting a formal rental would be difficult for the same reason. Sensing a direction to take, Alex went to his desk where a computer terminal stood, as with all the desks. He began the search with property licence details with the local council. Within moments he had the details displayed.

"Interesting," he murmured. "Who the hell is Kensington Mutual?"

Finding the answer was equally simple. The corporate structures of companies were public domain details and Kensington Mutual was displayed as a privately held company with interests in property, finance and a pair of companies specialising in pest inspections. It showed ownership of six houses in the region. Six directors were listed. Alex didn't recognise any of the names. He noted them down and switched to the police records data base.

The first three names provided no information. But the fourth did.

James Parker had some interesting data attached to the name.

"Well, James," said Alex aloud. "You're quite a naughty boy, aren't you? Breaking and entering in your teens, a couple of Grievous Bodily Harm cases, a bit of DUI. I wonder if that directorship is legal?"

He scrolled down and found some further comments.

"Suspicions, but unproven of loan-sharking, eh? That's not nice. And the same with prostitution, especially of under-age girls. This is getting ugly, James. Are you doing this all on your own?"

Further down the file, Parker's familial connections were listed. Parents were dead, there was one sister, he was unmarried and there were three uncles shown. Alex entered each name in turn and found nothing in the police data base. He pulled out of the system and called up a regular search engine for the names.

He glanced at his watch. It was after nine in the evening and he was getting hungry.

"Just these three," he muttered, "and then take-away Chinese on the way home."

The second name made him sit up.

Timothy Bradshaw was the director of one of Australia's largest banks. The picture showed a stern-faced, slightly over-weight man in his fifties, a graduate in Economics of Melbourne University and a post-graduate Business Degree five years later from the same establishment. The name was also one of the directors of Kensington Mutual.

"Well, well, well," said Alex. "What do we have here?"

He wrote a short summary to hand to Melanie in the morning, closed down the computer and went to his car, feeling cheerful about the evening's work. The

Chinese take-away would go down really well, he decided.

* * *

"Great work," said Melanie. "Nobody would have followed up those connections before the shooting, that was good initiative."

"Thanks, Sarge," said Alex. "It was just nagging me, a feeling that a murder was only part of the story."

"I gave your notes to D.I. Comley. He said well done also. Lots of good Brownie points in your dossier. He's passed them on to the Director of Public Prosecutions in Sydney, they suspect all those houses are being used as brothels, the entire board of directors of that company will be facing charges."

Alex laughed. "I must admit, Sarge, I enjoyed finding that stuff out."

The door opened and Marie leaned her head in.

"Good morning, Sarge," she said. "Alex, we're due on the road."

Alex stood up and gave an exaggerated sigh. "Just another day of shootings, DUI arrests, high speed chases and stuff. Dead boring. I'll have to work at it to stay awake."

Melanie laughed and waved him away.

Chapter 24 – The Ninth of August, 2022

At ten in the morning, Peter Fleming discovered that he was dead.

The first indicator of his death was when he tried to log into the internet on his computer.

"Incorrect Identification," said the message on his screen.

"What?" he said aloud and re-entered the details.

The result was the same.

"This is goddamned silly," he muttered and picked up the telephone to call his internet provider.

The phone line was dead. No dial tone, nothing. He rebooted the modem and the computer and after the few minutes that it took, he tried again.

No dial tone. No internet service.

He picked up his mobile phone, tried to dial the internet provider but the result was the same. No dial tone.

"What the fuck has happened?" he said with considerable volume. "Has war broken out? Have the aliens landed?"

As he spoke the power went off.

"This is fucking insane," he said, even louder. He went out to the fuse box on the back deck and raised the lid. All the fuses indicated "On" but there was no power. He picked up the mobile phone again but as before, was unable to call the electricity supply company with the dead phone. Trying to suppress the rising panic, he decided he would drive round to the supermarket and do some food shopping. "Maybe this whole shitstorm will have faded by the time I get home," he said aloud, working hard to convince himself and not succeeding.

The car started at first kick. "Well thank Christ that worked," he said, backed out into the road and drove the short distance to the small shopping centre. There was little that he wanted and it was only fifteen minutes before he placed the shopping basket by the self-serve check-out terminal and fed his purchases past the scanner. At the end, he extracted his customer card and placed that before the scanner.

Instead of the usual displayed message, *'Your card has been accepted,'* the little screen said, *'Your account is not recognised. Please see the customer service desk.'*

"Oh fuck you," he said under his breath and pressed the *'Pay'* option, placed his credit card against the reader.

'Invalid account,' said the message.

Peter found his heart was beating and he was breathing hard.

"Can I help you?" asked the young girl who monitored the self-service check-out terminals.

"My God, I hope so," said Peter with difficulty. "I've been shopping here for six years but suddenly my customer card is rejected and my credit card is declined."

"That's weird," said the girl. She passed her security card over the scanner and entered a code. The screen displayed a message.

'Customer account closed.'

"Never seen that before," she said, took out her mobile phone and began to speak with a supervisor. She looked briefly at Peter a couple of times and seemed embarrassed when she put her phone back in her pocket.

"Mr Fleming, your account was closed last night, according to the computer. My supervisor said that they had received a note from your doctor that you were dead."

"I'm what?"

"That's what he said."

"Okay, let me leave these things here, I'll go and draw cash out of the ATM outside."

"No problems. I'll look after your bag."

He strode out of the supermarket to the line of ATMs by the entrance. He inserted his card into the slot and waited to be asked to enter his four-digit identification code.

'Invalid Account,' said the screen. *'Card retained for security purposes.'*

"Oh my God, what is happening?" he begged an unseen divinity. He felt tears start running down his cheek. He took a seat on the bench inside the doors and tried to calm himself. After a few minutes, he got up, went to his car and drove round to the bank. A young man sat at the customer service desk and he smiled and stood up as Peter approached him.

"My bank account has been closed, my credit card has been cancelled since yesterday. Can you explain why?"

"Please sit down," said the young man. "I'm sure we can clear this up. Your name?"

"Peter Fleming."

"Can I have your credit card?"

"No, your ATM swallowed it when I tried to draw money out a short while ago."

"Okay, let me find you on the computer." The man tapped a few entries and studied the screen. "Mr Fleming, your account was closed down yesterday after we received a death certificate from your GP, Doctor Holland."

Peter felt his insides churn.

"A death certificate? Do I look dead?"

"No, indeed you don't. Something horrible has gone wrong, there's no doubt."

"Can you somehow give me some money from my account? I'm without cash."

"If there had been any money in the account, we probably could. But the account had been cleaned out before the death notice was received."

"What!" Peter felt stunned.

"Mr Fleming, does our bank manager know you personally?"

"I've been banking with this organisation for over twenty years, six at this branch. We've met a few times."

"Would you write your signature on this paper, please? Give me four or five examples."

Peter wrote several examples of his signature on the paper and handed it back.

"Good. Let me check." The man consulted his screen and took several long looks at both the screen and the paper. "That's definitely your signature," he said. "Can I see your driver's licence?"

The customer service officer stared hard again at the licence, comparing the picture with Peter's face. "And that appears to be you. Please wait."

He got up, went through the security doors and vanished. Twenty minutes later, he returned.

"I've talked to the manager," he said. "Identity theft has happened before, but we've never encountered this degree of it. But we do know you and I'm sure it can be cleared up. The manager has authorised me to give you a hundred dollars emergency funding, as we expect that your account will be returned eventually. We've informed the police and they'll be in touch."

"That's a godsend," said Peter. "I'll go and see my doctor right away."

"Good idea," said the customer service officer.

Peter returned to his car and began the drive home. But the nightmare was not over. He saw the police car pull in behind him and felt his throat run dry as the flashing lights came on. He pulled in to the side of the road, wound down his window and waited.

The peaked hat leaned by the window.

"Good morning sir, do you know why we stopped you?"

"No officer, I don't. I was within the speed limit and I don't think I did anything wrong."

"That's correct sir, but there's a problem. We scan every car's licence plate automatically and we got a warning that this vehicle is no longer legally registered."

"Oh my god, not again."

"Again what, sir?"

"Officer, since this morning, my electricity service has been cut, my internet service is cancelled, my telephone account is dead and my bank account has been frozen. And now this."

The officer seemed undisturbed. "May I have your driver's licence, please?"

Peter reached into his back pocket and hauled out his wallet, extracted his licence and handed it over. The officer took it back to his car and sat there for a few minutes before returning.

"And that's not your only problem sir. This licence was cancelled yesterday."

"Oh my god." Peter hid his face in his hands and leaned against the steering wheel. Dimly, he heard the officer's radio click.

"Control to two-four."

The officer moved away from the car as he held a short conversation with the controller. Then he returned.

"It seems we've been informed of the banking difficulty, probably some form of identity theft. But the problem remains. Legally this car cannot be driven without registration or insurance and your licence is invalid. It will have to stay here for now. But my office said I can drive you home."

"That will be a help, Officer." Peter got out of the car, locked it and followed the officer to the patrol car. He took the back seat, received a nod from the woman behind the steering wheel and waited to move off.

"I've heard of identity theft,' said the first officer, "but never to this degree. It might take some time to clear up."

"Will you drop me at my doctor's office?" Peter felt unwilling to discuss the situation further.

A few minutes later, he entered the clinic where he had been a patient for six years since moving to the small town.

"I certainly didn't issue a death certificate," said Doctor Holland. "Let me look at your record." He keyed a code into his computer and stared at the screen. "Bloody hell, but there is one here. Peter, I have no idea how this happened. Somebody has clearly hacked the system."

"Somebody bloody brilliant," mumbled Peter. "My bank, the electricity company, the internet company, the supermarket, driver's licence, car rego, I've been killed off totally. I don't even want to think about my tax file, passport and I probably can't even get into my club to have lunch!"

"I'll contact all the agencies involved and keep the record for the cops. Will you get me your account numbers for everything?"

"I'll have to go home to get them."

"As soon as you can."

Peter walked home in a daze. When he got in, there was no power in the house. He fell on the bed and sobbed his heart out.

* * *

Twelfth of August, 2022

"Just brilliant," said Nona. "I would not have thought of an identity killing like that. What a brilliant concept that was."

"It was amazing," said Jean Worrall. "But could somebody really hack into all those systems?"

"I certainly could," replied Allen Miller.

"That's interesting," said Carl Hitchcox. "Just what is your background, Allen? You've never told us what you did in the USA."

"Let's just say that I did some amazing break-ins. Maybe one day, I'll tell you about them."

"So what will happen to Fleming?" asked Bella Langer.

"It will take several court orders to restore his life. He'll have to bunk in with a friend for maybe three weeks while it happens and borrow some cash from him, but eventually he'll get his life back."

"Well, it was bloody clever," said Tanya. "When we started this project, I would never have thought of a digital killing like that! Well done, Allen."

"Okay, next month's project," said Nona. "Who's in the hot seat?"

* * *

"Like I told you, it's not really needed to kill somebody physically."

Allen Miller was standing over Nona as she packed up her notes. She shrank back a little, remembering the nightmares, knowing this was her first failure in domination.

"You certainly made your point," she said. "Where did you learn to hack into computer systems like that?"

"That will remain my secret. Just remember, if I can do it to one person, I can do it to others."

She shifted in her chair. "Allen, are you trying to threaten me?"

He smiled, a cold, thin smile. "No, I'm not. But that was just to remind you, I know what you are. Don't try any of those party tricks on me again."

"Allen, I promise you, I won't."

"Good," he said and walked out.

Nona sat where she was for a few minutes, trying to gather herself and wondering if she had ever hated somebody like she hated this man.

"I am the Goddess of life and death," she said aloud. "Decima, Morta, where are you, my sisters? It is time to cut this man's thread of life."

She picked up her bag and left, the slight sickness in her gut leaving her uncertain of how to proceed.

Chapter 25 – The Fifth of September, 2022

"Hey there, Detective Sergeant Melanie. How's the world of crime solving?"

The young man in the tan suit took the seat opposite Melanie Carter in the Queanbeyan coffee shop, placing a document holder on the side of the table.

She smiled with delight.

"Probably as dull as life in the coroner's office. Nothing but bodies, bodies, bodies stacked to the ceiling."

"Yeah, I know what you mean. Sometimes the smell gets a bit extreme."

"Jeez, I wish you hadn't said that. I was just about to order lunch."

They smiled at each other as old friends do and examined their menus. After the waitress had taken their orders, they started the conversation again.

"So, Andrew, what caused this amazing event?"

"Come on, Melanie, we do this every month."

"Yes, I know, but you sounded a bit tense when you called. Something up?"

"I dunno. There may be." He opened the document holder and extracted a single sheet. "One of my jobs is looking at statistics of sudden deaths."

"You always were a bit of a numbers man, even when we were in junior school. Top of the class in maths every term. It got irritating. Every month it was, *'Top of the class, Andrew Fellowes.'* It gave me a serious attack of the runs."

Andrew's serious expression didn't change.

"I have access to all the Bureau of Statistics files, as well as the Institute of Health and Welfare data bases," he said. "And I spend a lot of time going through them for various reports. Last week, something caught my eye, not really sure why, but I started running some analyses of the data."

"And you found something interesting?"

"I did. I looked at the homicides and accidental deaths in the State and also in Canberra, ran some trend analyses, played with a few assumptions and all the brainiac stuff I do so well and I came to this conclusion. If we take the accidental deaths that were maybe not all that accidental at all, put in some probability statistics, then we've had between six and ten homicides all within twenty kilometres of here."

"Explain that probability thing."

"Simple. There were a number of accidental deaths reported to my office, but with a little bit of imagination, some could be homicides. So I ran the analyses placing a probability of anything from fifty percent to eighty percent that each of them was a homicide and the figures didn't vary much at all. They all said the same thing. You've had at least six homicides, possibly as many as ten on or near your patch, all of them unsolved."

She stared at him.

"Holy shit, it's not that they're unsolved," she said. "Even with those that are genuine homicides, we haven't a single fucking clue as to the killers. Somehow, they've been covered up like professional gangland killings. And with the rest, it's even worse. If they're really homicides, they've been disguised so thoroughly that they've fooled both the New South Wales and Capital Territory cops completely."

"And that's why I called you. I just pulled this last sheet off the computer. Have a look."

They were interrupted by the arrival of their lunches and Andrew returned the sheet to the holder. "Later," he said.

"Okay, give me an example," said Melanie.

"That one you attended, the bloke who died in the sauna," said Andrew, carefully spooling his spaghetti on the fork with his spoon. "It just didn't seem right. The medical examiner's report certainly said he was obese, not healthy, but not so infirm that he couldn't have tried getting up, opening the door and getting out of the heat. And yet you found him lying outstretched on the bench thoroughly cooked and dehydrated."

Melanie concentrated on slicing a portion of her fish, adding some tartar sauce and transferring it to her mouth. Around them, the sounds of conversations and clatters of plates had faded into another world. She felt she and Andrew were in a cocoon of their own.

"So if he could have got up, even with great difficulty, he could have got to the door and pushed it open, even if he then just fell onto the floor in the corridor," she said. "At least he would have cooled off. So what are you thinking?"

"Even at a probability of fifty percent, that looks suspicious. Did he have any form of emergency call system, like a pendant round his neck? I know a lot of people who do."

"Oops," she muttered. "We did find one, but it was in a desk drawer in his study. Let's go along with this theory for a moment. How do you see a murder working?"

"I'm an analytical bastard as you know and I've seen some imaginative murders in my years at the Coroner's Office. So let's suppose this. The killer knows that Jensen takes a sauna every morning at about the same time. He comes in soon after Jensen is comfortably relaxed..."

"He?"

"Could be a she, certainly. He or she comes in, turns the heat up to maximum, jams the door shut and quietly leaves. The doctor reckoned Jensen was in the sauna for a whole day. If he couldn't get out, that's a certain death."

"One problem. If he was able to get up and try to get out, why was he found lying flat out on the bench?"

"I thought of that. What if the killer returned the morning he was found, opened the door, hauled Jensen to the bench and then turned the heat off and called you in?"

Melanie found that she had lost interest in her lunch.

"The cleaning lady," she muttered.

"She had a key?"

"She did. And I'd say she was strong enough to get Jensen back on the bench."

"And no marks from her hands would be left on the body, given the burned and blistered skin," said Andrew. "One more thing. The doctor estimated the time of death the day before he was found, that puts the murder, if indeed it was a murder, on the ninth."

"Is that significant?"

"It is, because every other one of the possible murders also took place on the ninth of the month and all within twenty kilometres of your little town."

"Okay, that's one. Do you have another that fails your smell test?"

"That accident where an elderly lady had gone off the road and into the ravine."

"Why is that suspicious?"

"It wouldn't be if I hadn't already got my smell detector going. But she was an elderly woman, early seventies, not renowned for driving like a hoon, dry road, almost new Michelin X tyres. Unless she fell asleep, that one fails my sniffer test. Her GP reported that she was quite fit and didn't suffer from sleep apnoea, so she was unlikely to have fallen asleep, even at eleven at night. Her family reported that she was quite the night owl, rarely going to bed before two."

Melanie put down her knife and fork.

"I think I have to get back to the office."

"I think you do. Go on, bugger off, I'll handle the bill."

She touched his shoulder as she walked out.

"I'll keep you informed," she said.

Chapter 26– The Sixth of September, 2022

"I really appreciate your help in this matter," said Melanie.

"My pleasure," said the insurance clerk. "We're always happy to help a police investigation. You're following up on that tragic accident for some reason?"

"We've received some information that suggested we should. So I'm relieved the insurance company has kept the file."

"We keep them open for a year before we put them in the archive. So what is it you want?"

"Did your adjuster take all the pictures?"

"Oh yes, every inch of the car, let me get them out of the file."

A few minutes passed while the insurance agent laid out twenty or more photographs of the wrecked car on the table.

"My god, what a mess," Melanie said under her breath.

"It fell twenty metres onto rocks. It was just scrap metal and the driver died instantly."

The detective took a magnifying glass from her handbag, something she always had with her.

Carefully she examined every photograph. Something caught her attention. "What's that?" she asked.

The agent looked at the back of the photo where a paper had been attached.

"That's the left front shell, between the bumper and the headlight."

"And that mark?" She pointed at a scratch on the red metal. It was about five centimetres long and something had dug into the paint and revealed the metal underneath.

The agent took the magnifying glass and looked carefully.

"Something dug into the metal," he said. "I think we concluded it was a sharp edge of rock."

"Probably right. Do you have these pictures scanned?"

"Sure do. Let me bring them up on the screen." He turned to the computer and took a few moments to find the pictures. He referred to the file and brought up the one that the detective had been examining. "All yours," he said and moved away.

Melanie took a seat in front of the monitor and began expanding the picture, focussing on the scratch. Eventually it filled the screen. It appeared to be about a centimetre wide and was as first thought, deep enough to reveal the raw metal.

"Can you print me a copy?"

"Sure."

Melanie spent another hour going through the pictures but nothing else caught her attention. She stood up and collected the envelope with the copy she had requested which the agent had placed on the desk a few moments earlier.

"Where's the wreckage?" she asked.

"Our storage garage. I'll give you the address and a letter of authorisation and I'll send you our best accident investigator to help. He's a retired cop who used to do this full time."

"Thank you so much. You've been a wonderful help."

"Like I said, Sergeant, that's my job. Do you think you've found something suspicious?"

"Hard to tell. I'll go and see the wreck and that might tell me more."

"You'll let us know if anything turns up? It could likely change the policy payout and impact on any other insurances she had."

"I certainly will. But on that point – who benefits from the insurance? Did she leave a will?"

The agent looked at his monitor.

"Yes she did. Everything was left to the local hospital."

Melanie left the insurance company's office in deep thought. There was always a major question with a homicide – who benefits? The whole situation had become more complicated.

*   *   *

The pathetic pile of red scrap lay in one corner of the concrete yard. Several other severely damaged cars stood around, some worse than others. But the red Toyota was by far the worst. Barely a fragment existed that couldn't be lifted by a single person.

"It's probably the worst I've ever seen," said the accident investigator standing next to her. He had introduced himself as Rod Crowe. "Is there something specific you're looking for?"

"The bit under the left headlight," replied Melanie.

"Let's see." The investigator began carefully checking each piece of metal, pushing rejected pieces to one side. "Better stay there, Sergeant," he said. "You're not dressed for this."

Twenty minutes passed then the investigator let out a loud "AHA!" and came back, carrying a battered piece of red metal with a broken headlight on one corner. "Is this what you're looking for?"

"I think so." Melanie took out the magnifying glass and examined the deep groove. She couldn't identify it any more than she could that morning. "What do you think that is?" she asked the investigator.

He followed her example and studied the metal through the magnifying glass. After a minute, he put the metal down and returned the magnifying glass.

"Steel cable," he said. "About a centimetre wide. I'd say the car hit it an angle at some speed, perhaps fifty or sixty and that was enough to deflect it to the right. The cable was probably strung across the road at an angle. Sergeant, something very nasty happened here. What the hell made you suspect it?"

"Not me. An old friend of mine in the Coroner's Office said it was a bit smelly."

"He needs a reward," said Rod. "Can I help further?"

"Will you write me a report confirming what you said? And do you have any idea what sort of cable? What would it be used for?"

"Maybe in a shipping yard? Towing another boat perhaps? Or possibly in the docks, used with a crane? I'll do some asking around."

"Rod, I owe you," she said. "You may just have helped crack something very ugly indeed."

He grinned cheerfully. "I'll call you if I get anything," he said. "And you have to promise me you'll let me know how all this works out."

"I promise," she said and returned to her car on the roadside.

* * *

"Rod, this is a pleasure. Do you have something for me?"

"I do, Sergeant. About that cable. Can you meet me at the Belleville airport?"

"Yes, I can. Say half an hour?"

"I'll see you there. Go to the little hangar at the south end."

"So why have you called me out here, Rod?"

"Do you know that this field is used by a gliding club at weekends?"

"I do. I've come out a couple of times and watched them. It looks fabulous fun."

"Did you watch them do a winch launch?"

"Is that where a bloody great big engine at one end of the field hauls a glider into the air at the other end of a hell of a long … Oh shit, Rod, is that what the steel cable is?"

"I'm pretty sure of it. Mate of mine flies here and he gave me a key to the hangar. Let's have a look."

A few minutes later, they stood before the huge engine that was the winch. A control cabin sat above two enormous drums on which were wrapped steel cables. Melanie put a cautious hand on one.

"That looks like the size of the groove, alright. How would one cut a length of that?"

"No need. My mate says that a cable break is a common event during the launch. Pilots practice the recovery at various heights, they drop the broken part attached to the glider by pulling the release in the cockpit, people come out and re-attach the two bits, cover the knot with heavy duty tape and carry on."

"But how would somebody get a length that you think they would need to cause the accident?"

Rod didn't answer but began walking round the hangar.

"Here," he called out. "Some loose bits. My mate said that if the break occurs near the glider, they don't repair it, they just add the connection bit to the cable and throw away the short bit. This is where they store some of those smaller lengths and eventually recycle the metal."

"So if this really is a murder, the killer is a member of this club?"

Rod shrugged his shoulders. "Not necessarily. There are a couple of clubs in the region, maybe it was somebody who knew about this sort of cable, somebody who had come to watch the gliders and saw a cable break and got the idea from that."

Melanie stared down at the couple of broken lengths of cable on the floor. She took out her notebook and pen, laid a piece of the cable across a blank page and carefully drew a line on each side to indicate the width of it. As an additional check, she placed her driving licence alongside the cable for comparison and took a photograph.

"I think I have to go," she said.

The investigator nodded. "And I bet I know where," he said. "I'll come with you."

"This is where the car went over the edge," said Melanie. "From the tyre marks, she was driving west. If our theory is right, the cable would have been hung a bit to the east of the collision point and across the road a little to the west, so forcing the car to the right and over the cliff."

She began walking east alongside the trees by the road, examining each tree that would have been solid enough to be an anchor. Rod crossed over the road and started walking in the same direction, making the same examination.

"Sergeant," he called. "I have it."

She looked at where he was pointing and walked a little further. Then she saw it. The tree was solid, probably half a metre wide and on the edge away from the road was a deep groove in the bark, exactly as would have been made by a steel cable wound round it when a solid object hit the cable and made it dig into the tree.

She took her phone from her pocket and photographed several shots of the damage then walked across to where Rod was standing by a similarly damaged tree. A line between the two would be at about a forty degree angle across the road.

She and Rod looked at each other.

"Well shit, eh?" he said.

"Exactly," she said. "It's murder. I'll get the scene of crime people out to collect the rest of the evidence."

* * *

"It's murder," she said to her boss, Detective Inspector Russell Comley a little later in the day.

"Fill me in," he said. The big man in the untidy suit lounged in his seat behind the desk that was strewn with papers. Melanie had always wondered how he kept anything in order, but his mind didn't seem to be like his desk.

She went through the process of examination of the car accident and he sat silently throughout, looking intently at the photo of his wife and son on the corner of the desk.

"Yes," he said when she had finished. "It's murder."

"That's not all," said Melanie and repeated the conversation she'd had the day before with Andrew Fellowes of the Coroner's office.

"Let's see if I've got this straight," said Comley. "If your pal is correct, we've had at least six murders on our patch, one every ninth of the month, even though some of them have been ruled accidental deaths, or in one case, suicide?"

"That's about it, Sir."

"They're all with a different MO. I've never heard of a serial killer using a different MO with each killing, have you?"

"No sir. We examined a number of murders, especially serial killings during Detective School at Goulburn, but there was nothing like that."

"I tell you what is does remind me of," said Comley. "Remember a few years ago, we had all those serial killings around the country? Each batch was by the same MO but all the different series were different. We had a few in Sydney, a couple in Melbourne and Perth. It had the country baffled and we took a lot of crap from the media."

"I remember those, sir. I think it was D.I. David Hunter from the Parramatta Homicide people who worked on that."

"It was. And he cracked it when he realised the same thing was going on all over the world. So even though each series was done by a different killer, they were all controlled by one person in each country."

"Could we get D.I. Hunter to help on this, Sir?"

Comley shook his head. "No chance. The whole thing almost destroyed him, came close to killing him and he retired, went north to become a farmer. But I think I know who may be able to help."

He stood up. "Melanie, this could be the biggest thing in your whole career. I'm still tied down in Canberra and the whole country is short-staffed after that damned pandemic, so you're on your own still. I suggest you pull in that bright kid Alex Welland as your assistant, we'll transfer him temporarily and I'll let you know if and when this idea of mine works. But read up about that whole story of D.I. Hunter. And when you're done, go up to Parramatta. I'll arrange for David's old team to talk to you."

He waved and walked out, leaving Melanie in a mixture of excitement, exhilaration and being swamped by the demands on her.

* * *

"Detective Sergeant Carter, I'm Detective Inspector Bill Hamilton. Welcome to Parramatta, home of the Homicide Group."

"Good morning, Sir. I've read the reports of the investigation you ran with D.I. Hunter and Doctor Jack Savage."

"And we've read what you're facing down south. You've got a tiger by the tail, there."

"It certainly feels like it, Sir."

"Come on in, meet the crowd that worked with David and Jack on that dreadful story."

She followed him into the small conference room to see three faces looking at her with interest.

"Detective Sergeant Carter, meet Detective Senior Constable Rachel Norman."

A medium height woman of stocky build and bad complexion extended a hand and smiled.

"You have a real handful down there, Sergeant," she said. "I wish we could come down and help, but we're short-staffed here and a bit overwhelmed."

"That seems to be the case everywhere," said Melanie. "I'm lucky that my boss has asked Jack

Savage to come and help. I really need that sort of expertise"

"Oh yes, we'll talk about Jack," said Norman.

"And this is Detective Sergeant Jerry Bowler," said Hamilton.

The young man in the military blazer with a crest on the breast pocket couldn't help the admiration showing in his face.

"Great to meet you," he said, a slight flush showing in his cheeks.

Melanie hid a smile at the reaction that was so common with young men.

"I heard about the work you did with D.I. Hunter," she said.

"And finally, Detective Senior Sergeant Barrie Roche."

The forties, tall man with a shock of black hair smiled at her. The admiration in his face was obvious but he didn't blush.

"Thank you all," said Melanie. "I've studied that whole episode you all went through, and D.I. Hunter was obviously fortunate to have such a team. I'm sure I can learn a great deal from you."

"Let's take our seats," said Hamilton. "This group went through some horrors then and we were all affected. And in private, the formalities get ignored. Can I call you Melanie?"

"I'd be delighted, Sir."

"Okay, from now on we're Bill, Rachel, Jerry and Barrie when we're in this room. Okay?"

"Absolutely." Melanie began to relax. She sensed the expertise and support in these four people.

"So, run through what you've got," said Hamilton.

"What we've got is a series of deaths, some of which we first thought were suicide or accidental, some of which were obvious murders. The first was a poisoning of an old lady on January the ninth, initially thought to be a heart attack, but a very clever medical examiner found a weird, almost unknown drug in her system. I'll tell you more about that later."

"Is that the Rosary Seed we read about?" asked Barrie Roche.

Melanie nodded. "Then on February the ninth, another old lady drove her car off the cliff and died instantly. That was assumed to be accidental death, but for reasons I'll go into later, we've since determined it was murder. Somebody had strung a steel cable across the road, angled to direct her to the cliff."

"The ninth again? A coincidence?" Rachel looked sceptical.

"More on that later," said Melanie. "There's a reason why I'm holding back some information for now, all will become clear."

"I'm intrigued," said Hamilton.

"On March the ninth, an old man had his throat cut in his back garden. Lots of blood, but not a single clue to be found, other than just some possible signs that the killer had entered over the fence by the river and left the same way."

"No clues at all?"

"Not a single damn thing."

"And the ninth of the month again," said Jerry Bowler.

"Indeed," said Melanie and smiled at him. The slight flush reappeared. Rachel saw it and hid her smile with a wink at Melanie.

"In April, a fisherman drowned in the local lake. He wasn't wearing a life jacket, the ruling was accidental drowning."

"And no doubt that was on the ninth?" said Barrie.

"You're getting it. In May..."

"On the ninth?" said Rachel.

"On the ninth. A very old, fragile man took a severe overdose of a prescription pain killer, a heavy narcotic, washed down with a lot of brandy. His wife had died the week previously and it was initially ruled a suicide. In June, yes, on the ninth before anyone asks, an old man died in his sauna, ruled accidental death. He had heart issues. No signs of any struggle and he was lying on the bench. His cleaning lady found him when she came for her regular session. Then in July, an obvious murder, a woman beaten to death with a baseball bat, again on the ninth. But I have to admit, I didn't get the common date because not all the deaths were reviewed by me. Some were just handled by regular uniforms."

"Nothing in August?" asked Hamilton.

"Not so far that we've found."

"So how did you discover that this whole story was one of murder, not suicide or accidental death?" asked Barrie.

"That was some clever work by an old childhood friend of mine, Andrew Fellowes, an information specialist with the Coroner's Office. He'd been playing with data from various sources and spotted the common date. He suspected that it was not coincidental and looked further. Having seven deaths all on the ninth of the month, all leaving absolutely no clues, all within twenty kilometres, it all seemed a bit out of whack. He was particularly suspicious about the February death where an old lady had gone off the road at night. There were no drugs or alcohol involved, she was known as a night owl of very high mental competence. There was no reason for the accident."

"So you investigated?" asked Rachel.

"I did. The insurance company had detailed pictures of the wreckage and each part of the car. One thing looked strange, a scar on the metalwork. An investigator and I went to examine the wreckage and it looked like the scrape of a metal cable. We found the same scrapes on two trees on opposite sides of the road, at an angle that would have diverted the car to the cliff."

"There are two things that grab my attention," said Bill. "The first is the significance of the date. Why is somebody committing a murder on the ninth of the month? Is there some religious or other symbolism to the ninth? The other is, if all those seven deaths were actually murders, including the ones so far ruled accident or suicide, how come there were zero clues left? That never happens, killers can't help but leave some traces behind, blood, bits of clothing, footprints, something."

"But boss, that was a problem with the serial killings we investigated with David," said Jerry. "Not a trace of anything. Nor was there any motive that could be identified. Nobody benefitted from any of the killings. A lot of them were just homeless old men."

"That's right," said Bill. "And when David went undercover and was accepted as a killer, he was given instructions, very detailed instructions on how to hide his tracks. The whole protective gear that our scene-of-crime people wear to avoid contaminating the area, coverall, gloves, shoes, masks. The killers were advised in detail what to do."

"Oh my god, are you suggesting that somebody is guiding these deaths?" Melanie felt cold.

"Almost certainly," said Barrie. "They can't be by one single serial killer. The modus operandi are all far too different, even a really clued-up serial killer couldn't vary the MO that much."

"And that means some interest in why hasn't there been a murder in August?" asked Rachel. "My nasty suspicious mind says there has, but you haven't identified it yet."

"That's a horrible thought," said Melanie. "And it could mean that I can expect more over the next few months. How long will this go on?"

"This you will have to put to Jack," said Bill. "He's good at these mind games. But I remember that when we found the whole global serial killing thing, we found it was a competition and there was a time limit for how many killings the powerful players could get. This could also be a game of some sort. It seems obvious that you'd better look very hard at those poisonings and suicide deaths also. If they were on the ninth, assume they're murders, regardless of what the evidence suggests."

He checked his watch and was about to say something when the door opened. A large, overweight man entered. His face seemed set in a permanent look of disapproval. The detectives rose to their feet. Recognising senior authority, Melanie did the same.

"Sir," said Bill, "this is Detective Sergeant Melanie Carter. Sergeant Carter, this is Chief Superintendent Stavely."

"Good morning, Sir," said Melanie, feeling uncomfortable. There was no welcome in the senior officer's face."

"I understand you're having a number of homicides in your region," said Stavely. It was a statement, not a question.

"Yes, Sir," replied Melanie.

"Well, Sergeant, it's your problem. Don't expect any help from my team here, they have more important things to do."

Melanie felt something welling up inside her, some anger, some sense of wrongness and also some exhilaration. She looked directly into the big man's eyes.

"Sir, my understanding is that the Parramatta operation is responsible for all homicides in the State. I came here under orders from my supervisor to request guidance."

The Superintendent glared at her and for a moment she was sure he was about to flare up in anger. But he didn't. She watched as indecision crept into his eyes, she sensed the growing doubts and insecurity in him and he moved away from her.

"Well, er... yes, I suppose we can offer some support. Contact the Inspector here if you need anything."

He turned and walked out.

Melanie looked around the room. They were all staring at her.

"What the hell happened there?" asked Bill, confusion in his face. "That bastard can't tolerate women in the force and makes no effort to hide it. He replaced Charlie Perkins who was the boss when David was here, and he's never shown any real decency to any of us. What did you do to him?"

"I've no idea," said Melanie, uncertain herself of what had happened.

"Well, it was a joy to see," said Hamilton. He looked around the table. "Okay children, time for lunch. Melanie, you're our guest today."

Later that afternoon, Melanie drove home, greatly comforted by the support shown to her, though disturbed by the indications that Andrew had been right, all those deaths on the ninth of the month were really murders. And she still couldn't work out what had happened with her meeting with Chief Superintendent Stavely.

She looked forward to meeting Jack Savage when he arrived in the next few days.

Chapter 27 – Melanie Carter, 2010

"Mind if I join you?"

The young man sitting reading a book with a mug of coffee in the students' lounge looked up, startled.

"Er... yes... of course. Melanie, this is a surprise."

"It's deliberate, Scott. Any time I join a group when you're there, you always make some excuse and walk away. It bothers me and I'd like to know why. Do I scare you, or something?"

Scott looked embarrassed and stared down at his coffee mug.

"Well actually, yes, you do. And I've never been the sort that hangs around beautiful women to drool all over them and beg for a little attention. When I see the mob around you, I walk away."

"So now you'll have all my attention. Will you please relax?"

Finally, the young man seemed to ease the tension in his body and smiled.

"That's better," she said. "I really would like to talk to an intelligent man without the whole conversation pointing towards getting a date."

He laughed. "I imagine life can be quite complex for a beautiful woman. It could be like being a multimillionaire, wondering if people like you because of who you are or because of the millions."

"Exactly. I can't talk to a man without him always trying to impress me, leading up to asking me out. There's nothing involving actual friendship."

"Have you been on a date with anyone recently?"

"A couple. But they always end up struggling to avoid a slap and tickle session and I have to get away."

"That's horrible. But what about the women? There's usually a bunch of them in the group surrounding you."

"I think they're hoping some of what I've got rubs off on them. And sometimes I sense real hostility under the smiles."

"Christ, I never thought of all that. Being beautiful can be a real curse, eh?"

"That's what my mum told me. I can't help it, I don't know where these genes came from, but they do complicate life. Most people can't accept that I have a brain as well as the other stuff."

"Okay, now we've got that out of the way, I promise I won't drool all over you or ask you out on a date. So why are you studying psychology?"

"Because I want to do something useful. I've got high intelligence, I know that, psychology is really fascinating, maybe if I become a practicing shrink, I might help a few people. How about you?"

"Similar idea, though I think I'd like to specialise in children's psychology. I really like dealing with kids."

"That sounds good, too. Looks like we have a class in ten minutes. Scott, let's talk more. Now, about that date thing."

"I said I wouldn't ask you out."

"Yes, you did. Would you mind reviewing that decision?"

He laughed. "Okay, but only because I like your mind."

"That's the best reason I've heard all term," she said.

"Tell you what," he said. "My dad gave me an amazing car. It's astounding, super performance, you'll love it and while I'm driving, I have no chance to try for some slap and tickle. Come out with me this Saturday, we can drive to the Blue Mountains, have a pub lunch and I can return you unscathed to your place."

"It's a date," she said.

* * *

2011

"Mum, I've got engaged."

"Melanie, that's wonderful! I'm assuming it's Scott?"

"Of course, Mum. We've been together for nearly two years."

"I'm thrilled to bits, lass. We liked him from the start, a truly good young man. When will you get married?"

"Not until we've graduated. We both want to get first class honours and that means a lot of work."

"That sounds good. Make sure you keep us informed."

"Of course, Mum."

* * *

2011

"And the Degree of Bachelor of Science in Psychology with First Class Honours goes to Melanie Carter. Congratulations, Miss Carter."

* * *

"Doctor Phillips, you asked to see me?"

"Melanie, yes! Please sit down. You're familiar with that seat after three years of tutorials in this office."

"Oh yes! I think I've left a deep imprint in that chair."

"Ha! Indeed. Couple of things, Melanie. First, congratulations on the first class honours. Fully deserved, I must say. It's been a pleasure to teach you. Can I ask one thing though?"

"Of course."

"You once said that you had wanted to study medicine and I'm pretty sure you'd have made a success of that. But why didn't you?"

"I think in the end it was a matter of spending so many years as a student. My parents are not well off, I needed to graduate and start work so that I could help them a bit."

"That's sad. But now that you've graduated, any ideas of what you want to do?"

"Well, that thesis I did for you on the mind of the serial killer really got to me. I think criminal psychology could be the way to go and I wanted to ask you what you thought and how to start."

"Interesting that you should say that. The real reason I wanted to talk to you was the call I got this morning. It was from a Professor Declan Allinson, he's a lecturer in criminal psychology at the police academy in Goulburn."

"The police academy? What could he want?"

"For you to consider a career you almost certainly have never thought of. Become a police detective."

"You're right, I would never have thought of that."

"Like I said." The professor smiled at her. "But while you would have to spend some time as a constable, the fast track process for graduates would see you entering detective training quite soon and promotion would be rapid, given your educational achievements."

"Actually, that sounds interesting. But there's a problem. Scott and I are planning on getting married this year and if I'm a cop, I could be posted anywhere. That's not a good thing for a marriage."

"That could certainly be an issue. But will you at least talk to Declan and see what he has to say? There may be ways around it."

"That can't hurt."

"Good, I'll set up a meeting with him for you."

Chapter 28 – The Ninth of September, 2022

"She's the perfect target," said Tanya from the front passenger seat of the panel van. "I know from her prescription in the shop that she's been on this drug Midazolam for a week now because she's had such difficulty sleeping. When she brought the script in, I rang her doctor to make sure I was advising her correctly on how to take it, so I know she would have taken her dose about an hour ago and she'll be totally out of it now."

"How long for?" asked Ollie next to her.

"Four or five hours. But I'll slip her another pill when we pick her up and that'll make sure for another couple of hours."

"Okay, the road's empty, it's two in the morning, nobody's about, let's do it."

They opened the car doors without light escaping, Ollie having sealed down the switches on both doors that morning, and walked up to the house. Like many houses in this small town, it was set well apart from the nearest home and the very wide streets made it almost isolated.

Tanya and Ollie walked round the side of the house to the rear door. Ollie cracked the rear window with the small hammer he had brought for the purpose, reached in and opened the door from the inside. A few moments later, they were looking down at the old woman on the bed. She hardly raised a bump under the covers and her breathing was almost inaudible.

"Poor old bitch," said Tanya, not bothering to lower her voice. She grinned at Ollie's reaction. "She can't hear a thing," she said. "That drug is bloody powerful. Okay, let's get her out."

With little difficulty, they lifted the old woman out of the bed, still wrapped in the blanket she had over her and carried her out of the back door and out to the panel van. Ollie held her on his own while Tanya opened the back door of the van and they gently laid the woman out on the floor.

"Let's go," said Ollie and slid behind the wheel. A few moments later, they were on a country road and continued along it for a few kilometres before turning onto an unsealed track and followed that, reaching a small collection of old sheds where they stopped.

"Wait while I slip the old biddy another pill," said Tanya and moved round to the back of the van, taking a small bottle of water from her pocket with a single pill. It was easy to put the pill in the woman's mouth and pour a small amount of water in. She swallowed instinctively and resumed her deep sleep.

Ollie joined her and they carried the woman out to one of the sheds, laid her out on a bench and Ollie tied her hands behind her and then to a solid wooden pillar.

"Okay, nobody will hear her and nobody comes this way," said Tanya. "So she'll probably last a day or two at the most because she won't get the other pills she needs for her heart and blood pressure."

Without a further word, they returned to the van, both grinning widely.

"Okay, time to get home, burn these coveralls and shoe covers and stuff, have breakfast and get to the library," said Ollie. "I'm looking forward to telling them about this."

"And you wore the protective clothing at all times?" asked Nona.

"We did," said Tanya. "But that was very early this morning, so well inside the ninth, but we didn't have time to write the story. We'll send it by email when we have it done."

"How can you be certain nobody will find her?" asked Bella. "It's going to take a couple of days for her to die, what if somebody finds her?"

"I've known those sheds for years," said Ollie. "They've been left to rot as long as I've known them. And the nearest property is five kilometres away. And anyway, what if she's found? She's not going to last more than a day, according to Tanya and anyway, we've left no trace at all."

"No, this worries me," said Bella. "The idea was that the victims would actually be killed on the ninth. This one could take a couple of days to die and there's always a chance somebody might find her. Nona, I don't think this qualifies."

"I'm with Bella on this one," said Mitchell. "It's risky, not within the rules and if she's found, it's not a killing and could cause problems. Are you certain she couldn't have any idea of who did this?"

"I'm quite sure," said Tanya. "I know the sleeping pills she took, and my boss said she'd be out cold for several hours with just the one. And I shoved another one down her throat anyway."

"And how about traces?" said Allen. "You're quite certain you were completely protected?"

"Damned sure," said Ollie. "Full coveralls, shoe covers, head cover, gloves, the whole lot."

"And nobody saw you?" continued Allen.

"It was after two in the morning," said Tanya. She revealed her irritation at the questions with a slightly louder and higher-pitched voice. "No lights anywhere, nobody was up and about."

She looked over to Ollie for support and he showed some anger also, his lips tight.

"Nobody saw us," he said. "For Christ's sake it was after two, that road is just a few houses, all of them old people. None of them would be up and about at that time."

"Well, that seems pretty good," said Nona. "We're on schedule, one death on the ninth of each month, though this last one may not actually be dead on that date, but I think we can accept kidnapping is in the rules. Well done, both of you, you stepped up to the plate when we had the gap and you can both take pride in having done two killings to everybody else's one."

A ripple of applause went round the table. Despite the apparent approval, Nona looked at each of the group in turn, her super-sensitive awareness of emotions telling her all was not well. Some of the group, as well as Mitchell and Bella Langer looked a little worried. She knew she would have to do something.

"Let's have coffee," said Nona, "and then Mitchell can tell us how he plans to do his chapter for next month."

* * *

Annie Blaydes had been breeding alpaca for three years and had loved every moment of it. The animals were hugely friendly and were more like pets than a source of income. The wool she obtained from the dozen animals more than covered the vets' and shearers' fees. Finding that the alpacas were wonderful watch animals and established friendly relationships with the cows that they also maintained was a source of great pleasure to both her and her husband.

But that morning, Annie discovered a problem. The animals were also highly intelligent and one of them had managed to slip out through the fence around their paddock.

Setting off with Tallis, the Welsh Border Collie that was almost a family friend, she let the dog follow the scent of the alpaca. He seemed to be heading for the old sheds that had been part of the small hobby farm some friends had run for a time a few years ago, before abandoning the rural life and returning to Sydney.

The loud, energetic barking from Tallis indicated the search was over and Annie followed the sound to the elderly sheds. Sure enough, the alpaca was grazing peacefully near the structures and Tallis was wagging his tail in friendly companionship.

"Silly old critter," she said to the alpaca and slipped the rope round its neck to begin leading it home. But another sound caught her ears, almost a child's sob.

"What the hell…?" she muttered and followed the sound inside. A moment later, she reached for her mobile phone.

* * *

"In shock and still very groggy from the sleeping pill," said the doctor. He and Melanie stood by the window looking into the hospital ward where the old woman was lying awake but not moving. "But not in danger at all and she was able to tell me her name and address. She's Jennifer Samuels, lives out along the Belfort Road."

"How long would she have been there?" asked Melanie.

"Since very early this morning."

"So she was taken today, the ninth." Melanie felt a small shiver run through her.

"Just a few hours, right," said the emergency ward doctor. "I talked to her GP and he said she would have taken a dose of Midazolam, that's something like Valium, probably about nine last night. Given her condition, I would have expected she'd be more wide awake than she is, so it's probable that whoever took the old dear gave her another dose of something similar. But she was able to drink some hot soup and we gave her the other pills she normally takes for blood pressure and cholesterol. Let's keep her here overnight and she should be okay to go home tomorrow morning."

"Can I talk to her?" asked Melanie.

"Best not while she's in shock. Anyway, there's nothing she can tell you. She went to bed and woke up in that place, all tied up."

"Then can I see the clothes and the covering she had?"

"That I can do," said the doctor. "Ask the nurse, she'll give you everything. We'll take her home by ambulance, so she won't need them."

Melanie collected the bag and drove to the address of the old woman. On the way, she called for assistance.

The broken back window was immediately obvious.

"Somebody knew she wouldn't hear that," said Constable Alex Welland.

"Which means somebody also knew she had taken a heavy-duty sleeping pill," said Melanie. "Alex, check her bathroom, see if she has any more prescription pills. In fact, she will, the ER doctor said she takes stuff for blood pressure and cholesterol."

Without a word, the constable found the bathroom and opened the cabinet.

"Just as you said, Sarge," he called out. "Wilson's Pharmacy in town."

Melanie joined him. "And the prescription will say who the GP is. The doctor didn't tell me."

"Doctor du Plessis at the local clinic."

"Good. Nip round and see both of them. Find out just who would have known of her condition and drug usage. I'll see you back at the station. When you get back, organise the standard door to door questions. Not likely anyone saw anything, but you never know your luck. And maybe the scene of crime officers will find something at the shed."

* * *

"Sarge, Doctor du Plessis says the only people who could see the medical file would be the three other doctors in the practice and the nurse who does stuff like regular injections."

"Did you talk to them?"

"I did. All of them have perfect alibis for the night of the kidnapping."

"What about the pharmacy?"

"Just the pharmacist in charge, one Forbes Hunter and the assistant who doles out the drugs, a woman called Tanya Roberts."

"Alibis?"

"Not really. Hunter was in bed, it was sometime after midnight, after all, he's single, so no alibi. Tanya Roberts says the same, single, in bed alone, no alibi."

"Okay Alex, write up the file. Let's see what the laboratory says."

* * *

"Detective Sergeant Carter, this is Irene Chang at the lab."

"Yes, Irene, do you have some information for me?"

"Sure do, Sergeant. We found two sets of fibres on the old lady's night dress. One is just a very common broadloom, the sort of thing you find in waiting rooms or the floors of vans and cars and things. Not easy to identify, but it could well be the vehicle she was carried in. There was a certain amount of dust as well, mixed with the fibres."

"And the second?"

"More interesting. It's the fibre from protective coveralls, the sort tradies use for painting and general protection, you can buy them at Bunnings any time."

"As you say, interesting. Thanks Irene, you'll send me the report?"

"It should be there already Sergeant."

"You're a treasure, Irene. We'll have to repeat that Dim Sum feast we had last year in Canberra."

Replacing the phone, Melanie sat back, deep in thought. The ninth? Protective coveralls? Things were falling into a pattern but what it said was almost beyond her belief.

Chapter 29 – the Tenth of September, 2022

The tap on the open door of her office pulled Melanie from her deep thoughts about the kidnapping of the old lady. Was it supposed to be a murder? If so, it had failed, so would there be another attempt? Was it just a coincidence that it happened on the ninth of the month? And what the hell was the motive for each of the other murders? How were they all connected?

She looked up and saw a man perhaps in his seventies looking down at her with a smile. He was dressed casually, jeans, a golf shirt, his hair looking like it badly needed a meeting with a barber.

"Jack Savage," he said in a pleasant baritone voice. "Your boss Russell asked me to come and talk to you."

"Oh yes," she said and stood up. "Detective Sergeant Melanie Carter."

"Yes, I know that," he said, placing a finger on her nameplate on the office door. "But it took my two doctorates and years of working with you lot for me to deduce it."

She couldn't help but laugh and waved him to the seat across from her desk. "I'm very glad you were able to come down. This situation is getting terrible.

We've had eight probable murders this year, but yesterday we had a kidnapping that probably would have been murder if we hadn't got lucky with a witness."

"It took a lot to pull me away from raising alpacas and grandchildren in Queensland," said Jack. "But this sounds very weird indeed. I couldn't resist it, apart from the chance to talk to another alpaca breeder and compare notes. Let's have a look at each of the less obvious murders, the ones that were initially ruled accidents or suicide."

"Can I start with the one my friend in the Coroner's office identified as a likely murder?"

"Sure."

"We call it the Sauna killing."

Melanie went through the details of the discovery of the dead man in the sauna and Andrew's suspicion that it didn't smell right. Savage stared out of the window the whole time and didn't make a sound, but when she had finished, he looked back at her.

"An obvious thing to look for," he said. "That blocked door out of the sauna. Is the house occupied now?"

"I heard it had been sold a few weeks ago."

"Let's go and see. Got a magnifying glass?"

She nodded and picked up her handbag.

"Let's take my car," she said. "I think you'll like it."

They walked out of the building to the parking area and as often occurred, there were three young men staring at her car.

"What the hell is this?" said Savage, looking wide-eyed at the beautiful machine.

"It's a Gordon-Keeble," she said, hiding her smile.

"Never heard of it," he said.

"Not surprising. There were only a hundred ever built way back in the sixties."

"And how come you have one?"

"A long story. Get in, buckle up and I'll treat you gently for your first time."

He was still laughing as they arrived at the house where the sauna killing had occurred.

* * *

"Good morning. "I'm Detective Sergeant Melanie Carter and this is my colleague in CIB, Jack Savage."

The young woman at the doorway looked puzzled. She was in her thirties, dressed in a tracksuit and trainers and looked very fit.

"Good heavens," she said. "Have we done something wrong?"

Melanie smiled. "Not at all. We're making inquiries about a death that took place in this house before you bought it. Did you know about it?"

"Oh yes, that poor old man who died in the sauna. The estate agent who sold us the place did tell us about it, but we loved the house and decided we wouldn't let it bother us. How can I help?"

"Could we just come in and look at the sauna again? There's something we may have missed."

"Sure, come on in. My husband had to go in to work, some weekend exercise, he's in the Auditor General's office in Canberra, he'll be interested to hear about this."

A few moments later, they were all by the sauna. Melanie took out the magnifying glass she always carried with her and looked at the door.

"I think this needs closer examination," she said, lowered herself to her knees and then stretched out at the foot of the door. Carefully, she examined the bottom edge, centimetre by centimetre, tracking with one finger. About a hand's width from the front end, she applied the magnifying glass and carefully studied the bottom edge. She stopped, pulled a whiteboard marker from her shirt pocket and made a tiny mark on the door. A second mark was made about ten centimetres along from the first. She continued the examination and repeated the process, so that two sets of marks were made about twenty centimetres apart.

Melanie got up from the floor and handed the magnifying glass to Jack. "Can you have a look?" she said.

He took the glass. "It'll be a bit of a creaking and groaning, but I guess this ancient body can still manage it," he said and repeated her actions.

When he stood up, he nodded. "Two wedges placed to prevent the door being opened."

"Then it really was murder," she said.

"Curiouser and curiouser," said Jack Savage. "I'm really glad I came down."

"So tell me about this amazing car," said Jack as they drove back to the station.

She hesitated a moment.

"British," she said. "Great big V8 engine on a tubular steel frame, Bertone body in fibre glass, supposed to have a top speed of 145 miles per hour, but a British motoring magazine had a top racing driver try it out on the German Autobahn and as he described it, he put his foot down and it was still accelerating at 168 miles an hour when he ran out of nerve."

Jack laughed. "And what have you done in it?"

"I took it to racing driver school," she said. "I had two weeks of training and the men there couldn't keep their eyes or hands off it. I sympathised."

Jack laughed again. "It's the same problem you have, is it?"

She didn't reply.

"Sorry," he said. "That was unnecessary. So how did you end up with it?"

"It belonged to an ex-boyfriend."

"He gave you this treasure?"

"A long story, Jack."

Savage recognised the conversational guillotine and concentrated on studying the interior of the extraordinary vehicle.

Chapter 30 – Melanie Carter 2011

The Sydney Morning Herald, June, 2011

Another senseless killing occurred at the Cross last night when a young man was hit by a single punch outside a restaurant. Scott MacAdam, aged 22 was leaving the restaurant with his fiancée, Melanie Carter when a thug walked up to him and landed a single punch to the head. Mr MacAdam collapsed, hitting his head on the concrete. A bystander called an ambulance and several others tackled the thug and held him until the police arrived. But the victim was pronounced dead on arrival at St Vincents Hospital. He and his fiancée had graduated recently from Sydney University and were planning to get married later this year.

* * *

Twenty-Third of June, 2011

"Miss Carter, thank you for coming in to see us."

"I'm puzzled. Why have you asked me here?"

"We're the solicitors acting for the family of Scott MacAdam."

"Scott's family? Oh my goodness…"

Melanie sat back in the seat across from the desk of the young man who had met her at the reception desk of the legal office. Tears rose in her eyes and she pulled out a tissue to wipe them.

"I'm really sorry to have to distress you like that, Miss Carter. We have acted for Jerome and Cathie MacAdam for some years and we knew Scott very well. A fine young man and we all feel so sorry for your loss."

"But why am I here?"

"Scott had made a will a few months ago. You may not realise it, but the MacAdams were very wealthy people. They had asked Scott to make a will as soon as he turned twenty-one and had assets of some value. One of those is his trust account."

"I don't want Scott's money. We never married, that would be horrible."

"Indeed, Miss Carter and the family would not have put you to that stress. The trust account is transferred to his younger brother, Geoffrey."

"Good. This whole thing has been horrible for them. I met the family a few times and they were all so nice."

"I said there was another asset. You know it, his Gordon-Keeble car."

"You don't mean..?"

"I do, and the whole family endorses this with great enthusiasm. The car is now yours and with it, $5,000 purely for maintenance purposes to cover your costs until you have secured employment."

This time, Melanie could not stop the tears.

* * *

"Professor Allinson, what you describe sounds very interesting."

"I think it will suit you very well, Miss Carter."

"As you know, I was planning on getting married this year and what you suggest might not have been possible, given that I could be posted anywhere after graduation, but..."

"I heard about the tragedy, Miss Carter and I am truly sorry."

"Thank you. But now that problem doesn't exist, I'd like to take you up on the offer. Becoming a police detective and encountering the sorts of minds that I wrote about in my thesis might be a form of poetic justice."

"I accept that it's for all the wrong reasons, Miss Carter, but on a personal basis, I'm really pleased that you'll join us."

"I'll see you in Goulburn, Professor Allinson."

Chapter 31 – The Twelfth of September, 2022

"Let's review all the deaths you've so far identified as occurring on the ninth of each month and see what we have."

Jack Savage looked like the archetypal university professor standing before the pair of whiteboards in the conference room of the police station. His blue jeans were faded, his light sweater was dark blue, his hair was way past needing professional help.

Melanie and Constable Alex Welland sat in front of him, notepads and tablets available. Alex looked comfortable in civilian clothing rather than his uniform, having been temporarily transferred to the Criminal Investigation Branch as a detective.

Jack turned to the whiteboard, a black marker in hand. He spoke as he wrote.

"The first murder that we are sure of was on January ninth, the bizarre poisoning by the seed of a Rosary vine. Very weird, I've never heard of that one before."

"Credit the Doctor Mortimer with that one," said Melanie.

"Indeed," said Jack. "Number two is the car crash over the ravine, initially assumed to be accidental death until your very clever young mate in the Coroner's Office cast some doubts on it. Then you and the investigator from the insurance company showed that it was also a murder, also on the ninth of the month, this time February. That was clever detective work, I must say."

"Thank you, kind sir," said Melanie, struggling to hide a laugh.

Jack wrote the details on the board, started a new line and wrote, *'March 9th.'*

"And so to March. On the ninth of March, an elderly man had his throat sliced by an intruder in his back garden. No signs left by the killer, not a single worthwhile clue, other than the sign that the killer had come in over the back fence."

"That's what got us," said Melanie. "No footprints, no fibres on the victim's clothing. One of the guys on the crime scene investigation team suggested the killer was wearing the same sort of protective clothing that they were, including shoes, gloves, hood, all to avoid contaminating the scene, only in this case, to avoid leaving clues."

"Which suggests considerable planning and preparation," said Alex.

"And then on April the ninth, we had another death deemed accidental, the drowning of a fisherman, but it was also on the ninth of the month and that's now enough to arouse suspicions."

"Oh! Something has just come to my mind," said Melanie. "Something about that drowning. Alex, you remember we examined the boat the dead man had been using?"

"Yes, Sarge. We gave it a good going over."

"But there was one thing we might have overlooked. We found the man's life jacket in the boat and we assumed he hadn't put it on. A lot of people do that, they don't think it's an issue in a calm lake. I've just remembered, the jacket was almost all dry, but there was just a small wet patch. So what if he had actually been wearing his jacket, a killer hauled him out of the boat, drowned him and then removed the jacket and threw it back into the boat? The sun had been up a couple of hours, so the jacket was mostly dry, but just this bit on the underside was left still wet."

"Ordinarily, I'd say that was a bit far-fetched," said Jack. "But now? Hell, it's suddenly possible. The date was right."

"Doctor Savage, sir," broke in Alex. "Can you clarify something for me?"

"Sure, but only if you call me Jack. I hate being called Doctor, people immediately start asking me to diagnose their symptoms."

Alex stifled a laugh. "Thank you, Jack. You keep referring to a serial killer. Is there a specific mindset or characteristic of a serial killer that's suggested here?"

"Good point, Alex. Alright, let's review, shall we?" Savage folded his arms. "The classic background is amazingly common. More than eighty-five percent of serial killers are white males, the greatest majority under thirty and often quite intelligent."

"IQ usually between 105 and 120," said Melanie. "I remember this from my university days. In fact, it was from one of your textbooks, Jack. The serial killers usually come from dysfunctional families, miserable childhoods, spends a lot of time day-dreaming, heavy-duty masturbators.”

Jack smiled. “I’m glad you’ve read the materials. Alex, does that give you a picture?”

“It does. Thank you, Jack.”

“Let’s move on. May the ninth, there is a death, but so far it looks like nothing but a suicide. An old man, distraught at the death of his wife only a few days earlier, commits suicide by taking a seriously heavy-duty pain killer drug together with lots of brandy.”

“We had a look at the scene,” said Melanie. “But we found nothing to indicate any other conclusion. We did note that the back door was open, but it hadn’t been forced, so we assumed the old man had left it, being in a seriously disturbed state as he decided on suicide.”

“Okay, for now, we can leave that,” said Jack. “In June, we had the murder in the sauna. We only discovered that it was murder on Saturday morning, three months later, after you and I went out there, Melanie. In this case, we did find some sort of clue, the wedge marks under the door, but absolutely no signs of any breaking and entering.”

“For now, I’ve got my sights on the cleaning lady, this Jean Worrall,” said Melanie. “But I have nothing to tie her into it, other than opportunity. Just as with all the others, we’ve seen no motives for any of the killings. Nobody has benefitted from the wills of the deceased, other than charities.”

"Let's look at July," said Jack. "Some similarities with the throat-cutting murder, a woman battered to death with a baseball bat, no motive, no clues, again the probability that the killer wore the same protective clothing as the previous one. But definitely a murder and definitely on the ninth of the month."

"The date seems to be the only thing linking all this," said Alex. "What's so important about the ninth?"

"An interesting question," said Jack. "But it does link them, so it could be symbolic of something. We may get a clearer idea as we examine the details or get more information."

"What do we know about the victim?" said Alex.

Melanie looked at her tablet. "Caroline Collins, aged thirty-eight," she said. "Divorced, worked as a book-keeper for a garden supply firm in Queanbeyan. No social life that we could find, just a member of a writers' group in town where she was the secretary. That's all. Rather an empty life, it seems."

"A bit sad," agreed Jack. He turned back to the whiteboard. "We appear to have no killing in August, or maybe we haven't identified one."

"Jack," broke in Alex. "There's something…"

The other two looked at him.

"I read a report a few days ago. Sarge, do you remember that weird event of that bloke, Peter Fleming? He found his identity had been wiped, driving licence, internet account, bank account, all because a forged death certificate had been sent to all the authorities. It took him days to clear it all up and it looked like one brilliant case of hacking. Our techie gurus in Sydney examined everything, couldn't find a trace of who might have done it."

"But he wasn't killed," said Jack.

"Not physically," said Melanie. "Alex, that's brilliant! What if this is a digital killing? More than just identity theft, but in many ways a murder? A man is totally wiped from a number of systems, he has no identity, almost no life."

"Holy shit, eh," said Jack. "What was the date of that?"

"August the ninth," said Alex.

"Good grief," said Melanie. "Could that be linked to the others?"

"If it is, then it shows one thing," said Jack. "This is all either by one demonically clever person, or more than one person is involved."

"Not the profile of the average serial killer, then," said Melanie.

"Not at all. This is getting better and better," said Jack. "I'd like to get back to the digital murder a little later, but let's keep on this track for a while longer. And now this week, just three days ago on the ninth, a kidnapping of an old lady, no motive, but maybe it's a failed killing," said Melanie. "Another day or two, she would have been dead."

"And no clues, it seems, except for the interesting fact that the fibres from a protective garment were found on her clothing," said Alex. "Again, this one does have some links to a couple of the others. What if the two poisonings were done by somebody wearing all that protective stuff? What if somehow they got into the house, overcame the victims and forced the poison down their throats? Both the victims were very old people, they'd have been easy to hold down."

Jack grinned at Melanie. "A good idea bringing this kid into the team, Melanie. He seems quite bright."

"Don't overdo it, Jack," she replied. "The kid might want to be permanently assigned here and he can't until he makes Senior Constable."

"Then I'll have to work at it," said Alex, keeping his face straight.

"So we don't really have much," said Jack. "But a couple of things are ringing bells. As you know, I worked with David Hunter on that horrible series of serial killings in Australia and then around the world."

"I do," said Melanie.

"And I read the report," said Alex. "The Sarge here told me to do so, as soon as we heard you might be coming down to help."

"Then, as you know, each episode of a serial killing had all the classic characteristics of such things. They never exceeded four in a row, but each one had similar victims, the same modus operandi and each one left some form of distinguishing mark on the corpse. But there was never any clue left behind, other than that signature mark and never a motive. And each individual series had a different MO."

"And eventually you and D.I. Hunter discovered that the killings in each country were managed by a single person, all part of some competition with people in the other countries," said Alex.

"That's right," said Jack. "What does ring the bell is that the killers all knew to wear protective clothing to avoid leaving any clues and there was one single link between all of them, in this case the tycoon or political heavy taking part in the competition."

"Pretty sick," said Alex.

"And it could have gone on a lot longer, except that David and I got a suspect in our hands because of a silly error on his part and we broke him down to admitting it was just a game."

"What was the error?" asked Melanie.

"A patrol car stopped this guy because of a broken tail light. The amazing thing is we had already interviewed him earlier because of his car which resembled one seen by a witness, but his alibi seemed cast iron. But when the guys stopped him, they found a cosh on his front seat. That's illegal, and we already suspected something like a cosh had been used on the Sydney series. They brought him in, David and I interrogated him and frankly, David broke all the rules and hit him. But that's when he broke down."

"So what do we get from all that?" asked Melanie.

"Something links all these murders. For now, let's assume that the suicide was another murder. In that case, we've had a murder on the ninth of each month, including that weird digital one, one considered accidental drowning and one failed one, the one yesterday. There's no motive of any sort in any of them that we can see, so there's a resemblance with the global serial killings David and I worked on. Something or somebody links these events, for what purpose I have no idea. But the usual indicator of a serial killer, the common MO isn't present here, every killing is different. This is not a serial killer at work, this is more like those global killings, linked by a single force behind them, but a different killer each time."

"So it seems we must expect another one each month of this year," said Melanie.

"And let's hope only this year," said Jack. "But my gut feeling is that there's a time limit on this thing, just as there was in the competition killings."

"We'll need to review all the cases that have so far not been identified as a murder," said Melanie. "Let's start with the most obvious one, based on what Alex said. Let's have a look at the suicide of the old bloke. We'll have to interview everybody who knew his wife took that drug and what his physical condition was. Alex, you go and interview the staff at the clinic that prescribed the drug, I'll talk to the pharmacist and staff that dispensed it."

"I can't be part of those interviews out of these offices," said Jack. "Not without some official authority. I'll look forward to your conclusions."

"I'll make sure that authorisation comes quickly," said Melanie. "We need you in those interviews."

* * *

"Tanya, can I call you Tanya? I'm Detective Sergeant Carter and I'm following up on the suicide death of Martin Fielding back in May."

"Oh! How can I help you? That was some months ago."

"Four months ago, almost to the day, that's correct. I understand this pharmacy dispensed the prescription drugs for both Martin and his wife, Maggie."

"Yes, we did. Martin came in every month."

"And you were the one that served him?"

"Most of the time. Sometimes the boss, Forbes did, sometimes the other girl who works here part time did."

"Could I see the drugs that you gave to both of them?"

Melanie was watching the woman closely and thought that a small expression of worry crossed her face. She noted it and left it for possible future reference.

"Er... yes," said Tanya. "I'll have to go to the computer."

"Please do."

Tanya turned to the screen on the counter and tapped a few entries. "There," she said. "That's the list for both of them." She turned the monitor so that Melanie could read the data.

"Take me through it," said Melanie.

"Martin had bad acid reflux, so that's for that problem," said Tanya, pointing at the first line. "He took that one for high blood pressure and that one there for cholesterol."

"Nothing else for Martin?"

"No," said Tanya.

Melanie noted down each of the drug names. "Okay, how about Maggie?"

"Maggie had severe arthritis and also osteoporosis in her left hip, so that one there is an injection she got every six months and the one next to it is an anti-inflammatory."

"And that last one?"

Melanie was sure now. Tanya was tensing up.

"That's a pain killer."

"Is that a restricted drug?"

"Er.. yes, what we term a Class "A" drug."

"Is it dangerous?"

"It can be. It's only prescribed for extreme pain and only for a limited period."

"Why was Maggie taking it?"

"She'd had a fall a few weeks before and broken several ribs. She was in a lot of pain."

"What was the date of her last prescription?"

Tanya studied the monitor. Melanie was certain now. Tanya was nervous.

"The twenty-eighth of April," she said.

"And that drug is given out how, in a box or a sealed packet?"

"In lots of twenty, in a small blister pack."

"And she would take one a day?"

"At night before going to bed."

"So if she took one on the twenty-eighth of April, there should have been at least fifteen pills left, if she died on May third as the doctor told us."

Tanya nodded. There was great anxiety in her face.

"What's the lethal dose of that drug?"

"Twelve would do it, when taken with lots of alcohol."

"Thank you, Tanya. I must ask you, where were you on the evening and night of the ninth of May?"

Melanie noted with interest the nervous gulp that Tanya displayed.

"I was at home," Tanya said. "I went to bed about ten."

"Anyone who can confirm that?" asked Melanie.

Tanya shook her head. "I live alone," she said.

She's definitely nervous, thought Melanie. *This needs following up.*

"While I'm here, may I follow standard routine and ask you where were you on the night of the eighth and ninth of this month, just a few days ago?"

Tanya looked shocked.

"Why?"

"Just routine. I'll be asking everybody locally the same question. It's about the kidnapping of an old lady."

"Why, what happened to her?" asked Tanya. "Is she alright?"

"She's fine. Somebody found her that morning and she's recovering in hospital now."

Tanya's eyes were wide. "I'm glad she's alright," she muttered.

"And just as a follow up, can you tell me your movements that day?" asked Melanie.

"That was Friday? I go to a writers' group in the library. I got there at ten, we meet until one and then I came into work. It's an arrangement I have with Forbes."

"Thank you, Tanya, I'll let you get back to work."

The relief in her face was obvious. Melanie drove back to her office in a thoughtful mood.

* * *

"She was lying through her bloody teeth," said Melanie. "How about your interviews, Alex?"

"All clear, as far as I could tell," said the young constable. "If not, they were all damn good actors. They were all quite unfazed by being questioned."

"And Tanya wasn't. Trouble is, I can't break her alibi, even if she had one. She said she was in bed that night by ten, there's no way of disproving it. But on the other hand, I'd swear she knew something about the kidnapping. She seemed very tense about it."

"I'd call that real progress," said Jack. "We have a real possible suspect."

"But it's still foggy," said Alex. "What the hell is the motive for any of these killings? They tell us at Goulburn that there are always three things needed in a murder, method, motive and opportunity. All we've got is method and even that is different with each one."

"That's the crisis David and I faced with the global series," said Jack. "We need a breakthrough and that could come at any time."

"Let's talk to Jean Worrall," said Melanie. "But before we do, there's something we need to arrange."

* * *

"Good morning Jean, remember me? I'm Detective Sergeant Melanie Carter and we talked the day you found Mr Jensen dead in his sauna."

"Oh! Yes, I remember you. What do you want?"

Melanie was sure, there was a reaction, but she decided anyone might react when the police appeared at their door.

"Can we come in, Jean? We have some questions about the accident. This is Constable Alex Welland."

"I thought I'd told you everything I know. I signed a statement at the police station the next day."

"Just following up on some things, if you would give us a few minutes."

Reluctantly, the woman opened the door and let the two officers in. They followed her into a lounge room, Alex and Melanie sitting opposite Jean who took her seat in the sofa.

"This is a nice house," said Melanie, looking around the room. It was spacious, the furniture looked good quality, an expensive rug lay on the floor between them and a well-polished sideboard against the far wall held some photographs in ornate frames.

"I have a number of cleaners working for me," said Jean. "Business is always good."

"Nice to hear," said Melanie. This was news to her. "Now, let's go back to the day you found Mr Jensen. That was on Friday, the tenth of June, according to my notes."

"Was it? I can't remember that far back. But it must have been a Friday, I did his house that day every week."

"And you hadn't been in the house since the previous week?"

"That's right."

Melanie was certain now, Jean was nervous. Her hands were tightly clasped together and her voice had a slight hoarseness to it.

"Jean, we did have some questions to ask you, but here's the real issue." Melanie took an envelope from her jacket pocket. "This is a search warrant to look through your house. There are some issues about Mr Jensen's death that have made us reopen the case."

"What?" Jean's face showed mounting dismay. "Search my house? But why?"

"Like I said, we have had reasons to reopen the case. Alex?"

Alex stood up and went back to the front door. Two uniformed officers stood there. Alex nodded at them and they entered and all three began looking through the rooms of the house.

"Jean, I want you to stay seated, this won't take long," said Melanie. "But I do have one more question for you. Are you by any chance a member of a writers' group that meets in the library on the second Friday of each month?"

Jean's face had gone white and her eyes were wide. She could only nod in reply.

Oh, hello, thought Melanie. *I only asked that as an accidental thought after Tanya had mentioned it. Have we stumbled on something here?*

The next fifteen minutes passed in silence until Alex returned.

"Just these, Sarge," he said and handed over an evidence bag containing a pair of overshoes of the type worn as protective covers by crime scene investigators.

"No gloves or coveralls?"

"No, Sarge."

"Okay, thanks Alex, Tell the guys to stand down."

She turned to Jean.

"I'll have to take these for now, Jean, we need to have the lab examine them. I'll return them as soon as possible. But I must ask, why do you need them?"

"Some of our clients are factories," said Jean. "Their places can be filthy."

Melanie nodded. "I can understand. Alright Jean, we'll leave you now, sorry for the interruption."

* * *

"She was certainly frightened, but there was no evidence of having killed Jensen," said Alex.

"We'll see if the lab comes up with anything on the shoe covers," said Melanie. "But her explanation for having those was perfectly rational."

"And no gloves," said Alex. "And no signs of the wooden wedges."

"She wouldn't need special gloves for this killing," said Melanie. "Any ordinary household rubber gloves would be adequate for hauling Jensen off the floor and onto the bench. And it was months ago, she'd have thrown those out a long time ago. Same with the wedges, they'd have been thrown out at the same time."

"We didn't find any coveralls," said Alex. "But she wouldn't have needed any, she's in that house legitimately every week, no need to hide her presence."

"So just confirmation that she's a member of a writers' group?" said Jack.

"That's about it," agreed Melanie. "And that was just a random thought. No grounds for charging her at this stage."

There was a knock on the door and a policewoman entered. She handed an envelope to Melanie who studied the contents.

"Very little on the shoe covers," she said. "Just some fibres from a carpet. Again, Jean could argue that she wore the covers when vacuuming the place."

"So just another pointer to a group of writers of which two of the women were members," said Jack. "I tell you what, if we do eventually find all the killers are members of a writers' group, it will make a fantastic paper for me to write for the professional journals. And it won't do any harm to your careers, either."

Melanie smiled at Alex. "Better prepare for your Senior Constable exams," she said.

Chapter 32 – The Thirteenth of September, 2022

"Tanya! Jean! What are you doing here?"

"Nona, I've got to talk to you. I've got problems," said Tanya.

"Me too," said Jean.

Nona studied the two women and sensed the panic in them both. "Then you'd better come in."

Nona led the distraught women through to her lounge and pointed at the armchairs.

"Now, what's so critical that you have to come and see me?"

"The police have been to see me about the poisoning of Martin Fielding," said Tanya, her hands shaking.

Nona was silent for a moment. Then, "What did they say?"

"It was a woman sergeant, said her name was Carter, I think. She asked me about the drugs Martin and his wife had been taking."

"And you told her?"

"Of course. I couldn't refuse. But she seemed most interested in the pain killer that Maggie was taking. It's the one I used."

"And you, Jean? What's your problem?"

"The same cop came and talked to me. She said they were reopening the case of Mr Jensen, but didn't say why. She had a search warrant and they searched my house"

"Did they find anything?"

"Just the shoe covers, but I can't see what they might find there."

"Did she imply at all that you were a suspect?"

"No, but the fact that they know it was a murder is enough. They're not going to stop looking for clues. We all thought we'd got away with it when the coroner ruled it was an accidental death."

Jean hid her face in her hands. "I wish I'd never got into this thing. I could end up in prison."

Nona reached over from her armchair and touched the hands of both women.

"Tanya, Jean, there's nothing to be worried about. The police often review suicides and old cases like that. There's nothing can tie you to it. You wore all the protective clothing like I told you?"

"Everything, the coveralls, gloves, shoes, mask, everything," said Tanya.

"And you, Jean?"

Jean looked up and nodded. "I only needed the shoe covers. I'm in the house every week, so no need to hide that. And I wore ordinary rubber gloves to move the body and I threw them in the rubbish bin after that."

"What about the wedges you used to block the sauna door?"

"They were thrown into a garbage bin in the park, nowhere near my house."

"Then there's no chance of them finding anything to link either of you to it," said Nona.

"Well, I had to leave the back door open," said Tanya. "It was the sort of lock you need a key to lock it."

"Again, not a problem. They'll just assume Martin was deeply distressed and about to commit suicide, he left the back door open accidently."

"But there's more, Nona," said Tanya. "She asked me about the night we kidnapped that old woman."

Nona sat up. "Really? I wonder why?"

"She said it was just routine, they were asking everybody."

"Did you tell them anything?"

"Of course not. I just said I was asleep in bed that night. But she told me the old woman isn't dead! She said somebody found her that morning and she's in hospital, recovering."

Nona went silent for a moment. "Several people said that was a possibility, didn't they? Maybe it wasn't such a good episode. But again, you and Ollie both wore all the protective gear?"

"We did."

"Did you speak to each other at all?"

"Just a bit, but I knew she was out cold from the drugs she gets from my shop, and I gave her another one. She wouldn't have heard a bomb going off."

"Okay, Tanya, Jean, look at me. There's nothing to worry about, that cop was just following routine. They know who dispensed the drugs, so it was natural they'd talk to you. Now look at me. Look at me."

She stared into the eyes of the two women and slowly saw the familiar effect, the slightly glassy look and the tension easing from their bodies.

"Now go home, both of you, don't talk about any of this to anybody, okay?"

Tanya nodded, got up and left. Jean stayed a moment longer, her head in her hands but finally she looked up, tears running down her face and also left.

Nona stayed up late, thinking hard about the news the two women had brought but eventually assumed that there was nothing to worry about and went to bed herself.

Chapter 33 – The Eighth and Ninth of October, 2022

At ten that evening Harry Jones started wrapping long, thick strips of towelling around every inch of the heavy kangaroo-protection bar on the front of his Land Cruiser. He had raided the stock of bath towels from the bathroom cupboards and cut them carefully into equal-width pieces earlier that afternoon.

By eleven, the big protective frame was covered with the towelling and Harry returned to his lounge room to pour himself a slug of rum in preparation for the task ahead.

Soon after midnight, Harry completed his task by carefully spreading some mud over the front and back number plates and then drove the Land Cruiser out of the garage, down the two hundred metre unsealed path to the stock route that led to the road. He had carefully selected a spot about two kilometres away, where very occasionally, he had seen people walk their dogs from their homes and into a small park. He stopped by the side of the road under some trees and settled down for what could be a fruitless wait or the fulfilment of a strangely exciting fantasy he'd had for years.

At about 1:30 in the morning, he was beginning to feel irritated and bored. He'd seen people on other nights by this time and he'd expected he'd be home again by now, making further inroads into the rum. Then he saw it. A light came on in a distant house at the end of one of the driveways and a few moments later, a figure appeared leading a large dog that seemed to be straining at the leash with its eagerness to get to the park.

Harry watched as the figure, probably a man by the shape reached the park, bent down and released the dog who bounded away with wild enthusiasm. The man stayed by the roadside, strolling slowly along the side of the grass.

Harry switched on the engine, turned on the headlights, put the vehicle in gear and accelerated sharply. He stayed on the road until he was just a few metres from the man and then flicked the wheel to the left, striking him with the middle of the roo-bar. He felt the thump, saw the body fly forward and a little to the left. To make sure, he swerved left to run over the body again and then continued accelerating up the road and toward his house.

Still breathing hard but with a great sense of fulfillment, he drove into his garage and began donning the protective coveralls he had bought at Bunnings a few weeks ago. He added the shoe covers, the gloves and raised the hood over his head, finishing with the mask over his nose and mouth. Then he took the big box cutter from the work bench and began slicing into the covering at the front of the car. There was a lot of blood over the towelling and he took a great deal of care as he unwrapped it to ensure none was left on the metal bars. It took twenty minutes before he was able to take the towel strips to his barbeque pit that he had prepared the previous day, light the fire and feed all the material into the flames. The strips were followed by the mask, coveralls, gloves and shoe covers. Finally, he returned to the garage, removed the blade from the box cutter and immersed them both in the basin of bleach-filled water and scrubbed them as carefully as he could. Only then did he enter his lounge room and start work on the bottle of rum.

* * *

"Some time just before two this morning," said Doctor Mortimer. "He was struck from the side, his entire left rib-cage is crushed, one rib penetrated the heart causing instant death. The left hip and upper leg are both shattered, so is his left arm."

A full moon illuminated the awful scene as the doctor knelt by the body and two scene-of-crime officers investigated the immediate area. Three obviously distraught people stood nearer the roadside.

"Who discovered him?" asked Melanie.

"Those people. They heard his dog howling and came to investigate. They said that was a bit before two. That's why I can give you an accurate time of death."

"And that's why I was called out just a little later. That's dreadful. What's happened to the dog?"

"One of the neighbours has taken it."

"My guys have started door to door questions, so we'll get as much as we can there. But can you estimate the sort of vehicle?"

"A damn great big one," said the doctor. "And travelling at some speed. But the injuries look like they were caused by a 'roo-bar, so probably on something like a Land Rover or a Land Cruiser or a similar sort of four-wheel drive. Those are as common as muck around here, so you'll have your work cut out identifying it."

*　*　*

Fourteenth of October, 2022

"Great story," said Jean. "Where does the name Harry Jones come from?"

"Nowhere in particular," said Mitchell. "Just a simple name."

"You certainly took care of the details," said Allen. "I particularly like the towelling cover over the 'roo-bar. That would take care of the blood spatters and by the time you used the protective covering, burned that and the towels and scrubbed the box cutter, there's no way in hell anyone could link your car to the killing."

"It's certainly got the cops baffled," said Gabrielle. "I heard on the news the same day that they were appealing for witnesses. So you got it done on the ninth and it looks like you didn't leave a trace."

"The cops did come round yesterday," said Mitchell. "They'd obviously worked out it was a big vehicle with a 'roo-bar and they would have checked out every vehicle like that in the region. They went over mine with a microscope, they wiped bits of the bar and the radiator and I imagine they did all that *'Silent Witness'* stuff and tested every atom, but they haven't been back, so I agree, I think they've found no clues. You know what, they even looked in my barbeque pit, so they must have some idea that protective gear was used, but I kept the fire burning high for a couple of hours, so there was no trace at all in the ash."

"This has been brilliant," said Nona. "Ten down, two to go, all of them on the ninth and the cops have no idea who did any of them and they don't even know that some of those 'accidental deaths' or 'natural causes' were actually killings."

"It's sure as hell been exciting," said Tanya, "just like we all imagined. Every time I see a cop car, I get a real rush, knowing they'll never work out what we've done."

"Coffee break time," said Nona. "I brought a lovely sponge cake, so dig in everybody. Then we'll talk about next month and who's in the hot seat."

"That'll be me," said Bella. "Mitchell and I have always done everything together, so it has to be my turn."

"Great," said Nona. "Have you worked out what you'll do?"

"I have. I think you'll find it original."

"We'll all be looking forward to hearing about it," said Nona.

Chapter 34 – The Eleventh of November, 2022 11:15am

"Make sure the gun is broken and held in the crook of your arm," said Anthony Clarke.

"Yes, Dad," said Bella, checking the shotgun.

"Now, we walk alongside each other and I'll decide who gets the shot when we see a fox or a rabbit, okay?

"Yes, Dad."

Father and daughter set off into the woods at a gentle stroll. Bella felt so happy being with the father she almost hero-worshipped and being trusted to learn how to shoot. They said nothing, walking very softly and Bella copied her father's way of walking, sliding her feet forward so as not to crack a twig and frighten a potential target.

"There," said Anthony. "A rabbit. Your shot, Bella."

Softly, Bella closed the shotgun, aimed and fired. The rabbit collapsed, its middle torn to pieces.

"Great shot," said Anthony.

Bella grinned in huge delight. She felt a warm flush of excitement run through her body and she walked up to the dead rabbit and stared down at it, fascinated.

"Leave it for the crows," said Anthony. "Now, replace the shell, leave the gun broken and let's move on."

"Yes, Dad."

Five minutes later, Anthony held up his hand and they both stopped.

"A fox," he said in a whisper. "Look, about fifty metres off to the right. He's standing by the pine tree."

Bella looked hard and finally saw the red shape half hidden by the lantana bush at the base of the tree.

"My shot," said Anthony, raised his rifle and took aim. The bullet hit the fox in the head and it became motionless.

"Great shooting, Dad," said Bella and ran up to the animal, staring down with a similar sense of excitement at the bloody corpse.

An alien noise invaded the quiet of the woods. Bella looked up and saw a strange shape flying above the trees, a noisy engine sounding ugly to her.

"It's an ultra-light," said Anthony. "A tiny little aeroplane, just two seats, they fly very low and very slow. There's a flying club just a few kilometres away and they often fly over the woods around here."

"They're noisy," said Bella with a look of distaste. "I don't like them."

"It's a free country," said Anthony, "and they don't do any harm. I rarely see more than a couple of them when I'm here."

"I still don't like them," said Bella.

"Let's carry on," said Anthony.

"That's a nice start," said Nona. "It sets the scene very well. How old were you then?"

"Twelve," said Bella. "That was the first time Dad took me out shooting."

"Interesting," said Nona. "Sorry, do carry on reading."

Returning from her father's funeral, still wiping tears away, Bella looked for his keys which she knew he kept in a desk drawer in his office. With the bunch in her hand, she selected the one she knew opened the gun cabinet, though she had never been in the room when he opened it.

Breathing a little harder with the sense of being about to make major discoveries, she opened the solid steel door and swung it aside. Her breathing accelerated into a huge gasp when she saw the contents.

Two shotguns and she knew about those as she had gone hunting with her father on many occasions since the first time six years ago. Three rifles, one she had seen before from the very first time they had gone out together, and she knew that the smallest one was a .22 calibre. But the other two seized her attention. They were much larger and heavier and she had never seen either of them before.

There was a slot in the side of the cabinet and it contained a brown envelope. She took it and found the permits for the guns. She leafed through and identified the permits for the two shotguns and the .22 rifle, naming her father as the licensee. The last sheet identified one of the guns as a Winchester .308 and the notes again identified it as her father's but this time as a licenced kangaroo hunter. She found another key, unlocked the chain through the trigger guards and pulled one of the rifles out, looking for the registration number. Checking against the licence, she realised that she was holding the .308. It was beautiful, with a polished redwood stock and gleaming metal. It was a bolt-action rifle and she tried moving the bolt out and back again, sensing the perfectly machined craftsmanship. It had a telescopic sight and she peered through that and tried to imagine seeing a large animal like a kangaroo through it. The excitement within her grew stronger.

The last gun gave pause for thought. It had no accompanying licence. It was about the same size as the .308, again with a telescopic sight and with the same perfectly machined metal parts. The click-click of the bolt as she moved it back and forth was immensely satisfying.

There was a second steel cabinet in the room, bolted to the brick wall like the first and this she knew contained the ammunition. She found the key and opened it. There were several boxes of ammunition and magazines on four shelves. Those for the little .22 rifle she could identify immediately. She had no difficulty with the shotgun ammunition, having used the weapon frequently. The two top shelves were labelled '308' and '338' and she decided that the slightly longer rifle was a .338 calibre. She took a magazine from the top shelf and opened a box of the cartridges. They easily slotted into the magazine and when she tried adding the magazine to the rifle, it clicked into place with the same satisfying precision of the bolt. She lifted the rifle to her shoulder, looked through the telescopic sight, completely lost in the almost erotic sensation of perfection, imagining a man in the sight.

Breathing hard and feeling her whole body flushed with heat, she replaced the pieces of the weapons back in the safes and locked them away.

Later that evening, she sat up with a shock. She realised that the police would soon learn that the gun licensee was dead and they'd be coming to get the weapons. There was nothing she could do about it, but if there was a licence for each gun, could it be that the big .338 rifle was not declared and the police would have no knowledge of its existence? She moved back to the gun room, unlocked the safes and took out the .338 and the ammunition, removed the '338' label from the top shelf, relocked the safes and thought about it. If the cops had no idea that another rifle existed, she was probably safe from discovery. She smiled as she realised the best course of action. There was a secret place she knew about...

Next morning, she went round to the police station and reported the death of her father and the presence of his guns. Pretending to be frightened by the idea and still distraught by her father's death, the desk sergeant was sympathetic and promised to send a patrol car round at once.

An hour later, the licenced guns were taken away. Bella went to the secret hiding place she had found for the bigger gun and the ammunition, took them out and held them affectionately and began to daydream.

"Excellent," said Ollie Simpson. "You've really set the scene perfectly. I can't wait to see what happens next."

"How old were you then?" asked Tanya.

"I was eighteen."

"And did you keep on shooting?" asked Allen.

"I did and quite legally," said Bella with a cheerful grin. "I joined the local gun club, completed the training program and applied for a licence. I got one for a .22 rifle and a shotgun, no problem because I was legitimately hunting pests in the woods. But I kept shooting foxes and rabbits with that big .338 rifle, it really made a mess of them, but one day I encountered a feral pig and I was glad of the heavy calibre. But nobody ever questioned me about it."

"Amazing," said Gabrielle. "So tell us, what happens next?"

Ninth of November, 2022

The forecast had been for a mild, sunny, windless day and Bella got up at five, went to the secret hiding place and took out the big rifle, put it and the shotgun in the car and carefully dressed in jeans and tee-shirt under the protective coveralls before setting off for her favourite spot for vermin-hunting. The light was good by the time she had reached her regular parking spot and she took both guns and began walking into the woods to a clearing that had usually provided good targets. But today, she wasn't interested in foxes or rabbits, not even feral pigs. She wanted bigger game.

She didn't have long to wait. Soon after seven, she heard the popping noise of the little motor that powered an ultra-light aeroplane. She quickly loaded the rifle, put on the gloves, face mask and hood and waited. Minutes later, the little aircraft appeared over the trees, a single person in the pilot's seat. Bella took a deep breath, worked to keep her composure and raised the rifle.

The image was astonishing. She could have been just a couple of metres from the man flying the plane. He looked young, maybe in his mid-twenties, his face under the safety helmet and goggles almost hidden. Bella moved the muzzle down to focus on the pilot's heart, held her breath and pulled the trigger. She saw the bullet strike the flying suit exactly where she had aimed, the man sagged forward, clearly dead and the aeroplane began a steep dive as the control column was pushed forward by the body. Seconds later it crashed into the trees.

"But Bella, surely the alarm would have been raised almost immediately," said Jean. "What if the pilot had been able to radio that he'd been shot? Or how soon would a search have been started when he failed to return? It was two days ago, they must have been looking for clues for some time."

"No problem," said Bella. "I knew my shot had gone straight into the heart, so he didn't have a chance to radio back. I had time to drive home, clean the rifle and hide it in a very secure place I made years ago. Then I burned the coveralls, gloves and mask in the barbeque pit and took a shower."

"What about the shoes?" asked Carl.

"Not a problem," said Bella. "Everybody knows I go shooting there quite often, so my prints will be all over the place. The main thing is not to have any blast powder from a heavy rifle anywhere on my clothes, face or hands."

A round of applause ran around the table, Bella shook her fists above her head like a champion.

"The cops will certainly be round to see me some time," said Bella. "They'll be talking to all the local shooters and anyone who was in the woods at the time. But they'll know I only have licences for shotguns and the .22 rifle, not a sniper's rifle like the .338, so they probably won't be interested in me."

"But what if they want to look in the gun cabinet?" asked Jean.

"No problem," said Bella. "Like I said, I hid that where I had before, in a space under the garage floor. They'll never find it."

"Well done," said Nona. "I'm sure we'll all be looking out for news of this event and once more hear how the police are completely baffled by it. Okay, everybody, time for coffee and cake!"

Chapter 35 – The Ninth of November, 2022
2:30 pm

"A bloody great big bullet," said Doctor Mortimer. "I called up a military acquaintance in Canberra and he came and looked at it, said it's a .338. Apparently it's considered to be a military sniper's gun, not something you find in people's gun cabinets."

Melanie Carter took out her phone and called the office.

"Alex, look at the gun registry. See if anyone has a licence for a .338 calibre rifle and start checking the gun shops for any sales of bullets of that size. Thanks, get back to me when you have something."

She put the phone back in her bag. "And it's a clean shot, straight to the heart?"

"Deadly accurate," said Doctor Mortimer. "That's a professional sniper's shot if ever I saw one. But it probably wasn't too difficult. From the angle it hit, the gun was fired from the ground and the people at the flying club said it was standard practice to fly over the woods not much above the trees. That's apparently the most fun."

"Something of that power would have gone right through the body," said Melanie. "How come you found it?"

"Through the body alright, through the solid webbing of his seat strap, through the same webbing of his parachute and stopped in the solid packing of his seat," said Mortimer.

Melanie took out her notebook from her handbag and was about to start noting some of the details but stopped with a jolt.

"It's the ninth of the month," she said.

"It is," said Doctor Mortimer. "Is that significant?"

"Something a friend of mine said to me a few days ago. He's with the Coroner's Office and he said that there have been several murders this year all on the ninth and a few accidental deaths or natural causes also on the ninth, all in this region. You did the postmortem on all of them."

"I remember the obvious murders," said the doctor. "There was the throat cut, the poisoning by that strange seed and the one with an overdose of a heavy painkiller and the baseball bat killing. What others?"

"A few weeks ago, I examined the wreckage of that car that went over the cliff. I found signs that a steel cable had been strung across the road, sending the car over the edge. I found the marks on the trees where the cable had been strung."

"You were going to tell me about this?" Mortimer stood immobile, every atom of his body radiating tension.

"Of course. It's hardly your fault, your job was to examine the body and report on cause of death. I only heard about this back in September. I'm preparing a report for the Coroner and of course you'll get a copy."

Mortimer eased up a little. "And you think there could be others?"

"I need to review the deaths. And I'll be asking my boss for resources to start re-opening some cases."

"Obviously, I'll give you all the help I can."

"I know that Doc, and I'll be grateful. What's bothering me is that each death has been different from all the others. Even the two poisonings were with quite different drugs and methods."

"So probably not a serial killer," said Mortimer. "They tend to use the same method each time, but these were, as you say, all different. Something very strange is going on."

Melanie's phone buzzed.

"Yes Alex?"

After a couple of minutes, she returned the phone. "My office says there is no licence anywhere in the state or in Canberra for a .338 rifle and no local gun shops have sold that calibre bullet. Nobody even stocks it. There are three local licences for .308 rifles, all for approved kangaroo hunters who are able to go out on official culls when needed. One of them used to live around here, an Anthony Clarke, he died over twenty years ago. His daughter reported the death and we sent people round to collect his guns."

"Not a likely killer, but I suppose you'll have to talk to her?"

"I will. Doc, thanks for all the help. I'll call you as things develop."

"Good luck, Melanie."

She waved as she left the mortuary.

Chapter 36 – The Ninth of November, 2022
4:00 pm

"Haven't we been here before?" asked Constable Alex Welland, turning into the lengthy driveway.

"Last month," said Melanie. "After that dreadful hit and run death. We checked out every large SUV with roo-bars and this was one of them. Mitchell and Bella Langer. It checked out clean."

They stopped at the front door of the homestead. The owners were standing on the deck, waiting.

"G'day," said Melanie, displaying her warrant card. "I called you earlier, I'm Detective Sergeant Melanie Carter, this is Constable Alex Welland."

"And why are you here?" asked Mitchell Langer.

"Just routine, Sir," said Melanie. "Have you heard about an accident in the woods this morning?"

"Yes, we have," replied Bella. "It was on the local news a little while ago, but they didn't say what the accident was. What has that got to do with us?"

"Were either of you in that area between seven and eight this morning?"

"Yes, I was," said Bella. "Everybody around here knows that I hunt there frequently. I shoot pests like foxes and rabbits."

"Yes, we do know that. Also that you are the legal owner of a shotgun and a .22 rifle. Do you shoot anything bigger than foxes and rabbits?"

"No, for two reasons. One, it's illegal to shoot kangaroos and wallabies and two, I don't have a gun big enough."

"So you don't have something like a .338 rifle?"

"Good god, no! Why would I want anything that heavy?"

Melanie was sure, Bella Langer showed some reaction to the question.

"While you were in the woods, Mrs Langer, did you hear a heavy calibre gun go off?"

"No, I didn't. The trees are dense all over there, a gunshot wouldn't be easy to hear."

"And did you fire either of your guns this morning?"

"I didn't. I didn't see a single rabbit or fox and I came home about nine."

"I know that we have checked your gun cabinet just a few weeks ago, Mrs Langer. May we have another look now?"

"By all means, though I think you need a search warrant. I mean, why would I want a gun big enough to shoot down a light aeroplane?"

"What brought that up, Mrs Langer? Nobody has said the plane was shot down."

"It was on the news, that's why."

"Okay, let's have a look at your cabinet."

The two detectives followed Mitchell and Bella to the gun room and waited while Bella found the keys and opened it up, unlocking the chain through the trigger guards.

Melanie took out each of the shotguns and the rifle in turn, carefully examined them but saw no signs that they had been fired recently.

"Thank you," she said, nodded at the constable and they returned to their patrol car, driving slowly along the dirt track back to the road.

"What do you think?" Melanie said.

"That stank like week old cod," said Alex. "Something spooked them both."

"I agree. They were tense as hell. Call the office, get a search warrant. I want to go over that place like a diamond cutter checking out the Koh-i-Noor diamond. Get a couple of extra officers, too. And call the local radio stations. Ask if their news broadcast said anything about a gunshot bringing down the ultra-light, rather than just reporting an accident."

Alex lifted the microphone.

* * *

Soon after six that evening, two police patrol vehicles arrived at the Langer home. Melanie was the first out and she advanced on the front door, exercising the knocker with some enthusiasm. Three more constables also emerged and began donning protective clothing.

Bella Langer looked astounded when she opened the door.

"What the hell are you doing here again?" she said, much louder than normal speech.

"Mrs Langer, I have a warrant to search these premises. Please allow my team and me full access."

"A search warrant? Why the hell do you want a search warrant?" Bella's voice climbed another notch as her husband appeared behind her.

"What the hell's going on?" he shouted. "Why are you bastards harassing us?"

"As I told your wife, Mr Langer, we have obtained a search warrant and that's because we have reason to believe you may know more about the shooting of an ultra-light pilot over the woods this morning."

"How the hell do reckon that?" said Mitchell, his voice hoarse.

"Because we checked with the ABC and the local stations and none of their morning news broadcasts mentioned an ultra-light aircraft. But Bella, you said you'd heard it, so there as no way you have known about it unless you were there. Now, may we proceed, or will I have to arrest you both for obstructing the police?"

The Langers stared at her for a few seconds, both wide-eyed then stood back from the doorway.

"Thank you," said Melanie and nodded at the two officers who had arrived in the second car. "Bedrooms and living quarters," she said. "Alex, you're with me, gun room and garage."

She put on her own coveralls, shoe covers and mask and the two of them moved through to the gun room. "Please open the gun cabinet," she said to Bella and waited while she found the keys and opened the steel door. There were only the shotgun and the .22 rifle locked securely. Carefully, Melanie checked the registration numbers of the guns with the licences and nodded.

"Thank you," she said. "And now the ammunition cabinet."

The process was repeated and Melanie counted the boxes of ammunition and checked the calibres. She looked up at the top shelf and something caught her attention.

"Bella," she said. "There's a lot of dust on those top two shelves and traces of something having been there, probably boxes of cartridges from the shape and size. Can you explain that?"

Bella's voice was hoarse. "That's where I had some of the other boxes. I put them in the lower shelves a few days ago."

Melanie lifted one of the boxes of .22 bullets and laid it on top of the traces she had seen. It was clearly smaller than the dust trails indicated. She looked at Bella and saw the signs of panic in her face.

"Oh! No, I've just realised, that must be from when I had my father's .308 rifle and the cartridge boxes were up on that shelf," said Bella. "I've never dusted them."

Melanie stood back. "Thank you," she said and let Bella close the cabinet. She caught the eyes of Alex who was checking filing cabinets and they moved well away from Bella to the far end of the gun room.

"Something's not kosher," she said. "I'll never be able to prove it and she'll clean up when we've gone, but I think there's been a heavy calibre rifle somewhere here, other than the one her father had owned. See what you can find."

He nodded as Melanie moved away and went to check on the other two officers. They looked up from where they were going through books and papers on the shelves. One shook his head.

"Nothing, Sarge," he said.

Something drifted into Melanie's mind like a fish rising to the surface of a pond. "Did you see any protective coveralls like we're wearing now?"

"No, Sarge. But I was once at a crime scene where a killer had worn stuff like this and he'd burned it. We got him from other evidence, but not that."

"Interesting," said Melanie. "Okay, I think we're done here. Bring a large evidence bag and come with me. You may have something."

She led the way out and to the rear of the house where a large barbeque pit stood. She opened the furnace designed for wood or coal and saw a pile of ash. A small shovel used for cleaning out the furnace stood nearby.

"Collect that lot, will you?" she said. "I'll talk to the lady of the house again."

She found Mitchell and Bella in their bedroom. They glared at her with huge hostility.

"Bella, is what you are wearing now, the jeans and tee-shirt the same as you were wearing when you were out in the woods this morning?"

"Yes, why do you want to know?"

"Then I want you to give me those two items, so please change into something else."

"What the hell? You've got no right..." shouted Mitchell.

Melanie raised a hand. "I have every right. Now, please do as I say."

She waited while Bella undressed and handed over the two items before taking a bathrobe from the wardrobe and donning it. Melanie took out a plastic evidence bag and folded the items into it. She returned to the barbeque pit where the other two officers were talking in soft tones.

"Good job, guys," she said. "Last thing I want, call the office, get a truck here. Load that Toyota Land Cruiser and take it to the lab. There's something I want to check."

"Yes, Sarge," said one of the officers and touched his radio switch. As he spoke, Alex joined them. "Look at this," he said and beckoned her to follow.

Back in the garage, one of the heavy cabinets on one wall had been pulled away. Alex bent down and pointed to a thin line where the cabinet had been. "There's something under there," he said.

"Let's move it," said Melanie and the two of them were able to pull the heavy cabinet well away from the wall. The line now took the form of a rectangle about a metre long and half that wide. At the far end was a notch. The two of them looked around and then Alex said "Aha!" and brought a crowbar, fitted it in the notch and lifted up a concrete layer. Underneath was a space containing something long and thin. Alex lifted it out and unwrapped it to reveal a beautiful rifle with a telescopic sight.

"That's a .338," he said. "I've got a mate in the infantry. He let me fire his once when I visited his base with a squad of police trainees. It's beautiful, and it's the rifle of choice for snipers."

"And that looks like ammunition," said Melanie, bending down and picking up one of several cardboard boxes from the cavity. "And that's what it says on the box."

She walked out back to the patrol cars and called the two men over.

"Alex has found something really interesting. Will you go and help him load it into the car? I have to talk to the Langers again."

She waited while the rifle and cartridge boxes were transferred to the patrol vehicle then she and Alex found the Langers standing tensely in their lounge room. Bella was now fully clothed again in jeans and a sweater.

"Mr and Mrs Langer, I have impounded your vehicle and it's being taken for further examination at our laboratories. Mrs Langer, I am arresting you for the possession of an unlicenced weapon which we found in your garage in a well-hidden space. Do either of you have anything to say?"

Bella looked almost catatonic with shock, staring at Melanie with wide open eyes, her face chalk white.

"You bastards," shouted Mitchell and jumped at Melanie. He didn't get far, as Alex caught him round the neck and hauled him backward.

"Mitchell, I could make this worse by arresting you for attacking a police officer, but I won't if you behave yourself. Alex, let him go."

Released, Mitchell collapsed onto the lounge and hid his face in his hands.

"Let's go," said Melanie. Outside, she watched as Alex put Bella into the back of the patrol car and slid in next to her. The other two watched with satisfaction.

"Okay guys, when the truck arrives, follow it to the labs and check everything in. I think we can call this a good day's work."

The two officers bowed courteously with wide grins. "Great job, Sarge," said one and watched as she climbed into the patrol car and set off down the track.

Chapter 37 – The Tenth of November, 2022

"Holy crap, Melanie, but you've got some serious jackpots here," said D.I. Comley. "After your phone call last night, I came straight up, stayed at my place and came into the lab early. The forensic chap said he'd be ready as soon as we got here."

"And I'm true to my word," said a short, stockily-built man entering the room where the detectives were waiting. They all knew each other so they got down to business immediately.

"You've kept my team up all night," said Andrew Blake. "That's the most work we've ever had at one time. "Let's start with the coveralls. Two things here. First, we went through the ashes you collected from the barbeque pit and we found three tiny fragments that had survived, none of them more than a centimetre square. Then we put the jeans and sweater under the microscope and found a number of tiny threads from something worn over them. And guess what?"

"All from the same pair of coveralls," said Melanie, feeling excitement from this process. She had never taken the lead in a murder case before and the evidence pointing to a successful discovery was making her heart thump.

"Indeed they are," said Blake. "But that only proves she had worn the coveralls over her clothing at some time, not necessarily that morning, so it's not proof of guilt."

"But we will certainly want to ask her why she had burned the coveralls," said Comley.

"I'm sure she'll be stressed out when you do," agreed Blake. "But now for the king hit. The bullet that killed the pilot came from the rifle you brought in. Look at these markings."

He touched a switch and an image appeared on the wall, transmitted from a small device hanging from the ceiling. Two outlines of a bullet were shown.

"The one on the left came from the body," said Blake. "The one on the right is the one we fired into a thick mass of gelatine last night. You can see from the striations, they're the same."

"No chance that they came from different rifles?" asked Melanie. She knew the answer but was relishing the process of uncovering a murder.

"None," said Blake. "I'm sure they taught you in Detecting 101 that striation marks are as unique as human fingerprints."

She smiled. "I just wanted to hear you say that," she said.

He nodded, straight-faced. "And you did. Now, this is still not one hundred percent conclusive. A good barrister could probably cast some doubts as to whether it was Mrs Langer or her husband that fired the shot, but she's already admitted that she was in the woods at that time and everything points to her. I doubt she'll resist interrogation for long. And so, let's turn to the Toyota."

Melanie felt a rush of excitement again. Something in Blake's voice indicated satisfaction.

"Now I know that a couple of scene of crime officers investigated that vehicle after the hit and run killing last month and found nothing. But with the new evidence about the gun, we got hugely suspicious and we tore into that vehicle like a virologist looking for a new infection. Here's the first thing we found."

He pulled a small evidence bag from his shirt pocket and slid it across to the other two. Comley looked at it first, said nothing and passed it to Melanie. At first sight, it seemed like just a tiny smear around a dot the size of a rust-coloured pinhead. She looked at Blake, one eyebrow raised.

"Blood," said Blake. "We found it buried in the gap between the windshield and the frame. It's been there quite some time, very dry and took some hi-tech examination, but there's no doubt, it's the same group as that of the dead man. Again, still not one hundred percent conclusive because we couldn't get any DNA from it."

"So we're still not totally barrister-proof," said Melanie.

"No, but we're getting there," said Blake.

Melanie was certain, he was about to reveal something critical that completed the case.

"We got under the vehicle," continued Blake. "We spent three hours going through every millimetre of the underside and we found this." He passed over another small evidence bag. Both detectives bent over it, heads touching. Inside was a tiny fragment of something hard and white, perhaps a centimetre long.

"Bone fragment?" asked Comley.

"Bone fragment," said Blake. "And this time we did get DNA."

"And it's from the body," said Comley, grinning widely. "Melanie, congratulations. You've solved two murders in one day. You can arrest Langer on a charge of murder and you can charge his awful wife with murder, as well as owning an illegal weapon. Go get 'em, girl!"

Chapter 38 – The Tenth of November, 2022

Melanie pressed the record button on the interview room system. A high-pitch whine sounded for a few seconds and then stopped.

"It is now 9:32am on Thursday, the tenth of November, 2022," said Melanie. "Present in the room are Detective Sergeant Melanie Carter, Doctor Jack Savage, psychologist assisting the police, Mr Graham Wall, acting for the accused and Mr Mitchell Langer."

She looked at Mitchell. "Mr Langer, do you understand the charges against you? Has your solicitor explained your options and rights?"

"No comment," said Langer.

Melanie looked sideways at Jack and exchanged a glance that said, *So it's going to be one of those interviews, it seems.* She looked back at Langer.

"Mr Langer, on Sunday, the ninth of October, sometime between midnight and four am, your vehicle, a Toyota Land Cruiser was involved in a hit and run incident in which Mr. Lloyd Freeman, aged sixty-two was struck and killed. Do you have anything to say about that?"

"No comment," said Langer.

"Then let me tell you what we found when we examined your vehicle over the last two days. First, we found a minute drop of blood embedded in the space been the windscreen and the frame of the vehicle. It was tiny, but our technicians were able to identify it as B Positive, the same blood group as the victim. Can you explain that?"

"No comment."

"The second find was a very small sliver of bone found stuck into the underside of the vehicle. On testing it, the technicians found it had the same DNA as that of the victim. Do you have anything to say about that, Mr Langer?"

Langer stared at her, his eyes wide and his jaw dropped. He said nothing. Melanie looked at his hands and they were trembling badly.

"That seems to have caused you some distress, Mr Langer, but I'm sure you will understand that when these details were submitted to the Office of the Director of Public Prosecutions in Sydney, they quickly decided that you would be charged with murder, contrary to the New South Wales Crimes Act of 1900. Do you have anything to say about that?"

Langer's face was white, his lips were trembling, his hands were now tightly clenched together.

"The details will be presented to the Coroner's court for an inquest today, but there can be no doubt that a finding of murder will be reached. At that point, formal charges will be read to you."

"Mr Langer," said Jack. "I'm intrigued. Did you know the victim, Lloyd Freeman?"

Langer stared at him and shook his head.

"So why did you kill him? When did the idea come to you that night? Was it just an impulse?"

Langer said nothing but a white tinge had appeared in his cheeks and neck.

"Or was it by some arrangement?" continued Jack. "Was this some pre-planned event, part of a program?"

Melanie recognised the line of questioning. Jack was looking to see if there was any similarity between the motivations for this murder and the global series of serial killings he had uncovered with David Hunter, and also if there was any connection to the other killings that had been committed on the ninth of each month this year.

"You see, Mitch," continued Jack, "I can't help but notice that you killed this man on the ninth of October. Your wife has been arrested on another charge of a murder that took place yesterday on the ninth of this month. Is there any connection between the two or was it just a coincidence?"

Langer's breathing had become coarse, strained and close to being sobs.

"Detective Sergeant, my client needs to stop this line of questioning," said the lawyer. "As you can see, he is in great distress. I must ask you to stop."

Melanie nodded.

"Of course, Mr Wall. He will be returned to his cell and I will have the police doctor examine him. This interview is concluded at nine fifty-one."

She reached over to the recorder and switched it off. She nodded at the camera that was watching the room and a moment later, a uniformed constable came in and led Langer out.

"Mr Wall, I'm intrigued by something," said Melanie.

"What's that, Sergeant?"

"You came here this morning, unannounced and declared yourself as the solicitor for both of the Langers. Nobody here knows you, so you are not in practice locally. But a quick search shows that you are in fact a barrister from Melbourne. This is unusual. Would you explain?"

"I presented my credentials, Sergeant, you are not entitled to any more than that."

"I am well aware of that, but common courtesy suggests..."

"Common courtesy has nothing to do with it. My task is to defend my clients against these ridiculous charges and I will certainly lodge a protest with the highest ranks of the police and the State government."

"Of course you will. I'll look forward to the result."

"You shouldn't, Sergeant. And talking of courtesy. Why is a psychologist present? What right has this man to be present?"

"Doctor Savage is employed by the New South Wales Police as a criminal psychologist. He is entitled to be present if we wish it."

"He may not be for much longer if I have anything to do with it," said Wall.

"How long have you had this delusion of power, Mr Wall?" asked Jack, smiling pleasantly.

Wall turned on him, his expression furious.

"You had better be careful, Doctor." The last word was full of contempt.

"So who hired you, Mr Wall?" broke in Melanie. "Who is paying your fees? The Langers are not rich, I doubt they can pay for an expensive legal defence such as you provide."

"That is not your concern, Sergeant. Now, if we have finished, I shall return to my hotel. You will call me if the interrogation is resumed and when you intend to subject Mrs Langer to the same amateurish proceedings."

"You may count on it," said Melanie.

"There's something very ugly going on," said Jack when the door had closed behind the solicitor. "The fact that both of them committed completely motiveless murders on the ninth of the month, but a month apart, that stinks for a start. Then when I raised the issue that there could be some element of planning or arrangement in it, that shook him mightily."

"I saw that," said Melanie. "That kicked him hard in the goolies. Okay, we're interviewing his wife at twelve. That could get interesting."

"Let's have a coffee," said Jack.

* * *

Melanie pressed the record button on the interview room system. A high-pitch whine sounded for a few seconds and then stopped.

"It is now 12:02pm on Thursday, the tenth of November, 2022," said Melanie. "Present in the room are Detective Sergeant Melanie Carter, Doctor Jack

Savage, psychologist assisting the police, Mr Graham Wall, acting for the accused and Mrs Bella Langer."

She looked at Bella. "Bella, do you understand the charges against you? Has your solicitor explained your options and rights?"

Bella looked directly back at Melanie, defiance in every fibre. "Yes," she said.

Melanie looked down and consulted her notes. "Then you understand that there are two charges against you, the first being possession of an unregistered rifle, a Remington 700 MLR 338 Lapua Magnum for which you have no permit, and associated ammunition, all stored in an illegal manner. Do you have anything to say about that?"

"Is that what it is? I never knew. It was just a .338 as far as I was concerned. It was my dad's."

"Let's leave the issue of illegal possession for now. On the morning of the ninth of this month, a pilot flying an ultralight aircraft was shot and killed, crashing into the woods near to where you have said you were."

"I was shooting foxes and rabbits, as I said."

"Yes, you did. However, the bullet which was taken from the body of the pilot was found to match test bullets fired from that Remington .338 rifle."

"Don't be stupid, woman," said Bella. "If I'd fired that rifle, I'd have gunshot residue over my hands and body. You didn't find any, so obviously I didn't fire it. Now, you can get me for illegal possession, I'll cop that, 'cos it's such a beautiful weapon and it was my dad's so I wanted to keep it, but I never used it."

"You are quite correct," said Melanie. "We found no gunshot residue anywhere on your body, that's a fact."

"In that case, Detective Sergeant Carter, you have no case against my client." The lawyer stood up and pointed a finger at Melanie. "This farce must now cease and my client is of no further interest to you."

Bella smiled with contempt and also stood up. "Then can I go now?"

"Not quite," said Melanie. "Sit down, Bella. Mr Wall, I suggest you do the same. We are far from finished."

She waited while both of them regained their seats, Wall looking angry while Bella seemed disturbed.

"The issue still stands that the gun in your possession shot the bullet that killed the pilot," continued Melanie. "And now a second point. We took the ash from your barbeque pit and gave it to our analysts. They're pretty good at this sort of thing and they have some very snazzy hi-tech equipment."

"So?"

Melanie looked at her and thought she detected tension in Bella's body.

"So, what we found were a few very tiny samples of a material used in protective coveralls, the type you buy at Bunnings, very similar to the coveralls our guys use when examining crime scenes so as not to mess up the area."

"So what?"

"And you remember that I took away the clothes you had worn on the morning of the shooting?"

Bella said nothing.

"Our techies examined those clothes and they found fibres that were identical to the ones we found in the ashes. So why were you wearing protective coveralls, Bella?"

Bella stared at her. "I've no idea. Maybe I was doing some painting. I can't remember."

"We found no traces of any painting being done, Bella, or any other work that might have required protective clothing. So why did you burn the coveralls?"

Bella shrugged her shoulders, "I don't know, can't remember. Maybe I spilled too much paint on them."

"I'll repeat. We found no traces of any painting being done anywhere in the house. Let me ask you another question. What were your movements from the time you say you got home the morning of the ninth when you said you were hunting foxes and rabbits and when my team arrived to arrest you that afternoon?"

"How the hell do I know? I work at home, I'm a dressmaker, so most days are the same. I don't follow a calendar"

"No variations? No social life?"

"Not much. I do go to the library once a month, the second Friday, I'm a member of a writer's group..." She stopped abruptly and looked down at her hands.

"So that will be tomorrow, will it? What time do you get there?"

"We meet between ten and one."

Jack cleared his throat. "Bella, a couple of things intrigue me. Why the ninth of the month?"

"What's the date got to do with anything?" Bella snapped in anger.

"Possibly quite a lot," said Jack. "Your husband killed a man in a hit and run, also on the ninth, a month earlier."

"No he didn't," retorted Bella, a flush appearing in her cheeks. "What possible evidence do you have for that rubbish?"

"I can't tell you that," said Jack. "But enough evidence to convince the Office of the Director of Public Prosecutions to bring a charge of murder against Mitchell."

"You've done what?" Bella rose from her seat and leaned threateningly toward Jack.

"You heard him," said Melanie. "And they have also decided to lay charges against you for murder, given the fact that a weapon in your possession was used to kill a man."

Bella sat down hard as if a string holding her up had just been cut.

"So we have a murder committed on the ninth of October by your husband and a murder committed by you on the ninth of November," said Jack. "Why the ninth?"

Bella was silent for a moment.

"Just coincidence," she muttered. The defiance had gone.

"Really?" said Jack. "This year, we've had a murder committed on the ninth of each month almost every month. The two that remain in doubt may not have been murders, but we're investigating. So what's the significance? Did you two kill these people as part of a program, a challenge, or something?"

Bella collapsed in a fit of weeping, slipping off her chair and onto the floor where she fell into a foetal pose, arms around her head, legs curled up against her stomach.

Melanie got up to help and saw that Bella's skirt was drenched at the thighs. She signalled to the cameras and a moment later, two women constables entered and gently pulled Bella to her feet and led her out.

"I hope you're satisfied," said Wall. "Your actions have caused huge stress in my client, you have intimidated her with lies and I will be bringing charges against you."

"You do that," said Melanie. "Now, I suggest you return to your hotel or maybe a discussion with your employer."

The fury that crossed the lawyer's face told Melanie that her guess had hit a mark. Somebody local was behind this man.

"You are at great risk, Sergeant," said the man and stamped out of the room.

"Oh my," said Jack. "Talk about a psychopath in action. He was ready to attack you."

"Scary, I agree," said Melanie. "But it confirms some local influential heavy is involved in this whole sick story. Now I'll get the janitor to clean up this mess. Jack, another coffee?"

* * *

"A writers' group," said Melanie as they sat in the lounge with their mugs of coffee. "That's triggered something... Yes, Jean Worrall, the cleaning lady at the sauna killing, she mentioned a writers' group."

"That's almost too ridiculous for words," said Jack. "A bunch of killer writers? But then, having a few top tycoons around the world playing a game to see how many people they could get killed was beyond belief, also."

"Looks like Alex and I will have to visit the library. One killer as a member is not a problem. But now we have Tanya, Caroline, Jean and Bella, all members of the same group. One's not an issue. Four starts to smell badly."

"I'm Detective Sergeant Melanie Carter," said Melanie, showing her warrant card to the librarian, a slender young woman dressed in an autumnal coloured dress in dark red and brown. "And this is Constable Alex Welland."

"I don't think we've ever been visited by the police before. I'm Trisha Hale, how can I help you?" The librarian smiled and showed obvious interest.

"You have a writers' group meeting here every month, I understand?" said Melanie.

"Yes, the second Friday of the month, between ten and one. They have the biggest meeting room that we have."

"So the next meeting will be tomorrow?"

"Normally, yes. But the woman who runs it phoned earlier today and cancelled it."

"That's interesting," said Melanie. "How many people attend?"

"I don't really know. I just see people arrive and go into that room, but I've never actually been in there when they meet."

"How many people could the room hold?" asked Alex.

"About twenty, I think. There's a long table in the middle, it probably holds that many seats round it."

"Do you have a list of the members?" Melanie asked.

"No, we don't." Trisha shook her head and her shoulder length hair flew round her face. "But I did know one of them, Caroline Collins but she got killed, back in July. You must know about that, it was a terrible story. Caroline was writing a historical novel and she spent a lot of time in here."

Melanie glanced briefly at Alex.

"Yes, we know about that horrible episode," she said. "How about any other members?"

"She was the only one I knew to talk to," said Trisha. "But we do have the name of the chairman of the group, we need that to contact her if anything has to change."

"Could we have that?" asked Melanie.

"Of course. Just let me check the computer." Trisha turned to the monitor, tapped a few keys then looked back at Melanie. "Her name is Nona Markham and this is her address and phone number. I'll write the details on a card for you."

"Thanks, you've been a great help."

Trish grimaced slightly. "I don't envy you talking to her. I find her quite scary."

"Scary? In what way?" Melanie was amused.

"Hard to say. I've talked to her a few times about meeting room arrangements and she makes me feel really uncomfortable. She's one of those very domineering women, doesn't let anyone get a word in edgeways and always seems to be looking down at you."

"Sounds interesting," said Melanie. "Anyway, they're not due to meet for another month, so can I ask you, if anything changes, will you call me? Here's my card."

"Of course. Can I ask, what's all this about?"

"Just routine," said Alex. "We're following up on a few things that need tidying up."

"Very professional, Alex," said Melanie as they left the library. "A professional case of Bullshit Baffles Brains there."

"Well, thank you, Sergeant," said Alex, struggling not to laugh.

"But that news about Caroline Collins was interesting. We never picked up that she was a member of this writers' group. That mob is getting more and more critical."

"I'm sure we'll be interrogating them all before too long," said Alex.

"Count on it! Alex, I'll need to have Jack along when we interview this Nona Markham. If she's somehow involved, it will need a psychologist to watch her reaction. Three of us would be too many, it might be threatening and she could clam up."

"I understand," said Alex. "But aren't you a psychologist, also?"

"I'm an amateur. Jack's the professional. I'll sit back and watch him work. But don't worry. You're going to be busy interviewing amateur writers a bit later."

"I look forward to it, Sarge."

"Okay, I'll drop you back at the station, I'll get Jack and we'll go and see Scary Nona."

Chapter 39 – The Twelfth of November, 2022

"Nona Markham? I'm Detective Sergeant Melanie Carter, this is Doctor Jack Savage working with the police department. May we come in and ask you a few questions?"

The woman at the door stared at them. Melanie sensed some reaction to her words but couldn't identify it.

"Police? Why?"

"As I said, Ms Markham, we need to ask you some questions about recent events in this region."

"What events?" She continued to stare at Melanie, making no move to open the door. Melanie looked back, seeing a large, imposing woman dressed in a black leather skirt and a blue sweater, a face without make-up, wide mouth and large nose. Her eyes were dark, no pupils could be seen.

Melanie sensed a strange sensation of fear, felt a slight tremble in her hands and fought against it.

"Ms Markham, we can do this the easy way, we've arrived in an unmarked car, you can let us in and talk about the issues we have, or we can do it the hard way, with a police car, uniformed police escorting you out and taking you to the police station. Please make up your mind."

For just a few seconds, a battle of wills was fought on the doorstep but then Nona stood back and walked into the house. Melanie began to follow her but Jack held her back until Nona had reached the far side of the building.

"Interesting," he murmured in soft tones. "Was she shocked or excited to see us?"

"There was certainly a reaction," agreed Melanie in a whisper. "Could it have been excitement? Who gets excited when the cops come to call?"

"Let's see. Okay, after you Sergeant. You ask, I'll watch."

They followed Nona into the house and through to a room at the back overlooking a large garden. Nona was already seated in the lounge, leaving two armchairs facing her. She waved generally at them and waited until the visitors had seated themselves.

"Alright, you wanted to see me. Ask your questions."

Melanie studied her. Nona was quite composed, showing no discomfort or unease. She sat unmoving, knees together, hands in her lap. Again, Melanie felt the slight unease in her stomach. *There was something about this woman...* She recalled the librarian, Trisha calling her "scary" and understood why.

"Ms Markham, I understand you are the chairwoman of the writers' group that meets in the library every month."

"You are correct. Is there a problem with that?"

"There appear to be some unusual events occurring with your members. Are you aware that we have arrested Mitchell and Bella Langer on charges of murder?"

"Yes, I am."

"May I ask, how do you know? We only arrested them yesterday and no announcements have been made."

"They called after one of your visits and I assigned my lawyer to them."

"So Graham Wall is acting on your behalf? And you will be paying his fees? Why is that, Nona?"

"The Langers are friends of mine and I know they're not well off. Mr. Wall is a top flight lawyer and he will kill off this nonsense."

"I see. I know that Bella Langer is a member of the group. Is Mitchell also a member?"

"He is."

"It seems that one of your group, a Caroline Collins was also a member but she was murdered in July."

"That was very tragic. Beaten to death with a baseball bat near her house, I believe."

"Quite correct. Now, let me ask you about two more people. Are Tanya Roberts and Jean Worrall members of the writers' group?"

"Why? Are they supposed to be murderers as well?" Nona leaned forward in her seat and stared hard at Melanie. Her eyes were unblinking, and Melanie felt a distinct wave of fear run through her.

This is insane, she thought and struggled hard, staring right back and forcing herself to stay calm. The short battle on the front doorstep was nothing to this, and Melanie fought to control the sickness she was feeling. She had no idea how long this lasted, but Nona suddenly sat back and looked down at her lap.

Melanie fought for breath and looked over at Jack. He was staring at Nona and Melanie could see the astonishment in him.

"Let me repeat the question," said Melanie, her breathing back to normal. "Are the two women I mentioned members of your writers' group?"

"Yes, they are." Nona's voice seemed a shade subdued. Melanie thought that she looked a little tired.

"Both of them are connected in one way or another to two deaths that occurred this year." Melanie looked down at her notepad. "In May, Mr Martin Fielding, a man in his nineties apparently committed suicide by overdosing on a powerful narcotic drug prescribed for his wife who had died a few days earlier."

"What's that got to do with Tanya or Jean?"

"The drug came from the pharmacy where Tanya works. She knew all about both the Fieldings, their health and their physical conditions."

"So is that supposed to be proof that she killed the old man?" Nona's expression was of somebody smelling something bad.

"No, it's not. It merely links her to the death."

"So you're not arresting her for murder?"

"No. Let's ask about Jean Worrall. Is she a member?"

"Yes. What's she supposed to have done?"

"She was the housekeeper for a Mr. Anders Jensen who died in his sauna when the door was blocked and he was unable to get out."

"Very tragic, I read about that. Jean was very upset."

"Yes, she was, I was the officer on the scene when we found the body after Jean had called us."

"So, if she called you, it's unlikely she had anything to do with Jensen's death."

"It would seem so. Can you tell me who are the other members of your group?"

"I could, but I won't. I don't want you running around accusing my friends of being killers."

"Then I'll have to find out for myself," said Melanie. "Perhaps Bella and Mitchell Langer will tell me." This time she was certain. Nona was disturbed.

"One last question, Ms Markham. Do you know what a Rosary Seed is?"

Once more, Nona was shocked. She swallowed, stared down at her hands and looked rigid.

"No," she said after a few seconds. "What is it?"

"That will do, Ms Markham," said Melanie. "We may have to ask you some more questions later, so please do not leave the area without telling us. Here is my card. We'll see ourselves out."

"Holy SHIT!" exclaimed Jack as he sat back in the passenger seat. He let out a long breath. "That woman is totally frightening."

"Tell me about it," said Melanie, starting the car. "I've never felt frightened of a person before the way I did when she stared at me."

"You handled it well. But she revealed a lot. I have no doubts now, the two women you talked about are guilty as hell, but we have no proof at all."

"And she knew what a Rosary Seed was, despite her denial. That seems to indicate that she was involved in the murder back in January of another old woman, Judy Henderson."

"But again, no evidence."

"Jack, I need a drink."

"Damn right."

She pointed at her phone on its base under the dashboard. "Call Alex, will you, his number is on the speed dial. Tell him to meet us at the pub. He needs to hear all this."

Chapter 40 – The Twelfth of November, 2022

"I'm a criminal psychologist," said Jack. "I've seen some of the worst things humans can do to each other. When I worked with David Hunter, I met rich, powerful people who thought nothing of hiring people to kill innocent victims as part of a competition. I interviewed killers who had killed small children and didn't have an ounce of remorse. I met people who had killed and eaten their victims. There were times when I wanted to kill myself, I was in such despair at the state of the world. But I have never met anyone who frightened me like Nona Markham frightened me."

He picked up his glass of beer and swallowed half of it.

"She sure as hell scared me, also," said Melanie. The three of them sat in the outdoor garden of the pub, well away from other drinkers.

"I wish I'd seen that, Sarge," said Alex. "It's hard to imagine either of you two frightened by one person."

"You'll meet her soon, Alex," said Melanie. "We'd better make sure you're not alone when you do. That goes for all of us."

"There's one interesting thing though," said Jack. "When you two stared at each other at one point, I could see the battle being fought. But you won, Melanie, she retreated and sat back. It makes me wonder what power you have in yourself."

"It was a close call," said Melanie. "And I nearly lost. I could feel her reaching deep down into my mind, trying to take over. I just decided I wouldn't let her."

"Which brings me to the professional stuff I want to raise and for which you are paying me vast sums," said Jack. He finished his beer and looked at the other two, with raised eyebrows. Both shook their heads and he stood up and went back to the bar, returning with a refilled glass.

"There are several types of personalities," he said. "Some people have more than one type within themselves, one usually dominates and the person presents most of the time as such a personality. The two types I want to discuss are the dominant and the submissive types."

"And I bet you're about to tell us that Nona Markham is a dominant type," said Alex.

"Bright kid, like I said," replied Jack, smiling at Melanie. She suppressed a grin.

"But I'm starting to see some connections between what's going on here and what I found working with David on the global outbreak of serial killings," said Jack. "Initially, we thought that all the killings in Australia, which is all we knew about at the time would have been committed by one person, a classic serial killer."

"And you did describe those characteristics," said Alex. "But I was young and foolish then and I can't remember. Can you bring me up to speed again?"

"All fairly well documented," said Jack. "Almost all male, usually between twenty-five and forty-five, a child of a broken home, certainly with little or no affection shown by parents, a serious day-dreamer and on a slightly odd side, a major league masturbator."

"So not a healthy individual," said Alex with a small smile.

"Indeed," said Jack. "But once we discovered that small runs of serial killings, almost all of them between three and five were occurring all over the world, we realised more than one individual was involved and we had to start looking at something outside standard pathology."

"We studied this at University," said Melanie. "It started to look odd as you identified some of the killers and they didn't conform to this standard pattern."

"What was the issue?" asked Alex.

"They weren't killing people because of their pathology," said Jack. "While all the killers had been identified as flawed psychopaths by the psychologists who were in the pay of the leaders of this game, they were doing it for money."

"That's what led to your other theory," said Melanie.

"Correct," said Jack. "I postulated that the psyche of the serial killer could be the same as the industry heavy, the sort of person that likes buying up companies, stripping them of all assets and wiping out the company. It was a sort of murder to them, they revelled in it and the only difference between them and the real serial killers was the socio-economic strata from which they originated. The rich ones killed companies, the poor ones killed people."

"And did that help?" asked Alex.

"It sure did. Once we had discovered that the killings were a game being played by very powerful people, we profiled a number of likely candidates. Increasingly, one of them stood out like a shag on a rock, the very same media baron who had been screaming fury at the cops for failing to find the killer."

"So how does this relate to our current problems?" asked Melanie.

"First factor here is that it can't be a single killer," said Jack. "There are too many differences between the M.O. of each murder and that is just too far out of possibility."

"And so?" prompted Melanie. She began to see where this was going.

"So just like the series of killings in each country by different killers were being controlled by one person, it seems to be the same here, one person is coordinating these murders in this small town."

"Nona, in fact?" said Melanie.

"Damn right, Nona."

"But Jack, is this possible?" asked Alex. "I know you've talked about dominant personalities and submissive ones, but could one person persuade ten or eleven others to change from being ordinary, regular people to being killers and condoning the murders of innocents over a whole year?"

"It seemed bloody impossible to me at first," said Jack. "So I started doing some reading. Can I suggest we get fresh drinks and then I shall give you the Savage Lecture on the mass influencer? My shout, I think"

"Sounds like a good idea," said Melanie and got up for a stretch then advanced on the washroom area of the pub.

"What the authorities call the DBS, the Dominance Behavioural System appears to be tightly linked to psychopathology," said Jack. "In simplistic terms, that sort of dominant behaviour is a sign of unhealthy psychology. It has been frequently found in the clinical diagnoses of mental patients who display abnormal behaviour."

He looked at the other two and saw that he held their full attention.

"Now we all tend to share one characteristic of DBS," he continued. "That's the pursuit of power. Even as children we display that and we all have a better or worse ability to spot the opportunity to gain power over others or control resources in something called '*Resource holding potential*' by the authorities. As we get older, this learning becomes a major part of our personality. Are you still with me?"

The other two nodded.

"Okay, just a couple more things to explain Nona," said Jack. "Part of the DBS is what we call *Dominance Motivation*, the desire to gain and extend dominance over other people. People with a very high dominance motivation tend to see the whole world as a framework in which they can spot opportunities for dominance or threats to it. They can be extremely sensitive to those signals."

"And this describes Nona?" asked Melanie.

"Almost perfectly," said Jack. "And conversely those with a very low dominance motivation, such as a submissive, they will not seek dominance, but rather seek to avoid it. So when you get a group of submissive individuals or even people who may not qualify as being submissive, they may all be those who seek to avoid power and will be drawn to somebody with a very strong dominance motivation."

"And we have the writers' group," said Alex. "But Jack, could she really change them so much that they will allow a year of murders by their own friends and associates?"

"That becomes the key," said Jack. "And that's what I'll be looking at for a paper to publish later. So let's look at recent history. There have been some quite astonishing examples of mass dominance. Take Adolf Hitler for one. He converts a nation known for world leadership in the arts, music and science and turns it into a Nazi state where mass murder is not only tolerated but approved of by the majority of the people. Friends, colleagues, even relatives were turned over to the Nazis for slaughter."

"I'll never understand that one," said Melanie.

"And Mussolini did the same in Italy," said Jack. "The country of opera, Michelangelo, composers like

Vivaldi, Botticelli and all the rest, it becomes a Fascist state of great cruelty and hatred."

He sipped his beer, thinking deeply.

"And in just the last few years, we had Donald Trump as president of the USA. His many millions of followers almost worshipped the man. The nasty underbelly of Nazism, racism, violence all crawled out into the open, with many of the country's leaders calling for people to swear personal oaths of fealty to him. Several Republicans even submitted bills in Congress and the Senate to declare the Democrats an illegal organisation that should be banned. Some Americans declared that liberals should be killed. It didn't reach the level of Germany under Hitler, but there were many who wished it to do so."

"Yeuch," said Alex. "And you see Nona with this capability?"

"Yes, she is not just a dominant, I'd call her uber-dominant. That's more than just charismatic, that's almost some form of psychological projection that stamps her authority over others."

"Jack, even if the writers are all submissives, could she actually persuade them to kill people?" Melanie was still sceptical.

"I've seen it happen," said Jack. "But always in the past, it's been a one on one relationship, one dominant, one submissive, often a husband-wife situation. I had a case exactly like that where the husband regularly beat his wife and eventually forced her to kill their two children."

"Good god!" said Melanie. "I just cannot imagine that sort of situation. I read about such cases in my university studies, but I never met anyone like that."

"Some form of mass hypnosis?" asked Alex.

"Not hypnosis, just enforcing one's dominance. The Jim Jones episode in Guyana is another one. One man persuades nearly nine hundred and ninety people to commit suicide together and kill their children at the same time."

"Having met her, I could well believe Nona has done this to her writers' group," said Melanie. "We need to identify the rest of that bunch. Okay, now I think I need another drink. Alex, your shout, I'll have a white wine."

Drinks replaced, the conversation resumed.

"But Jack, how could she persuade a group of normal people to kill innocents? I mean, just look at them? The Langers are just regular people, he's a farmer, she's a dressmaker. Tanya is a pharmacist's assistant, Jean, if she is the killer, runs a small cleaning business. Nona doesn't seem to do anything, but I ran a check on her, she inherited from a wealthy father. These people just aren't killers, though I wouldn't put it past Nona."

"I think there's more than just the dominant/ submissive thing going on," said Jack. "We all have elements of different personalities inside us. I once had a top psychiatrist examine me in detail, he looked at my writings, my history, everything and he concluded that I had a strong streak of violence in me. That shook me, I had no idea. But the more I thought about it, I realised how I occasionally day-dreamed about beating up my abusive father and then how I was drawn to the work I do, I saw that he was right. I just control it. But Nona might well have been able to reach down inside my head and turn the switch."

"Interesting," said Melanie. "I wonder if the very fact that they are writers, with highly creative imaginations could indicate that they have deeply hidden drives to murder?"

"I'd like to see the stuff they write when we finally identify them," said Jack. "But I strongly suspect that when we get the chance to talk more to them, we'll find some personality flaws that have allowed Nona to do what she has done."

"On that point, let's set up another interview with the Langers," said Melanie. "I'll call their lawyer, I'm sure he'll be difficult, but let's see if they can be made to tell us who the others are. Let's call it a day."

* * *

Alex was having a rare night in. The last few weeks working with Melanie and Jack had been exhilarating, exhausting and fulfilling, but the downside had been the decision by his girlfriend to abandon the relationship.

"What's the point of having a boyfriend if I never see you," she said. "And when I do, it's late at night, you're wiped out, all you want to do is sleep and you can't tell me anything about what you're doing. I could be dating a tailor's dummy for all the good you are."

"You know I can't tell you what I'm doing," he replied. "That's the rule in my job. But I've been given a job much bigger than I could have dreamed of, it's making a huge change for me and bumping my career along. I wish you could accept that."

"Well I can't," she said and picked up her handbag. "Good luck with that career, Alex, but my mum told me never to date a cop and now I know why."

She walked out of the apartment and a moment later he heard the sound of the elevator door opening. He missed her but he also knew that he wasn't going to give up on this amazing case he was engaged in. Sadly, he poured a beer, turned on the television and tried to pay attention to the evening news.

When the knock came on his door, his heart leaped. Was this Connie returning? Would she be all apologetic, extra sweet, forgiving? Would this mean a wild night in bed as had happened a few times after small disagreements? Smiling, he switched off the television, got up and went to the door.

It wasn't Connie.

He stared at the heavily built woman standing there. She looked to be in her forties, he thought, dressed in a black skirt and green sweater, brown hair with a hint of red. No makeup was evident. Something about her was disturbing, but he didn't know what it was.

"Yes?" he said, his throat suddenly dry.

"Alex?" she said. "I'm Nona Markham. May I come in?"

She was staring straight into his eyes. Alex felt impaled on her gaze, feeling his confidence diminishing. He desperately wanted to refuse her, she frightened him, but he couldn't. He stood aside and she walked in, sitting immediately in one of the two armchairs in his living room.

"Sit down, Alex," she said.

Feeling no control, he took the other armchair. His mind was whirling. He had never experienced anything like this before, this loss of control, the almost total subservience to another person. Not even facing one of the top police officers in the State had caused him this sort of confusion.

"Do you know why I'm here?" she asked.

He shook his head, sensing the first shiver of fear in his gut.

"You're working with Jack Savage and Melanie Carter, aren't you?"

He could only nod. *What the hell was happening?* he asked himself, his gut churning with bewilderment and growing fear.

"Why are you persecuting my friends, the Langers?"

He tried to speak but his throat was dry. He saw his glass of beer on the table and reached for it, draining it in one gulp.

"We're investigating a couple of murders," he managed to say, forcing the words out.

"They've done nothing," she said. "So Alex, I want you to consider something. If my friends have done nothing, you're under no obligation to follow the orders of that bitch, Carter. Do you understand? You can tell her to go fuck herself."

She leaned forward and stared into his eyes. He couldn't look away. He felt her presence work its way through his eyes, down into his soul. *Why not? Why should I obey that sexy bitch? What has she done for me? Why does she think the Langers are guilty of anything?*

But something was resisting. He felt the battle in his head. *Yes, Melanie is drop-dead gorgeous and I can't help staring at her when she's not looking. We've seen the evidence pointing at the Langers. What is this woman doing to me? Yes, I'd like to throw Melanie onto the bed and fuck her stupid. She's my boss, she's helping me get promoted, she's brilliant. This is terrible...*

"So, Alex, what are you going to do when you go to work tomorrow? I think you should tell Carter immediately she's a fool and her brains are in her tits. And then you can walk away from that silly job and do something sensible. You're a handsome young man, the world is all yours."

Alex had no idea how long they sat there, staring into each other's eyes. The turmoil within him grew stronger, the mixture of fear of the woman in front of him, the anger at Melanie Carter, the lust he felt for her, the anger at himself for letting this happen... he pulled away sharply. He felt the reaction in Nona.

"You're quite strong, Alex," she said.

He sensed some anger in her.

"Get the hell out of here," he said and stood up.

"No Alex," she replied. "We haven't finished."

"We have. Now get out before I arrest you for trying to interfere with police matters."

Looking astonished, she stood up and stared at him again.

"Alex, you will not say anything about this to anyone," she said and walked out without another word.

Alex stood still, staring at the closed door for another few moments, still feeling the sickness in his gut. He took another beer from the fridge and swallowed it rapidly. After half an hour, he switched the television on again and tried to concentrate on the happenings around the world but failed. It was after midnight before he went to bed and barely slept before the alarm went off at six the next morning.

* * *

"Alex, you look terrible," said Jack. "A bad night?"

"You could say that," Alex replied.

Before he could say more, Melanie appeared in the office.

"Good morning, gentlemen," she said cheerfully. "We have a busy day ahead of us."

Alex almost trembled. Multiple emotions ran through him, a mixture of anger and lust at Melanie, a terrible fear of what lay ahead and a massive conflict between a number of impulses. He found his usual seat opposite Melanie's desk and almost fell into it, grasping the arms as hard as he could.

"Alex!" said Melanie. "Are you unwell?"

"He had a bad night," said Jack. "No reason given why?"

Alex shook his head, trying to clear it. "No sleep," he mumbled.

"Why? Did something happen?" Melanie looked concerned.

Something leaped into Alex's mind and he couldn't stop it before some of it escaped.

"Go fuck..." he muttered.

"Okay, this is not rational," said Jack. "Melanie, leave this to me for a moment. This is right in my field. Alex, what happened last night?"

Alex shook his head, trying to speak.

"Nona," he croaked.

"What about Nona?" asked Jack.

Alex struggled, shaking his head.

Jack looked across the desk at Melanie who was staring at Alex, obviously hurt by his distress.

"He's been conditioned," said Jack. "The signs are obvious." He turned back to Alex and placed his hand on Alex's left shoulder. "Alex, did Nona come and see you last night?"

Alex began shaking, tears running down his face.

"Okay, relax," said Jack. "Nobody is going to ask you any more questions." He felt the trembling in Alex's shoulder die down and looked back at Melanie.

"This is a job for Super-Hypnotist Man," he said with a smile. "Nona may be a major-league dominant, but I don't think she can condition people against a professional hypnotist."

He turned Alex's chair to face his own, sat down and took out a gold fountain pen. "Now, Alex, concentrate on this pen, just look at it, keep looking at it..."

He moved the pen gently left and right and Alex followed it.

After a minute, Jack spoke again.

"Alex, you're going down a long moving staircase. You're just standing there, it's taking you further and further down, you can't see the end yet.... You're going further down... still further... further down..."

His monotonous tone kept on, the pen kept moving and then Alex closed his eyes.

"He's under," said Jack. "Melanie, don't speak until I ask you to."

She nodded.

"Now, Alex, it's perfectly safe for you to speak. You can tell me everything. Is that clear?"

"Yes," said Alex firmly, his eyes still closed.

"Did Nona visit you last night?"

"Yes."

"What did she tell you?"

"She said the Langers hadn't done anything wrong."

"Anything else?"

"She said I shouldn't obey Car... Detective Sergeant Carter."

"Did she tell you to say anything to Detective Sergeant Carter?"

"Yes. She said I should tell her to go fuck herself."

Jack shot a quick, amused look at Melanie who was smiling widely.

"And then?"

"She said I should walk away from the job and do something else."

"Okay. Now Alex, listen clearly. Nona can do you no harm, she can have no effect on you. She's frightened of all of us. And now Detective Sergeant Carter has something to say." He nodded at Melanie.

"Constable Welland, this is Detective Sergeant Carter. You are doing an excellent job on this case and when you pass your Senior Constable exams you will be transferred to the detective force."

Jack nodded his appreciation.

"Now, Alex," he said. "I'm going to count to five. When I snap my fingers, you will wake up and you will remember nothing of the meeting with Nona. Now, one, two, three, four, five..." He snapped his fingers with a sharp crack and Alex opened his eyes.

"Good morning, Alex," said Melanie. "Ready to watch the interviews with the Langers?"

"You bet, Sarge," said Alex.

"Let's go," said Melanie.

Chapter 41 – The Thirteenth of November, 2022

"Mr Langer, after receiving the Coroner's finding, I am now charging you with the murder of Mr Lloyd Freeman, contrary to the New South Wales Crimes Act of 1900. You do not have to say anything, but it may harm your defence if you do not mention when questioned something which you later rely on in court. Anything you do say may be given in evidence. Do you understand?"

Langer nodded.

"For the benefit of the tape, Mr Langer has nodded his understanding. Now I have a couple more questions to ask you."

"Mitch, remember, you don't have to say anything at all," said the lawyer. He glared at Melanie. "I object to my client being subjected to this harassment," he added.

"Understood," said Melanie. "Now, Mr Langer, are you a member of a writers' group that meets on the second Friday of the month?"

"Hold it there, Sergeant," said the lawyer. "You have no right to ask such irrelevant questions, this is nonsense. I demand that this interview be stopped right now."

"Your demand is noted, Mr Wall. Please bear with me. Mr Langer? The writers' group?"

Langer stared at his hands and said nothing.

"I must tell you, Mr Langer that your wife has indicated that she is a member of a writers' group locally. I cannot find any other similar group within fifty kilometres of here, so I am assuming it is the group that meets at the library as I said."

Langer stayed silent.

"Let me add some more information. Do the names of Tanya Roberts and Jean Worrall mean anything to you?"

Once more, Langer remained silent, still looking down at his hands.

"Again, Sergeant, I demand to know the relevance of these questions," said Wall, banging his hands on the table.

Melanie glanced briefly at him. "It's coming Mr Wall." She turned back to Langer. "I asked you that because both those two ladies are members of the group in question and both are persons of interest in connection to murders that have occurred this year."

She waited a few seconds. "No? How about Nona Markham?"

This time, she got a reaction. Langer's hands shook and his shoulders hunched.

"I ask you that because Mr Wall is here at the request of Ms Markham and she is the chairwoman of that writers' group. There seem to be a lot of strings attached here, all tied to a writers' group that meets at the library."

"That's it, Sergeant," said Wall again. "I demand you cease this nonsense. I shall be levelling a complaint to your senior officer."

"One more question, Mr Langer. Do you know any of the other members of the group other than your wife and Ms Markham?"

She waited again. "No? Okay." She waved at the camera. "Take him back to his cell."

"Bella, you have already been charged with the murder of Griff Miller, the pilot of the ultra-light aircraft and you have been read your rights. Now I have a couple more questions for you."

"Sergeant, we've been through this before," said the lawyer. "Your questions are irrelevant and I must ask you again to cease this harassment of my clients."

"Your request is denied, Mr Wall. Now, Bella, at our last meeting you mentioned that you are a member of a writers' group. Is that the group that meets at the library on the second Friday of the month?"

"Yes, it is," said Bella, staring hard at Melanie.

"And that is the group of which Nona Markham is the chairwoman?"

Bella tightened her lips and glanced at the lawyer. "Yes, it is."

"Bella, please, don't answer any more questions," said Wall, his tones climbing in volume. She ignored him.

"And is your husband also a member of that group?"

"Yes, he is."

There was a loud exclamation of annoyance from Wall.

"So you will know the names of Tanya Roberts and Jean Worrall? They are also members."

"Yes."

"What other members do you know?"

"Not telling you," said Bella.

"Okay. One last question. Did you and your husband commit these murders as part of a project with other members of the group?"

That one hit home. Bella sat back hard in her chair as if pushed, a sharp gasp escaped her and she stared in appeal at Wall.

"Take her back to her cell," said Melanie.

An hour later, she was back in her office when the phone rang.

"Detective Sergeant Carter."

"Trisha Hale at the library, Sergeant."

"Yes, Trisha, how can I help you?"

"You said to call you if anything changed with the writers' group. Well, Nona Markham just called. She wants the meeting room for an hour. I imagine that's for the group."

"And have you set a time?"

"Tomorrow at ten," said the librarian.

"That's really good news, Trisha, thank you. Please don't say anything, but I'll be there with my constable assistant and another officer."

"There won't be any disturbance, will there? You're not going to arrest anyone, are you?"

"Not unless somebody gets silly, honest. No, I just want to see who's in that group. We will be asking them to identify themselves, that's all."

The librarian's relief was evident in her voice.

"Thank you, Sergeant. We'll be expecting you."

Chapter 42 – The Fourteenth of November, 2022

"Alright! Everybody, please settle down. We can't do anything if you won't stop talking."

Nona rang her ornamental bell again and again, but it took three or four minutes before the group in the library meeting room went quiet.

"Now I know why you are all worried," said Nona. "And I understand. Mitch and Bella have been arrested, this is true. I assigned them a top lawyer and he will do everything possible for them, but we probably have to accept what he told me, the case against them is strong. We may just have to say goodbye to them."

She waited while a sigh of worry ran round the room.

"But it has to be said, people, Mitch and Bella caused their own problems by not following the rules I laid out. Mitch didn't clean his car properly, they found a spot of blood that matched the victim's and they found a scrap of bone under the car. Without those bits, they'd have had no pointers to him at all."

There was silence around the table.

"And Bella was stupid, using a rare rifle with ammunition that could be linked to it. I know she hid it well, but she was careless about burning the coveralls, she should have done a more thorough job. The tiny scrap of fabric they found in the barbeque pit was the only thing that made the cops suspicious. Without that, they would never have bothered looking for the rifle."

She stared at each of them in turn, sensing the worry and somehow forcing them to be calm.

"Now I know that the police have been back to see Tanya and Jean, but they found nothing at all incriminating, there is absolutely no reason for them to think the coroner's findings were wrong, suicide in the case of Tanya's old man and accidental death in Jean's sauna story."

"But what about the old lady we kidnapped?" said Tanya, her voice high-pitched with tension. "She didn't die and somebody found her."

"Again, no cause for concern," said Nona. "Yes, it was unfortunate that somebody found her, it was a remote chance, but she was out cold the whole time and couldn't identify you in any way at all. You both wore full protective clothing, she didn't hear you speak, there is absolutely nothing to link you and Ollie to it. So everybody, stop worrying, you all did your assignments perfectly, there is no clue anywhere to link any of you to them. So we have a great set of stories we can publish just for ourselves and nobody will ever know any more about the other deaths."

The door opened and in walked Melanie Carter, Jack Savage and Alex Welland.

* * *

"Good morning, all you writers," said Melanie with a pleasant smile and walked to the front of the room, standing behind Nona. Jack followed, but stood in one corner, watching each individual. Alex stood by the door, his arms crossed against his chest in a stance that said clearly, *Nobody gets past me.*

"My name is Detective Sergeant Melanie Carter. I've met some of you already, Tanya, Jean, Nona..." She smiled at Tanya and Jean, noting their white faces and wide-open eyes. "The young man guarding the door is Police Constable Alex Welland and this gentleman to my right is Doctor Jack Savage. He's a psychologist, retired now, but once he was considered the best criminal profiler in the country."

Nobody turned their heads to look at the other two. Their attention was rivetted on Melanie.

"But we've been looking forward to meeting the rest of you," continued Melanie, "because we want to talk to you about this tragic series of deaths we've been having locally this year. I'm sure you've heard about them and as you probably know by now, we've arrested Mitch and Bella Langer for two of them."

She looked around the table. Some of them were staring at her, some were almost catatonic, looking down at the table top or their hands.

"Now there's something curious about these deaths," Melanie continued. "While some of them were obviously murders, like the poor old bloke who had his throat cut in his back garden and the terrible death of Caroline Collins who was beaten to death with a baseball bat on the river path... she was one of your members, wasn't she? Your club secretary, in fact? How did you all react to that?"

She smiled around the room, like a visiting speaker. "There are questions about a couple of others. You may remember the accidental death of the old lady who ran off the road and over the cliff back in February? That was ruled an accident by the coroner, but we reopened the case a few weeks ago and we've since decided it was actually murder."

One of the men at the table drew in his breath and sat back in his chair. Melanie noted that and knew that Jack would have seen it too.

"And of course, you will have heard from Jean about her terrible experience last June, finding Mr Jensen dead in his sauna when she came to the house for her weekly cleaning. Well, believe it or not, we've re-examined that one too, and would you believe it, we've decided that was murder, also."

She was looking at Jean as she spoke and there was no doubt at all, Jean was terrified, eyes staring, hands in front of her mouth, her face ashen.

"And way back in January, another old lady died in her home. Initially, we thought it was another case of natural causes, she was very old after all, but when our pathologists really got down to it, we found traces of an extraordinarily rare poison in her body. So, guess what, another murder."

She sensed the small tremor in Nona sitting immediately in front of her.

"There are a few common features about all these sad events," continued Melanie into the silence.

"There were no signs, no clues as to the identity of the killers, nothing at all. That's most unusual and our crime-scene investigators are really good at finding these clues. Quite a number of the victims were old and frail, which suggest some planning and target selection. But the main thing that interested us was that all the deaths we've so far identified, including a couple I haven't mentioned here, all occurred on the ninth of the month. Don't you find that interesting? We did."

She took a few moments to look around the table again. She had all their attention.

"Let me mention some other deaths on the ninth of the month," she said. "In April, a fisherman drowned on the lake nearby, we have no cause to think anything but that it was an accident, the man wasn't wearing his life jacket. And back in May, an old man in his nineties committed suicide with an overdose of a powerful narcotic. And two months ago, in September, another old woman was kidnapped and tied up in an abandoned shed, miles from anywhere. But she was lucky, a farmer looking for an escaped alpaca found her. So, does anyone want to comment on what I've been telling you?"

She waited a few moments, not expecting anyone to speak.

"What I find interesting," she said, "is that nobody here has asked me why I'm telling you this. Doesn't it strike you as curious that two police officers and a police psychologist would interrupt your writers' meeting to tell you about a series of deaths in town? After all, while we have two of your group in custody for two murders, we have no evidence that any of the rest of you are involved.

"But what we do find interesting is that you're having this meeting. Your normal program is to meet on the second Friday of the month. That was last week and it was cancelled. So why this meeting? Could it have anything to do with the fact that we interviewed Nona two days ago? So I'll tell you, it's quite simple, it's just that there are an awful lot of links between the deaths I've mentioned and this writers' group and that makes my detective's nose twitch a bit. Same with Doctor Savage here, his nose has been twitching severely."

She took a notepad from her bag, nodded at Alex who moved away from his stance by the door and extracted a similar notepad from his jacket pocket.

"We're going to ask each of you that we haven't met already for your name and contact details," Melanie said. "We will be calling on each of you over the next two or three days to discuss what we talked about here, mostly to eliminate you from our enquiries. However, let me stress that you mustn't leave town without telling me until we have talked to you."

There was still no sound from the people at the table.

"Good," said Melanie. "Alex?"

* * *

"Well, that was fun," said Melanie, bringing her coffee mug from the kettle and sitting down. "I felt like a detective in an Agatha Christie novel, summoning all the cast to the library to explain why it was Colonel Mustard with a pistol in the bedroom, or something."

"Except that you didn't," said Alex with a wide smile. "You just scared the living crap out of everybody there."

"It was very revealing, certainly," said Jack. "And I tell you what, not only did it show up some serious suspects, it also showed that you have some of that same dominant personality stuff that Nona has."

"Let's concentrate on the suspects," said Melanie, pushed a little off balance by Jack's comments. "What did you see?"

"First off," said Jack, consulting his notes. "Carl Hitchcox, he's the sixties guy, thin, dark, bald, wearing a red sweater and black jeans. He definitely reacted when you mentioned the car off the road murder."

"Yes, I saw that one," said Melanie.

"Nothing on him in the files," said Alex. "I just did a quick squiz, but no mention. Seems quite clean."

"Second," continued Jack. "Our pet dominant lady, Nona Markham. She twitched when you mentioned the Rosary Seed poisoning."

"I saw that one too," said Melanie. "And when we interviewed her the other day, she reacted strongly when I asked her if she knew what a Rosary Seed was."

"Third was unexpected," said Jack. "There were two reactions to the news of the failed murder-kidnapping. Tanya flinched, but so did that young guy, Oliver Simpson. He got quite disturbed and looked across at Tanya."

"So those two may have done it together? That's interesting. Alex, have you had a chance to look at him?"

"Just a quick glance again, Sarge. No form at all."

"Okay. And we're pretty clear that Jean Worrall is in the sauna killing up to her scrawny neck," said Melanie. "Anything else, Jack?"

"Another twitch, this time from Paul Johnson. He's the forties bloke, looks very fit, full head of black hair. Just a tiny twitch when you mentioned the fisherman's drowning."

Melanie looked across at Alex, received a shake of the head.

"Two more," said Jack. "But this is in the dog barking in the night category."

"Explain please, to us illiterate folk," said Melanie.

"Oh, I know that one," said Alex. "Sherlock Holmes and the Silver Blaze story about a stolen race horse. On the question of the dog in the night, Sherlock said the interesting point was that the dog didn't bark in the night and that was the critical clue."

"Constable, you're getting to be irritating," said Melanie, ignoring the guffaw from Jack.

"But the kid is correct," said Jack. "Two people there didn't react at all, they looked quite composed throughout. The first is Allen Miller, fifties, very dapper dresser, jacket, tie, trimmed moustache, looked a bit military. He sat there, unmoved the whole time, never spoke a word."

"And he stayed silent when I got his name and address," said Alex. "Not a peep out of him."

"And the last is the plastic blonde," said Jack. "Her name is Gabrielle Greenwood, suspiciously perfect tight blonde curls, similar make-up, immobile face, looked a bit Botoxed. First estimate late thirties but as I got closer, I'd say nearer sixty. Very fit, neat body, a true gym resident. She didn't like you at all."

Melanie smiled. "I'm used to that. So, if we're sticking with the assumption that the writers are the killers, then we might imagine that Tanya and Oliver together did the kidnapping, Carl Hitchcox was the diverted car killing, Jean Worrall killed Jensen in the sauna and Nona could have poisoned the old lady back in January."

"Which still leaves some blanks," said Jack.

"Correct. We still don't know who killed the old man by cutting his throat, who killed Caroline Collins, their club secretary by beating her to death with a baseball bat, who, if anyone, poisoned poor old Martin Fielding and who, if anyone drowned the fisherman. Those last two might not actually be murders, there's only the fact of the ninth of the month date to cause suspicion. And of course, that whole identity killing by computer, we still don't know if it's part of this saga or totally unconnected."

"Seems to be time to interview them all," said Jack. "Do you want to bring them in or meet them at their homes?"

"At their homes," said Melanie. "It might lull them into a false sense of thingy and there may be some clues as to identities and background that could help."

"Can I join you?" asked Alex.

Melanie nodded. "It's time you watched the professionals in action and a third pair of eyes watching them could be critical."

"Excellent," said Alex, grinning with delight.

"But run a check on all the ones we've just met," said Melanie. "I'm pretty sure they're all clean, but you never know."

Alex nodded and left the room.

Chapter 43 – The Fifteenth of November, 2022

"Mr Johnson, I'm Detective Sergeant Melanie Carter. We met briefly yesterday at the library during your writers' group meeting."

"I have nothing to say to you. I'm not involved in any of those killings you talked about."

"Of course, but we would like to talk to you to clear you from further interest, if you wouldn't mind. May we come in?"

Johnson stood still for a few moments then reluctantly opened the door.

"You know Doctor Jack Savage and Constable Alex Welland from yesterday, also, I presume?"

Johnson didn't look back as he led the way to a lounge room. He sat in one of the two armchairs and made no gesture to invite the others to sit. But Jack took a seat on the sofa and Melanie in the second armchair. Alex stayed standing by the sideboard, looking at the pictures and other ornaments.

"Can I ask your occupation, Mr Johnson?" asked Melanie.

"I run a sports store in Canberra. I sell sports equipment and also memorabilia, signed photos of sports stars, that sort of thing."

"And how long have you been a writer?"

"About five years."

"And what do you write, if I may ask?"

"I've written some articles on naval warfare for a number of history magazines and I'm working on a book about naval tactics and strategy."

"That must take some expertise and a lot of research, I imagine," said Melanie.

For the first time, Johnson's hostility faded and he showed some animation.

"A hell of a lot," he said. "I spend a lot of time on the internet and also at the War Memorial Museum in Canberra. I've even been to the Imperial War Museum in London and the National Navy Museums in Paris and Washington to do some research."

"That's amazing. You must have been in the Australian Navy then?"

"I was. I was a Chief Petty Officer."

"Then I'm impressed. My dad always said that the military is ruled by non-commissioned officers, especially those of that rank, like staff sergeants and flight-sergeants."

Johnson appeared to relax even more, but he looked over at Alex who had begun looking at the photographs on the sideboard.

"Paul, may I call you Paul? Can we just take a small amount of your time and ask you where you were on April the ninth?"

"That's months ago, so I can't be sure. But I imagine I was at the shop, it's where I spend almost all my time."

"But not today?"

"You said you were going to come and talk to us and you called yesterday afternoon to say you'd be here today. I arranged for my assistant to hold the fort all day."

"And your assistant's name is?"

"Jennifer Wilder."

"Thank you, Paul, that should be all we need. Many thanks for your time."

"Not at all. I hope you solve all those killings."

Without another word, Jack, Alex and Melanie left and returned to the car.

"He's our man for the drowning," said Alex from the back seat.

"Explain," said Melanie.

"A picture on the sideboard," said Alex. "Him in navy uniform, a CPO as he said, but he was posed by the sign saying HMAS Penguin."

"So why is that suspicious? Wouldn't he serve on a ship?"

"Penguin isn't a ship, it's a navy training base in Balmoral. I know because that's where I grew up. It's the main Diver Training School."

Jack turned in his seat and looked at him.

"Well, shit, eh?" he said.

"Exactly," said Alex. "Which means I can get access to military records if the Police top brass ask for them and I can check just what his record was."

"Alex, you are becoming intensely annoying," said Melanie, her smile wide. "Stop being so clever and showing up your Sergeant."

"Yes, Sarge," said Alex.

* * *

"Johnson joined the Navy in 1974 at the age of eighteen," said Alex. "At twenty, he asked for and was transferred to HMAS Penguin in Balmoral and trained as what they term a Clearance Diver. That's pretty intensive training, very hard, needing great fitness. They're actually part of Australian Special Forces and you don't get much tougher than that. Their job is clearing mines. Once he had been trained, he was assigned to a group called Australian Clearance Diving Team One based at HMAS Waterhen in Sydney. His performance was highly rated and he became a CPO in 1984. He retired in 1995."

"So swimming submerged for a lengthy distance and hauling a man out of a boat would be no big deal for him," said Jack.

"It would barely make him breathe hard," said Alex. "Even in his sixties, that bloke is steel hard. I sure as hell wouldn't like to take him on."

"So a hell of a likely prospect," said Melanie. "But we have no evidence."

"But a Navy CPO isn't going to be a submissive personality," said Jack. "Maybe he's part of this for his own reasons, not following Nona's lead."

"Could it be that he's a dominant in his own right, a bit of a danger freak, if that job of clearing mines is anything to go by and fancied the idea of killing somebody?" asked Melanie.

"It could fit," said Jack.

"I did the other check you asked, Sarge," said Alex. "I went to see his shop in Canberra. Very impressive.

Every sort of sporting item you could want, even baseball bats."

"Baseball bats? Like the one that killed Caroline Collins?" said Melanie.

"It's a popular sport in winter," said Alex. "Cricketers use it to keep their eye in. But that wasn't the part that was interesting. Johnson wasn't there, and I talked to his very dolly assistant, Jennifer Wilder."

"And?"

"She checked the records. He wasn't there on the ninth, but then, he's often out all day. Jennifer said she's on her own more often than not."

"Well done, Alex," said Melanie. "Good pointers, but not enough to prove he's the killer."

"Okay, who's next?" said Jack.

"I think the well-dressed Allen Miller," said Melanie. "Somebody who stays so cool, calm and collected while all sort of tension and panic is breaking loose causes my nose to twitch."

"Mine does too, but that's because he wears a jacket and tie to an informal meeting of a writers' group," said Jack. "It ain't natural."

"Do you even have a jacket and tie, Jack?"

"Haven't worn one in thirty years. I've forgotten how to tie a tie."

"Should be an interesting meeting," said Melanie.

* * *

Miller looked calmly at them. He was still quite formally dressed, a white shirt with a tie, dark slacks, dark brown hair with the hairline receding to the middle of his head.

Jack and Alex took up the same positions as the last interview, Jack in an armchair, Alex standing by the door.

"That was an amazing performance you put on yesterday," Miller said. "The idea that a group of writers could have organised so many murders is astonishing, I'm surprised your superiors let you continue this farce."

"Having found so many connections between the murders so far identified and the writers' group, my superiors are quite supportive of my work," said Melanie. "I can't quite tell that accent, is it American or Canadian?"

"I'm originally from the States," said Miller. "From Baltimore."

"And how long have you lived in Australia?"

"Over ten years, and I'm a citizen. Is this to be a witch hunt for an illegal immigrant?"

Melanie smiled. "Heavens, no. It's a murder inquiry and what we are trying to do is eliminate suspects."

"Then eliminate me right now. I've never killed anybody."

"I'm sure we'll be able to do that soon. So, Mr Miller, what is your occupation?"

"I'm independently wealthy, I made a lot of money in the States. But I'm a good investor, I spend most of my time trading stocks."

"And you're successful at it, I assume?"

"Indeed I am." Miller looked smug.

"What are you working on as a writer, may I ask?"

"Does that have anything to do with your farcical murder inquiry?" Miller looked annoyed and he crossed his legs in irritation.

"I don't know," said Melanie. "But I'd like an answer."

"If you insist. I'm writing a thriller about financial fraud around the world."

"And it sounds like you may have the background and knowledge for it." Melanie smiled and saw the effect she was having on Miller. He visibly melted.

"Excuse me, Mr Miller, Sarge," broke in Alex. "Sorry about this, but can I use your washroom? The morning coffee is having an effect."

"Upstairs, second on the left, and no pretending to find illegal drugs there," said Miller and waited until Alex had left the room.

"Mr Miller," said Melanie, "this is the point at which I should advise you, I have a warrant to search this house."

"Really?" Miller looked unsurprised. "And what do you expect to find?"

"I really have no idea," said Melanie. "But while Alex is upstairs, he will have a look around."

"No problems," said Miller. "You can all look as much as you like. And yes, I do have the background for the book. But I'm there to learn how to write fiction."

"Were you ever in the military?"

"No, I wasn't."

"What made you choose to come and live in Australia?"

"Oh, the usual. Climate mainly. I don't have family, I liked everything I had read or seen about Australia. When I checked with your immigration, I was still young enough and I could bring in a large sum of money, so I applied as soon as I could."

"And have you always lived in this area?"

"Sergeant, I don't wish to be rude, but what the hell is this line of questioning? This is more like a social call and it's wasting my time. There are trades I want to make, people I need to call, stuff I have to research. Can we end this nonsense?"

"Just about," said Melanie. "But while we wait for Alex, just a couple more social questions. Are you particularly friendly with any of the others in the group?"

"No, I'm not. I'm not there to be social, I want to learn how to write fiction."

"What do you think about the chairwoman, Nona Markham?"

"I think she's amazing. She makes us think, makes some great observations and keeps the meeting rolling along. Now, a question from me. Why is a psychologist here and does he have any questions for me?"

Jack laughed gently. "My job is to watch you while the Sergeant asks the questions and see if I can see anything suspicious."

"And have you now concluded that I'm a raving serial killer and a danger to society?"

Jack's laugh was louder. "No Mr Miller, I have not. You seem quite sane to me."

"Well, that's a relief."

The sound of a flushing toilet came from the upstairs and Alex appeared a moment later.

"Okay, Mr Miller, we have no more questions," said Melanie. "Thank you for your time."

Miller stood up and nodded, but said nothing as they left the house and returned to the car.

"Any thoughts?" asked Melanie as she drove back onto the road.

"He's hiding something," said Jack. "There was definite tension when you asked him about being American and what he did in the USA. And the interesting thing is that there was not a picture on the walls, not a photograph of anybody anywhere, no sign of an actual life."

"Same with the rest of the house," said Alex from the back seat. "I snuck into the two bedrooms and the study, there's nothing, no pictures, nothing. It's almost as if he didn't have a life at all."

"Interesting," said Melanie.

"But the reason for the loo call was a lie," said Alex. "I just wanted to see his bathroom."

"And what did you find?"

"Possibly something critical. As we saw, he's balding, so I wondered if his hairbrush might show anything. I studied it carefully and I found what I wanted, a couple of hairs still attached to the follicles. I've got them in this little bag."

"Which means live DNA," said Jack. "Melanie, you'd better hang on to this kid, he's useful."

"Yeah, not bad for a dumb cop," said Melanie. "But Alex, you realise, you can't transfer to the detectives until you're a Senior Constable?"

"I do, Sarge."

"Let's get those follicles to the lab and see what they make of them. Then we have some more people to grill."

"Who's next?" asked Alex.

"The Botox blonde," said Melanie.

* * *

Gabrielle Greenwood stared with open hostility at Melanie.

"What the hell do you want? And why are these stupid men here?"

"As I said at the library, Gabrielle, I'm Detective Sergeant Melanie Carter. This is Doctor Jack Savage and the young man is Constable Alex Welland. We need to ask you some questions."

"You don't look like a detective."

"Why is that, Gabrielle?"

The woman shrugged and waved a general hand in Melanie's direction. "You look more like a fashion model. You can't have the brains to be a detective."

"How long have you been a member of the writers' group, Gabrielle?" asked Melanie.

"About three years."

"And what do you write?"

"Short stories, usually about stupid men and the stupid things they do."

"Are you married?"

"Have been. Two utterly useless wankers, they didn't last long."

"By that, do you mean the marriages ended quickly or they died?"

"Don't try that crap on me, woman. Trying to imply I killed them? No, I didn't, they both got what was coming to them and disappeared."

"I see. Now, Gabrielle, are you part of an arrangement in the group to kill somebody on the ninth of each month?"

Greenwood opened her eyes in shock and shrank back in her seat.

"You... what?" she stammered.

"You heard me. Did you kill somebody on the ninth of one month this year? You look very fit and strong. Could you have beaten your club secretary to death with a baseball bat? How about holding down a frail old man and forcing enough narcotics down his throat to kill him? Or how about slicing the throat of an elderly man in the back garden of his house?"

Greenwood was pressing back in her seat as if trying to escape, her hands twisting and her face ashen white.

"No-o-o," she said in a rasp. "No, I couldn't do anything like that, how could you say so?"

"I'd like to look around the house, Gabrielle. Is that okay?"

She swallowed and coughed. "Don't you need a warrant for that?"

"Funny you should say so," said Melanie and took an envelope from her jacket pocket. "This is in fact a court order to allow us to search this property. I advise you to stay here while this is going on, we'll be out of here quite soon."

"Nothing at all?" asked Melanie as they returned to the car.

"Not a damned thing," said Jack, and Alex shook his head. "No protective clothing, no signs of any destruction of it."

"No photographs of friends or family, no signs of human contact at all," said Alex.

"I went through her filing cabinets," said Melanie. "I found the marriage and divorce records and she was right, nothing very permanent. First marriage when she was twenty, lasted nine months before they separated then she had to wait the standard twelve months to get the divorce. Tried it again at thirty-two, similar results. I've noted the names of the husbands, we may want to talk to them, see if anything interesting results."

"I found two framed certificates," said Alex. "Both for various qualifications in unarmed combat. She was pretty good, by all accounts."

"But again, nothing at all to tie her to any of the killings."

"She reacted strongly when you mentioned the throat-cutting," said Jack. "I think she was shattered by all the killings, maybe she realised what she had got herself into, but I couldn't swear to it that she reacted specifically to the one mentioned."

"Okay, then let's call it a day," said Melanie. "I need a drink. See you back in the office tomorrow morning."

* * *

"Mr Hitchcox, how long have you been a writer?"

"Several years, though only full time since I retired."

"When was that?"

"Almost twelve years now. I was a lecturer in biology at the University."

The scene was almost identical to the other interviews they had conducted with the writers. Alex stood by the door studying the room, Jack sat in an upright chair facing Carl Hitchcox who had taken an armchair next to a wood stove that was not lit this late spring day. He was wearing almost the same outfit as he had at the writer's group meeting in the library two days earlier, black jeans and a red golf shirt. His almost bald head reflected the light from the French windows that opened out to a small lawn.

Melanie had taken the matching armchair across from him.

"So, Carl – can I call you Carl?"

He nodded, his eyes watchful.

"Carl, what do you write?"

"I've got three murder-mysteries written, but I'm working on a science-fiction book now."

"My favourite genre," said Melanie with a pleasant smile. "Are the others published?"

Hitchcox frowned slightly. "No, I was never able to get a literary agent, they're all women and I was told by one of them that they only look at romance books. So I self-published."

"Yes, I've heard that. I do sympathise, I've always been told that getting published is one of the most difficult things in the world. Can I ask, what are your hobbies and other interests?"

Hitchcox looked confused. "I thought you wanted to ask me about all those murders you talked about in the library. I mean, I was horrified to hear about Bella and Mitch killing those people, but that doesn't mean the rest of us are murderers."

"It's just routine, Carl, it lets us eliminate you from our inquiries."

Hitchcox still looked uncomfortable. "Well, I can't do a lot now. My eyesight has deteriorated a bit, so I can't do much. I can still drive a car, but it's a restricted licence, I can't go more than fifty kilometres from home."

"Going back to those murders I mentioned, Carl. So you wouldn't, for instance, batter your old group secretary to death with a baseball bat, or cut the throat of some old man in his back garden?"

"Good god, no." Hitchcox wrapped his arms round his chest.

"How about forcing a woman off the road and over a cliff edge?"

Hitchcox drew in his breath sharply. Melanie stole a look at Jack and though his face was immobile, she sensed that he had noted Hitchcox's reaction with interest.

She took an envelope from her jacket pocket.

"Carl, still part of a murder investigation, but because the writers' group seems so involved and you are a member, I applied for a warrant to allow me to search the house."

She passed the paper across to him and he took it as if it offered something repulsive. She stood up and nodded at the other two and they split up and began looking in different rooms.

Melanie was in the master bedroom, having seen nothing that could arouse her interest when she heard the call from Alex.

"Sarge, Jack," he said. "Come and look at this."

They met up in what was a study. A computer sat on the desk, two different printers sat on a table next to it and a third table held piles of documents. It was the wall behind the desk that caught their interest.

"Well, well," said Jack as they stared at the collection of pictures. The main one was a large, framed photograph of Carl Hitchcox sitting in the pilot's seat of a light aircraft. It was taken from the right side, the door was open and Carl sat at the controls smiling at the camera. There were several other pictures of him walking round the aircraft, filling up the fuel tanks and checking the wings.

Three others were even more interesting. Two of them showed Carl in the back seat of a two-seat glider, each time with a very pretty girl in the front seat. The third showed him in a single-seat sailplane, not looking at the camera but studying the instrument panel.

"A glider pilot," said Melanie. "How interesting."

Twenty minutes later they met again in the lounge room. Hitchcox looked like he hadn't moved while they were away.

"You were a pilot then?" said Melanie as they resumed their positions.

"I was."

"Sailplanes and light aircraft?"

"Yes, I flew both. But I gave them away when my eyesight began failing.

"So where did you fly?"

"At the Camden club when I lived in Sydney, occasional visits to Narromine."

"How about the local club here?"

Hitchcox shook his head.

"Alright Carl, we'll leave you alone. Thanks for your patience."

"Thoughts?" said Melanie as they drove back towards the station.

"Guilty as hell," said Jack. "That reaction when you mentioned the car crash was so obvious a child would have noted it."

"And he knows the gliding scene," said Alex. "Why don't I do a bit of checking about winch cables and wotnot?"

"Good idea. And follow up on our American pal, see just when he got here and what the immigration people know about him. Maybe the lab will get back soon with a DNA analysis."

"It theoretically ties another killing to an individual," said Jack. "But again, no hard evidence. This is a bit frustrating, though your interview technique is showing results. Hitting them with asking if they had killed anyone or were part of a program to kill people, that shocks the hell out of them. These people are as guilty as hell, but proving it is still a problem"

"Let's just keep plugging away," said Melanie. "Maybe we'll get a lucky break soon and get the entire bunch of sick bastards."

Chapter 44 – The Sixteenth of November, 2022

"It took a while, lots of high-level backwards and forwards from the police top brass, some legal manoeuvring, but I was able to get access to the computer systems of a couple of the organisations affected," said the tall young man at the front of the conference table.

Melanie had introduced him as a software specialist at the Australian National University in Canberra, Brian Corday.

"I was able to examine the doctor's network first," continued Corday. "I found the forged death certificate and the transactions sent from there. Clever stuff, I tell you. I tracked it back to a server in Jakarta, from there to a server in Tokyo, on to Istanbul, to Budapest and then I lost it."

"Bloody hell," said Jack.

Corday grinned at him. "About what I thought. Then I was able to get to the bank's system, their IT people were fully cooperative after getting the word from on high, we found the authority to close the "dead" man's account and had the same wild goose chase. This time it was Kuala Lumpur, Singapore,

Delhi, Tashkent in Uzbekistan, Berlin and that's where I lost it again."

"A real globe trotter, eh?" said Alex, sitting at the opposite end of the table.

"It's brilliant," said Corday. "I've heard about such genius-level hacking, never encountered it before."

"And all those transactions, was there a common identifier at all?" asked Melanie.

"Several were used, but there were three most common ones," said Corday. "The name 'Romulus' appeared five times, 'Horatio' three times and 'Odysseus' twice. A bit of a classical bent, our hacker has."

"Any more?" asked Melanie.

"Just the Roads and Maritime people where his driver's licence and car registration were wiped out," said Corday. "Similar story, Jakarta again as the starting point, then Athens, Rome, Istanbul and that's where I lost it again. I have to tell you, this bloke or sheila is a bloody genius."

"And that's it for now?"

Corday nodded. "To be honest, no point in wasting money on looking further. I'd only find the same, transactions being switched around servers all over the world, somehow getting past all the firewalls and defences. This is one scary, world class hacker."

"Brian, many thanks," said Melanie, standing up. "That's brilliant. We may not identify him or her yet, but you've sure given us a great pointer. There can't be many people capable of that."

"Cheers everybody," said the young man, and walked out.

"Holy shit," said Jack. "I'd heard of people capable of doing this sort of thing, usually some identity theft because somebody has been careless, but this level of expertise? That's incredible."

"This whole case has become incredible," said Melanie. "Alex, what did you find out?"

"First, our flying fellow," said Alex. "I called Narromine and they'd heard of him, they checked their records, he'd flown there a few times, they said he was pretty good, flew something called a Hornet, a Mosquito and something called a Jantar. Those are all fairly high-performance planes. But they only fly aero-tows, where the glider is pulled up by a power plane, no winch-launches."

He sipped at his coffee.

"Then I called the club at Camden. Much the same story, he flew there a few times, same sort of aircraft, liked taking up passengers in the two-seater called a Blanik. Aero-tows only, no winches."

He paused for dramatic effect.

"The local club, they knew him, despite him saying he hadn't flown there. He flew there a lot, only stopped a couple of years ago, eyesight problems. They have a two-seater called a Grob, also a Mosquito and a couple of others. They do have a plane for aero-tows but they have two big winches as well."

"Which I saw," said Melanie. "That's when I found the type of steel cable that was ideal for the car accident. Later, I found the marks on the trees where the cable had been attached. Let's refresh our coffee, this is going to get interesting."

Later, coffee mugs refilled, Alex resumed his research results.

"I reviewed the record of Gabrielle Greenwood," he said. "She has form, though not earth-shattering. At eighteen, she crashed her father's car, total write-off, she was hospitalised for a couple of broken ribs and concussion. But the toxicology report showed some level of cocaine. She was charged with drug possession but served only a few weeks of community service as the judge felt it was just youthful silliness, no point in ruining her life.

"But four years later, something similar happened, crashed her car, charged with DUI. She got off because at the time she was dating some high-calibre legal character, he was able to get her community service again, no loss of licence."

"Not exactly a great example of a moral person," said Melanie.

"Hardly," said Jack. "When we talked to her, she was giving all the tell-tale signs of lying most of the time. I don't think I can believe anything she says."

"Good work, Alex," said Melanie. "Who's next?"

"Allen Miller, the American," Alex said. "Full cooperation from the Immigration people in Canberra. Born in Chicago, not Baltimore as he said, has a degree in Economics from Northwestern University near Chicago, an MBA from Illinois State, and he's unmarried. Worked as a consultant for KPMG in Boston but made a lot of money trading on the stock exchange. He produced all the required certificates and a letter from KPMG confirming his employment there. A clean record in everything. He immigrated here nearly twelve years ago, was accepted as a business immigrant with three million bucks in the bank, applied for citizenship eight years ago. No employment recorded, appears to have continued trading part time. Seems a perfect asset to the nation."

"But?" said Jack. "I'm sure there's a 'but' in there?"

"And the prize goes to Doctor Savage," said Alex. "I emailed the Admissions Office at Northwestern. There certainly was an Allen Miller there in the years shown on his record, but they knew he had died a year after graduation in a car accident."

"Whoops," said Melanie.

"Whoops indeed," said Alex. "Similar story from Illinois State, there's an Allen Miller shown in their records as having attended for a two-year MBA. But there was an interesting note on the email. The woman writing it said she'd been there for fifteen years. She was curious about my query and checked all the records. She said there were complete records of grades in the exams and the professors' grades for projects and class participation but she was curious about why I had emailed. So she went out to the corridor where all the graduation classes have their photographs, found the year he was supposed to have graduated, but couldn't find his name or face. She asked a couple of the professors if they remembered him and neither of them could."

"Whoops again," said Melanie. "As Jack would put it, curiouser and curiouser."

"And there's more," said Alex. "With KPMG, the person I contacted said they did have a record of an Allen Miller working for them in Boston. The record was there, complete salary details, even his name on a couple of projects he had been on. I emailed back and asked if there was anyone who remembered him and he replied, saying he'd asked several partners and senior consultants who had been there at the time, nobody could remember him. And when he checked the audit records, the salary details didn't appear. That letter the Immigration Department had, certifying his employment was on file, but the partner who was supposed to have signed it had no memory of doing so."

"So some international grade computer hacking by Mr Miller, it seems," said Melanie. "Does that ring a bell with something we heard earlier?"

"A bloody great big clanging bell," said Jack. "Have you got that DNA analysis yet?"

"Not yet, but when it does come, I'll be sending it to the FBI immediately."

"I suspect it will be curiouser and curiouser," said Jack.

* * *

"And as Doctor Savage said three days ago, it did indeed get curiouser and curiouser," said Melanie. She smiled at each of them. "I sent the DNA analysis to the FBI in Washington with a query. They couldn't have had it for more than a couple of hours when they called me at home by Skype. Unfortunately, that was at two in the morning, but I sure as hell woke up quickly. A Special Agent Donna Hamilton seemed very excited. It seems our Mr Miller is in fact called Daniel Keeling and they have been looking for him for some years. He vanished about the same time as Allen Miller emigrated to Australia."

"And he's one hell of a computer hacker, I assume?" said Alex, not bothering to hide a wide grin.

"Just about the greatest," said Melanie. "He is believed to have broken into the Defence Department computers and sold a number of war strategy plans to Moscow and Beijing for large sums of money. He broke into some large high-technology company systems and sold the details to organisations in China, North Korea and again, Russia. He syphoned off some millions from several banks using identity theft. The man is a brilliant hacker and the FBI has not been able to catch him."

"If he's that brilliant, how did they identify who had done all that stuff and how did they get a DNA sample?" asked Jack.

"I asked her the same thing. Actually, they haven't got definitive proof, but apparently the hacking leaves certain signatures and they all pointed to this one bloke. The signatures involved the names 'Horatio' and 'Odysseus.' I'm sure that will please you."

Jack laughed out loud and Alex just smiled with delight.

"Got him," said Alex.

"She said they did bring him in for interrogation," continued Melanie. "But a high-class lawyer got him out again. But in the process, they gave him a mug of coffee and they were able to get a saliva trace off the mug.”

“It’s been a source of amazement to me all my professional life,” said Jack. “Here’s this max-IQ genius, utterly brilliant in his field and then he makes this one stupid mistake, drinking the coffee during an interrogation. Surely he would have known they’d get a DNA sample from the mug as well as fingerprints.”

“It’s almost a biblical truth in the detecting world,” said Melanie. “The police apply massive, grinding, plodding investigative work and that solves ninety percent of cases, but so often the case is solved because the criminal makes one silly mistake like that one.”

“And so we’ve found a world-class criminal,” said Alex. “That feels pretty good.”

“Donna asked me when they could have Miller back but I told her that’s up to people on a higher pay grade than me,” said Melanie. “My boss said we may just extradite him, because his crime here was not actual murder and there’s no point in going to the cost of a trial and imprisonment. Let the Americans do it.”

“Seems a good idea. Are we going to arrest him?” asked Alex.

“Too late,” said Melanie. “Immigration said they’ll nab him in a couple of days when they have all the paperwork of an extradition order sorted. I think the next stage is to start looking for all the millions he’ll have stashed away in banks around the world.”

“Brian Corday may have a lot of fun with that if they let him help,” said Jack. “Okay, great work, that’s one criminal out of the way. Let’s see what’s next.”

"I think the young Mr Oliver Simpson," said Melanie.

* * *

"I understand everybody calls you Ollie, is that right?" Melanie said. "Can I do the same?"

"Sure." Ollie sat in an upright wooden chair, his knees wide apart, his hands together in his lap, his eyes fixed on Melanie's chest. His sexual interest had been obvious from the first moment she appeared at his apartment door with Jack and Alex. Melanie ignored it.

The apartment was a one-bedroom place, the main living room held little furniture, just a single armchair facing a large television against one wall and a little round table with two chairs next to the door to a kitchen. A small bookshelf had a few hardback books on one shelf. Ollie had taken one of the chairs by the table and Melanie had taken the armchair. The two men remained standing by the entry door.

"Ollie, as I told you at the library the other day, we need to interview everybody in the writers' group. Now although two members have been charged with murder, we must try and eliminate you from any further interest in several other murders that have taken place locally. Do you understand?"

"Yes."

"Good. Ollie how long have you been in the group?"

"About four years."

"And what got you interested?"

"I met Gabby Greenwood in the gym, we both worked out there, still do as a matter of fact and we got talking. She told me she wrote short stories and I wanted to do the same."

"What sort of stories?"

"I've tried a few action stories, usually about army life, combat, war, that sort of thing. The group's helpful, but one or two of the women have said they're a bit violent for their tastes."

"Were you in the army at one point?"

"Yeah, I joined after leaving school, not much else I could find."

"How long were you in?"

"Just three years. Then I left, got a job with a tyre company, learned how to fit tyres and repair them, I've been with them ever since, about six years."

"I'll get the name of the company before we leave, Ollie. We really do need to check everything."

Ollie shrugged his shoulders.

"Are you a violent man, Ollie? You said you write action stories with violence in them."

"No, I'm not."

"So have you ever killed anyone? How about beating a woman to death with a baseball bat?"

Ollie finally stared at Melanie's face, shifted to a more upright position and brought his knees closer together.

"No, I didn't."

"Didn't what?"

"You think I killed Caroline? Why the hell would you think that? I didn't."

"I'm not accusing you, Ollie, just asking."

"Well that's a horrible question to ask anybody."

"How about kidnapping an old lady and leaving her in the woods to die? Could you do that?"

Ollie was showing signs of distress, his fists clenched tight and his feet shifting. He no longer stared at Melanie, either her face or her chest.

"No, I couldn't," he said, his voice hoarse.

"Could you do it if it was part of a competition or some sort of arrangement between the members of the writers' group?"

Ollie swallowed, gasped for breath and shook his head.

Jack moved and bent down over the bookcase, examining the books.

"Ollie, do you have a car?" asked Melanie.

Ollie took a moment, breathing hard then answered.

"Yeah, I've got a panel van."

"May we examine it?"

"What for?"

"Just routine, Ollie. As I said, we need to check on everything. In fact, I've got a warrant to search this place."

"A warrant? What the hell for?"

"Because this is a murder case and you are definitely a person of interest. Would you like to see the warrant?"

He stared at her, his jaws clamped tight and shook his head.

"My colleague Alex here is going to check out your bedroom, then we'll have a look at your van. Could I have the keys? I'll return them as soon as we've finished."

Ollie stood up and reached for a set of keys hanging from a hook by the kitchen door. He handed them to Melanie. "It's the green van, right by the front door."

"Thank you," she said. "I'll be back soon."

She and Jack left, leaving Alex still searching through the apartment bedroom.

The van was untidy. Melanie unlocked it with the remote control, Jack began examining the two front seats, Melanie went to the back and opened the two doors. The floor was covered with a simple broadloom carpet, there was a box of tools strapped to one side, a few rags scattered and little else. The carpet was dirty and partially covered with assorted debris, some gravel, some sand and what looked like stale breadcrumbs. Melanie took a small plastic evidence bag from her pocket and used her credit card to shovel a sample of the debris into the bag. She checked the spare tyre and found nothing unusual.

"Nothing up front," said Jack, closing the driver side door. "How about you?"

"Could be," she said, closing the back doors. "Some muck and grime from the carpet. Let's see what the lab has to say. What do you think about the young and muscular Ollie Simpson?"

"Guilty as hell and awash in testosterone," said Jack. "He reacted to both bullets you fired at him. I'd say he could well have killed Caroline Collins with a baseball bat and he was frightened when you mentioned the kidnapping.”

“And you thought Tanya reacted to that trigger too, didn’t you?”

“I did. They could have done that together.”

“What were the books on his shelf? Anything informative?”

“Not really,” said Jack. “All war books, one history book about Hitler’s concentration camps, illustrated with some horrific stuff.”

“God, what a sick bunch,” said Melanie. “Jack, could you return the keys? I can’t face Ollie staring at my tits again.”

Jack laughed. “I’m sure he’ll be terribly disappointed. Hey, what’s Alex got?”

Alex emerged from the building looking cheerful, holding a baseball bat.

“Found it in the bedroom,” he said. “I gave him a receipt, told him we’ll return it in a day or two.”

“Good man,” she said. “Let’s wait for Jack to return Ollie’s keys, then we’ll get back to the office and visit the geniuses in the laboratory. I took some crap from the van, we’ll see if it shows anything.”

Chapter 45 – The Eighteenth of November, 2022

"I was able to review Ollie's military record," said Alex. "Sarge, I have to tell you, this is a hell of a lot more fun than directing traffic and chasing hoons in souped up Holdens."

"Really?" said Melanie. "I never got to drive one of those sexy patrol cars and chase hoons in souped up anything. It's probably too late now."

"I have to admit, that part of being a copper was fun," said Alex. "But I hope I can get to do this intellectual stuff on a more permanent basis."

"We'll look into it," said Melanie. "Now, about Ollie Simpson."

"As he said, joined the army straight out of school and spent the next eighty days at the training school in Kapooka, near Wagga Wagga. He was pretty good, showed excellent physical conditioning, adequate intellect and he graduated without a problem. He went to the First Armoured Regiment, trained as an armoured vehicle crew trooper, did fine, learned to use some impressive weaponry, got to drive a tank. All in all, a good record, should have had a good career."

"I detect another 'But' coming," said Jack.

"Yes, but nothing really serious. He was on report a couple of times for fighting, but that's not a major felony. The worst was when he did sexually assault a female soldier, but little damage was done and she didn't push it. But there's an interesting note in his file. They felt that he was simply not a leader. Good follower, good soldier, reliable and all that but was never going to be promoted to an NCO position. One comment was interesting Jack, because you used the term, his sergeant called him 'too submissive.' He did three years, then decided to quit."

"Rather sad, really," said Melanie. "Sounds like he had all the makings of a decent career, spoiled by this odd character quirk. And after that?"

"He joined this company, Stillwells in Queanbeyan as a mechanic, very well qualified, not just a tyre fitter as he said to us, but a good, all-round service technician, hardly surprising after his time with the Armoured Regiment."

There was a knock on the door and a uniformed constable came in. "One from the lab, Sarge," he said and passed her two envelopes. "The other one is from D.I. Comley."

Melanie opened the one from her boss, read the single sheet and laughed. "It seems our revered Allen Miller, also known as Daniel Keeling has been notified by the Immigration people that his residency in Australia has been cancelled. Extradition warrants have been served by the FBI in the USA and it will take a day or two to complete the bureaucratic arrangements. Until then, he is under house arrest. Later, he will be flown to Los Angeles and handed over to the FBI. D.I. Comley says they seemed hugely grateful and they extend their thanks to all of us.”

“Definitely an unexpected but grand consequence of this horror story,” said Jack. “That should help the promotion chances for both of you.”

“About that, Sarge,” said Alex.

“Don’t push your luck, Constable,” said Melanie and opened the second envelope. “The lab report,” she said. “The baseball bat was examined under the highest magnification they have. It had been scrubbed and bleached in an attempt to clean it, but some microscopic traces were found of plastic wrapping and also human skin embedded in the wood, but too small for DNA extraction. Similarly, no match could be made with the traces of plastic wrapping found in the skull of the deceased, Caroline Collins.”

“Disappointing, but not surprising,” said Jack. “The only surprise is that he didn’t destroy the bat completely. We won’t get him on that.”

“But there’s more,” said Melanie. “The stuff I scraped off the floor of his van shows the same material composition as the traces we found on the nightdress of Jennifer Samuels, the old lady kidnapped and left in the old barn.”

“We’ve got the bastard,” exclaimed Alex and smacked his hands together. “Another one down.”

“Alex, save me the embarrassment of having him perving all over me and anyway, you deserve this. Take some muscle along to help, use a nicely coloured patrol car, blow the siren a bit and arrest the bastard. Just charge him with kidnapping for now. We’ll talk about the murder when he’s here.”

"Thank you, Sarge." Alex looked like a little boy at Christmas.

"I think we'll have another little chat with Tanya as well," said Melanie. "But here in the station, not at her place."

"You ask the questions, I'll watch," said Jack. "I'll give it fifteen minutes before she cracks."

* * *

Melanie switched on the recorder.

"Today is the fourteenth of November at 3:15pm," she said. "Present in the room are Detective Sergeant Melanie Carter, Doctor Jack Savage and Ms Olivia Reynolds, public defender, acting for Tanya Roberts who is also present."

She looked across the table at Tanya.

"Tanya, I must advise you that we have arrested Ollie Simpson for the murder of Caroline Collins and also for the kidnapping and unlawful imprisonment of Jennifer Samuels."

Tanya's face was white and she seemed almost catatonic as she had been since being brought to the police station an hour ago.

"Tanya, I should also tell you that when we arrested Ollie and brought you in for questioning, we contacted Nona Markham and asked her if she wanted to assign Mr Wall as your solicitor. This is because she had done just that for Bella and Mitchell Langer. However, she declined, and that is why we have brought in a public defender."

Tanya remained silent, but a tear ran down one cheek.

"Tanya, we will be questioning Ollie Simpson about both the murder and the kidnapping, but I want to ask you about the latter. Were you involved in the kidnapping of Jennifer Samuels?"

Tanya stared down at the table, her hands at her mouth and shook her head.

"The medical examination of Mrs Samuels showed traces of a strong sedative drug, Midazolam in her blood. The pharmacy records where you work show that you called her GP when she brought in a prescription for this drug to confirm the dosage, so you obviously knew about her use of it and how she would react. So can you understand why we need to clear up your involvement in this episode?"

"That's a bit of a stretch, Sergeant," said the solicitor. "Tanya knows the medical records of many people but that's no cause to suspect her of murder."

"I agree, Ms Reynolds," said Melanie. "But there's another event we have noted, the apparent suicide of a Mr Martin Fielding back in May. Mr Fielding died of a severe overdose of a Class 'A' drug, a restricted narcotic, also dispensed by Tanya's workplace. There are connections that do arouse suspicions."

The solicitor did not respond.

"Tanya, I must now point out that after interviewing all the members of your writers' group, there are a number of connections between those members and several suspicious deaths in this region, all occurring on the ninth of each month since January. Are you part of some sort of agreement, or competition to kill a person on the ninth of the month?"

Tanya reacted badly. She covered her face with her hands and began sobbing noisily. After a few moments, the sobbing eased and she finally spoke.

"I didn't want to do it, I hated it, but Nona made me."

Melanie looked at Jack, then back at Tanya.

"Are you referring to Nona Markham?" she asked.

Tanya nodded, her face wet and streaked with mascara.

"For the benefit of the tape, Tanya Roberts has nodded," said Melanie. "And what is it you said you did?"

"Tanya," interrupted the solicitor, her voice pitched significantly louder than normal speech. "I strongly recommend that you say no more."

Tanya didn't look at her but continued.

"Killing that old man, Fielding," she said. "I didn't want to, but she somehow talked me into it."

"And did you also help Oliver Simpson kidnap old Mrs Samuels?"

Tanya nodded again and then collapsed into another round of sobs.

"For the benefit of the tape, Tanya Roberts has nodded again," said Melanie. She waited for the sobs to subside before speaking again.

"Tanya Roberts, I am now charging you with the murder of Martin Fielding, contrary to Section 18 of the New South Wales Crimes Act of 1900 and the unlawful kidnapping of Jennifer Samuels, contrary to Section 86 of the New South Wales Crimes Act of 1900. You do not have to say anything, but it may harm your defence if you do not mention when questioned something which you later rely on in court. Anything you do say may be given in evidence. Do you understand?"

"Yes," mumbled Tanya.

Melanie signalled to the watching camera and a moment later, two female constables came in and gently led Tanya away.

"Interview suspended at 4:12," said Melanie and turned off the recorder.

"Oh my word," said Olivia Reynolds. "That was very hard to watch. This is my first murder case and it was distressing. Are you saying that her writers' group has been killing people? Why the hell would they be doing that?"

"I can't tell you any more," said Melanie. "But your colleague is going to sit in as the Public Defender now as we interview Ollie Simpson."

The solicitor nodded and followed her out, tension showing in her face. A few moments later, a young man entered and showed his identity card.

"Frank Maine, Public Defender," he said.

"G'day Mr Maine," said Melanie. "I should warn you, this interview will reveal some ugly facts and will be disturbing. Be prepared."

The solicitor nodded without comment.

"Time to chat with Ollie," said Melanie.

* * *

"Ollie, you have already been charged with the kidnapping and unlawful imprisonment of Jennifer Samuels. Do you have anything you wish to add to that?"

Ollie looked frightened, but said nothing.

"Did you do that on your own?" asked Melanie.

"Yes, I did," said Ollie, his voice a croak.

"Ollie," said the Public Defender, "I advise you to say nothing else."

"The thing that interests me, Ollie," said Melanie, "is how did you know that Jennifer would be sleeping so soundly that you'd be able to wrap her up and take her out to your van without her resisting you?"

"I don't know what you mean," said Ollie, his voice still harsh.

"When we checked her in the hospital after we found her, the doctor said there were doses of a powerful sleeping pill in her blood. We talked to her GP who said there should have been some trace, because she was having trouble sleeping and he'd prescribed a sedative for her to be taken before bed. But the amount in her blood was almost double what he said should have been there, so it seems she was given another pill."

Ollie said nothing but stared at the tabletop.

"So let me ask you again. How did you know she'd be extremely sedated, and who gave her an extra pill to put her in an even deeper state of unconsciousness? Where did you get this extra pill? It's a highly restricted drug, you can't just buy it over the counter."

There was no response from Ollie but the tension in him became increasingly obvious.

"Let me suggest this, Ollie," said Melanie. "We know that you are well acquainted with Tanya Roberts, you're both members of the writing group that meets every month in the library. Tanya works at the pharmacy in town where Jennifer Samuels got her sleeping pills and she has access to the drugs there. So I think you and Tanya would have known that Jennifer was in a deep, drug-induced sleep, you kidnapped her together and Tanya gave her an extra pill to ensure she'd be out cold. We know that you were involved because we found traces of materials that we took from your van on Jennifer's nightdress and on the blanket she was wrapped in. So was it Tanya who helped you?"

Ollie's face was white and his jaw was clamped tight. His hands were rigidly clasped on the table.

"I think it's time to tell you then, that we brought in Tanya for questioning earlier today and she has confessed to having worked with you to kidnap Jennifer Samuels and leave her to die in the shed where she was found."

Ollie put his face on his hands and his body shook.

Melanie waited a few moments until he seemed calmer.

"Ollie," said the lawyer. "Again, I advise you to say nothing."

"Ollie?" Melanie said. "Any comment?"

"It was all Nona's fault," he mumbled, barely audible. "She made us do it." He looked at the lawyer, tears running down his face. "I want to tell them," he said.

The solicitor looked back, his face expressionless.

"Is that Nona Markham, the chairwoman of your group?" asked Melanie.

"Yes," mumbled Ollie.

"Will you please sit up, Ollie. I can't hear you properly like that."

Slowly, Ollie sat up again. His face was tear-stained and his eyes were red. His hands were now trembling.

"Are you saying that Nona Markham somehow persuaded you to kidnap and attempt to kill an old woman?"

"Yes."

"How did she do that? Did she tell you specifically to kill an old woman or did she just ask you to kill somebody, anyone?"

"She asked all of us. We were all supposed to kill somebody to make up a book."

Three sets of eyes, those of Melanie, Jack and the solicitor stared at him. Ollie seemed to shrink under the combined gaze.

"Again, Ollie, how did she do that?" Melanie asked.

"Dunno. She just told us and somehow we all agreed."

"So, did you kill Caroline Collins? We found traces of plastic covering and human skin on your baseball bat, even though you had scrubbed it."

"Shit!" exclaimed Ollie. "How did you find that? I thought I scrubbed that really hard."

"Our people are pretty good at that sort of stuff. Oliver Simpson, I am now charging you with the murder of Caroline Collins, contrary to Section 18 of the New South Wales Crimes Act of 1900, in addition to the existing charge of kidnapping. Right now, you're going back to your cell while we prepare the full evidence."

As two uniformed officers escorted Ollie out, Melanie said, "Interview suspended at 5:58" and looked at the solicitor.

"Some day, eh, Frank? Your first murder? I hope you sleep okay tonight."

The young man shook his head. "Talk about an insight into an ugly world," he said. He gave a small wave and walked out.

* * *

"What do you think?" asked Melanie. She sat in her office with Alex and Jack.

"I think my professional paper is developing," said Jack. "Tanya and Ollie are certainly classic submissives. Jean Worrall is the same, so is Bella Langer, despite her apparent defiance, and her husband is even more so. The others are not, but they display some interesting characteristics that make killing quite feasible."

"Take us through them," said Melanie.

"Paul Johnson, the Navy diver is the most obvious," said Jack. "Did a dangerous, very tough job in the armed forces, certainly capable of killing. By no means is he a submissive, but as an NCO, his inclination is to take orders from authority. We probably can't get his full service records but it would not surprise me in the slightest if there was some hellish episode that caused severe Post Traumatic Stress Disorder, PTSD, a disorder that can hit people who face danger and stress frequently. The effects vary, but if I could treat him for a while, I'd say I'd find an urge to kill, for one reason or another. He could easily have fallen under Nona's spell and agreed to join this game."

"And certainly fully capable of it," said Alex. "If he did kill the fisherman, it would have been well within his capabilities."

"Alex, will you talk to the boss?" said Melanie. "See if you can get permission to get more service details about Paul Johnson."

"Will do, Sarge," replied Alex.

"How about the Botox blonde?" asked Melanie. "I certainly felt she was interested in killing me."

"And anyone else who threatened her sense of superiority," agreed Jack. "You for obvious reasons, she wouldn't be the centre of attention if you were around, but I think she is totally self-absorbed, lacks all empathy for other people and a total man-hater. Again, if I could talk further to her, that last one may have come from two disastrous marriages. No man could be totally submissive to her, which is what she would want, and it would drive her nuts. If she did kill that old bloke, it would probably have been an immensely satisfying moment for her. She'd welcome Nona's granting permission to kill, especially to kill a man."

"And I always thought writers would be nice people," said Alex. "What a bloody eye-opener this has been."

"We all have our dark side," said Jack. "Looking back to the work with David, it was a real shock to discover how easily ordinary people could be persuaded to kill a totally unknown human for the reward of a few thousand dollars. And the other horrible shock was to discover how some highly successful people at the top of the social tree could engage in a game of having people killed. It all soured my perception of the human race and that's what caused David to retire and head north to become a farmer."

"I can understand that," said Melanie. "Okay, the last two. What about Carl Hitchcox, the pilot and biology professor?

"I really don't know," said Jack. "He didn't conform to any submissive personality trait that I could recognise. I'd have to spend a lot of time with him to work out his motivation. There was some resentment about not being published, but a lot of writers would share that and they don't become killers. He could also be a bit resentful that he never made full professor, but again, without some severe psychosis, I don't see him as a killer. I have to reserve judgement about him."

"And the genius hacker?" asked Alex.

"Not really a killer," said Jack. "It was just a game to him, I imagine, no permanent damage done. But there would have to be a massive lack of empathy to join in this game without suffering an attack of conscience at the very real deaths of innocent people. Anyway, he's the Americans' problem now. Let's concentrate on our own story."

"So we've got four confirmed killers out of a dozen writers, with Tanya having confessed to one killing and one kidnapping, and the same with Ollie," said

Melanie. "The rest must be considered probables, but we'd never get a case against them so far. The central figure in all this is Nona Markham. We need to talk to her again and see if we can find the buttons to press."

"Do we bring her in?" asked Alex. "And can I watch this time?"

"Only by the video," said Melanie. "She'll have that slimy Wall character and he'll raise hell about three of us harassing his client."

"I suggest you go and get her," said Jack. "You may be the only person here who could stand up to her."

"Jack, you say the sweetest things," said Melanie. "Alex, with me, and get two more uniforms in a patrol car to come with us."

"Sure thing, Sarge," said Alex.

Chapter 46 – The Eighteenth of November, 2022

"Sergeant, I will repeat my complaint, you have no right to harass my client like this and I shall be reporting you to the Commissioner of Police."

Graham Wall, the lawyer stood in the middle of the room, pointing an aggressive finger at Melanie. "And I must also register my objections to this unqualified, so-called psychologist being in the room."

"Thank you, Mr Wall, your objection is noted and of course you are free to object to anything. And as you have seen, this interview is being recorded. But Doctor Savage is legally part of the police operation on this matter and Miss Markham is here to be legally questioned about a series of murders during the year."

"Is my client under arrest?"

"No, Mr Wall, she is not. But given the nature of the case, I can arrange to have her held for twenty-four hours and if necessary, I will arrest her on suspicion of incitement to murder."

The lawyer stood silent for a few more moments then took a seat next to Nona.

"Ask your questions, Sergeant, but I have instructed my client to remain silent."

"She has that right, of course, but she may find it helpful to answer my questions."

Melanie looked hard at Nona who stared back at her. She sensed the same darkness in Nona's deep eyes and couldn't help a small twinge of distress.

"Ms Markham, I know that you are already aware of the arrests of Oliver Simpson and Tanya Roberts because we asked you if you wished to assign Mr Wall here to their support, something you declined. I must advise you that we have charged both of them with two murders and one unlawful kidnapping."

"So?" Nona maintained her direct stare into Melanie's eyes. "Why should I waste my money assigning them a lawyer? I have nothing to do with them."

"Then I must tell you that both of them have told me that you persuaded them to attempt to kill a Miss Jennifer Samuels. Together, they kidnapped this old woman and left her tied up in an abandoned shed some distance from any other habitation, expecting her to die."

"They're lying. I never gave them any such instructions."

"Tanya Roberts also confessed to killing Mr Martin Fielding by forcing him to swallow a lethal dose of a powerful narcotic mixed with alcohol. She claims that you persuaded her to commit a murder, but not any one specific victim."

"She's lying."

"Sergeant," broke in the lawyer. "This is outrageous. I demand that you end this nonsense immediately and let my client leave."

"Your request is denied, Mr Wall," said Melanie. "Now Ms Markham, Ollie Simpson confessed to the murder of Caroline Collins by beating her to death with a baseball bat. And again, he claimed that he did it under your orders."

"Then he's lying, too."

"Ms Markham, I understand that you are the chairwoman of a writers' group that meets…"

"You've been there, Sergeant, you know about my writers' group. Stop wasting my time."

"It's a fascinating group Ms Markham," said Melanie, fighting the slight sickness she was sensing in her gut. "We have Tanya Roberts confessing to the poisoning murder of Martin Fielding on the ninth of May. Then we have Ollie Simpson beating your club secretary to death on the ninth of July. And then both of them kidnapping Jennifer Samuels with the intent of letting her die on the ninth of September. On the ninth of October, another of your members, Mitchell Langer ran down and killed an old man using his large four-wheel drive vehicle and just over a week ago, his wife, Bella Langer shot and killed the pilot of an ultra-light aeroplane, also on the ninth of the month."

She paused and looked hard at Nona who stared back without expression. Melanie felt the sickness and fear increase. She struggled for self-control.

"So, between twelve people in your group, Ms Markham, we have four people who have admitted to four murders and one kidnapping and another member who was the victim of one of those murders. Do you have any comment to make on that?"

Melanie felt the room go deathly silent. Somewhere in the vacuum of sound, she sensed the lawyer speaking, but it was felt, not heard. There was nothing but the black, shadowed eyes of Nona Markham in front of her and she sensed the awful dark pit that was trying to draw her forward. She fought the sickness and the pull and began to feel stronger and the sickness subsided. She stared back at Nona, drawing power from somewhere deep inside herself, the pull of the blackness subsided and she felt the loss of strength in Nona.

Sounds returned to the room and Melanie turned to look at the two men at the table. Jack was looking astounded, his jaw dropped, his eyes wide, almost frightened. Wall was upright in his chair, eyes also wide in shock, much fear in his face.

"You don't know who I am," whispered Nona.

Melanie took a deep breath and felt calmness return. "Who are you then, Nona?"

"I am Nona, I am one of the Three Fates, I am the Goddess who spins the lives of all people. I and my two sisters decide how long people shall live."

"How long have you known that, Nona?" asked Jack.

Recognising the greater skills, Melanie sat back and let Jack continue. She examined her own internal reaction. The fear had gone but something had taken its place. She struggled to identify it and finally recognised it – it was exhilaration. She could not tell the cause of this and for now decided it must be the sense of having escaped great danger and survived.

She put the strange thoughts away and listened to Jack.

"I have always been Nona," said the woman.

"Tell us again," said Jack. "Who and what is Nona and who are the Three Fates?"

"I and my sisters, Decima and Morta, we spin the lives of every mortal and immortal from birth to death. Even Jupiter fears us."

"So why did you decide that the people in your group would kill somebody on the ninth of each month?" Jack's voice was soft as he concentrated.

"Because the ninth is a holy day," said Nona. "It is the day a child's name is chosen, nine days after birth. It is the number of the month that a child is born after conception."

"And is this why you are called Nona?"

Nona's face had become flushed, her eyes wide, her mouth open in a laugh.

"My mother could tell I was the Goddess Nona when I returned to earth and she named me with my true name."

"And did you order the deaths of these people?"

"I did not," she replied. "My servants simply understood that they should end the undeserving lives of the wicked, the old and the useless."

"And were all these deaths on the ninth of the month caused by your servants?" asked Jack.

Melanie looked over at Graham Wall. His eyes were fixed almost hypnotically on Nona, an expression of horror on his face.

"They were," replied Nona, her face in a trance-like state of exhilaration.

"And where are your two sisters now?" asked Jack.

"Decima is with the Gods for a long period," said Nona. "But Morta, ah Morta, she is here with me, soon she will remember who she is and she will join me in my work."

"And do you know where Morta is?"

Nona turned her eyes on Melanie and pointed at her.

"There!" she said. "There is my sister Morta."

Jack snapped his fingers with a crack that sounded like an explosion in the silent room. Nona jerked, stared wildly round the room and seemed to shrink.

"Mr Wall, take your client home," said Melanie. "Alternatively take her to hospital and either way, seek mental health care. Interview suspended at five fifteen."

"Holy crap, Jack, that was unnerving."

She, Jack and Alex had returned to her office. Jack sat across from her at her desk, Alex had moved a chair to a corner and sat silently, looking almost withdrawn.

"For all of us, I assure you," said Jack. "Do you know how long that battle between you lasted?"

"A few seconds, surely?" Melanie looked puzzled.

"Four minutes and twenty seconds," said Jack.

"What? Four minutes and...? Jack, that's impossible!"

"No, that's right, I timed it, having seen something similar at your last meeting. What the hell was going on?"

"Jack, it was terrifying. I felt myself being pulled into some sort of black pit and I had to fight like hell. But then I felt myself grow stronger and pulled out."

"Nona does have some extraordinary skills," said Jack. "There's no doubt she's a dominant, as we've said before, but I have never seen such dominance as that. It's almost as if she has some natural skill at hypnotism."

"You think I was being hypnotised? That's incredible."

"I think so. Even watching from the side, I sensed that process. I'm a pretty good hypnotist myself and I recognised what was going on."

"That is truly scary. I can see how some of the submissives in that group became controlled enough to kill somebody."

"But there's something else," said Jack. "You defeated her, you pulled back and in that process, you broke her. She failed to capture you."

"So what does that mean?"

Jack looked serious. "It means you are even more of a dominant than she is."

"Good god!" Melanie looked shocked. "But I've never done anything like persuading people to do stuff they wouldn't do normally."

"That's because it's not in your nature to do that. You're a decent person, not a tyrant."

"Jack, that's horrible. I don't want to do anything like that."

"It has a major professional advantage for you, if you think about it."

"What possible advantage could it have?"

"Have you ever thought about why you've been a successful detective?"

"Not really. I know I'm fairly bright and I have the academic qualification, not like yours but enough to help me analyse problems, but I've never really thought about it."

"It's your interview technique. I talked to your boss and he said you get more confessions from suspects than anyone else he knows."

"Good god, does that mean I force innocent people to confess crimes they haven't committed?" Melanie looked horrified.

Jack shook his head. "No, not that, all your solved cases have come with proof of the crimes as well. But you save a hell of a lot of time because the perps can't easily resist you. You break them down rapidly. It's an enviable skill in your profession. Look how quickly you broke down Tanya and Ollie and before that, the Langers."

Melanie sat back, deep in thought. A thought swam up from her memories... *the way she had somehow changed the attitude of the Superintendent in Parramatta, was that because she had used this strange ability without realising?*

"Another question, Melanie. When you defeated Nona, how did you feel?"

Melanie hesitated. "I think I remember feeling some excitement, some exhilaration but I can't think why."

"Probably two reasons," said Jack. "It's a well-known result of escaping great danger or possible death, the escapee feels huge exhilaration."

"And the other?"

"I think it's because you recognised that power in yourself. Hard not to be exhilarated by that."

"That's scary, Jack. I don't want to dominate my surroundings and the people there."

"Like I said, you're naturally a nice person, you won't be drawn to do that unless you're facing some danger like Nona. But I suggest you will need to be careful. You may find yourself in a situation and if you use that power without realising it, you could hurt somebody."

"And changing the subject, what was all that stuff about the Fates and her being a goddess? Did she just go over the wall there?"

"It was interesting, that's a fact. The Three Fates come from Greek and Roman mythology. Nona used the Roman names, Nona, Decima and Morta and as she said, they spun the lives of all mortals and immortals, so even the Gods were frightened of them. I suspect that her mother knew of these legends and gave one of them to Nona. She must have told Nona and she would have looked them up and they triggered a deep reaction in her. And then she adopted the role completely. She feels she has the right to dictate when a person dies."

"So why the hell did she say I was... what was her name? Morta?"

"Because she recognised the same power in you that she has. Her delusion worked overtime and she took you for one of the other Fates."

"Not a nice thought," said Melanie.

"Not at all. But all that stuff about the Fates dictating life spans makes me think that she probably did murder an old lady by poisoning with a Rosary Seed. Can you get Alex to review that case? It was in January, if I recall correctly."

"I'll do that. It was quite obvious that she knew about the effect of that poison. Alex?"

She looked over to the silent young man in the corner. He had not made a sound since they had come into the room and he seemed to be lost, staring at the carpet.

"Alex," she said again. "Are you alright?"

He raised his eyes to her. His face looked pale.

"Yes, Sarge," he said. "That was all a bit of a shock."

"I agree, it was for me as well."

Alex finally seemed to shake off the frozen attitude and he laughed. "I can well imagine, Sarge," he said.

"Did you get the bit about checking on that Rosary Seed poisoning back in January?"

He nodded.

"Okay, get the file, review it, see if anything leaps out at you if you make the assumption that it was murder and anything else you can find."

"On it," said Alex and left the room.

"Now that he's gone, can I ask you some personal questions?" said Jack.

Melanie looked worried. "Depends on what they are."

"Okay, let's try this one. Why are you a detective?"

Melanie sighed in exasperation. "Is this where we start that stuff about why aren't I a supermodel or film star? Jack I've had that shit since I was ten."

"I can well imagine. Will you go along with me a little? It might help."

"If you insist. I just became sick of all that adulation from the age of ten. All that, 'Oh Melanie, how beautiful you are, you must become a top model or a movie star' nonsense. The idea of having a job that consisted only of being beautiful gave me a serious attack of the runs. Nobody could see that I was fairly bright as well."

"But you could have become almost anything," said Jack. "Why the police?"

"You don't realise just what a curse it is to look like this. I got a first class honours degree in criminal psychology, but nobody wanted to interview me for a job. I applied all over the place for jobs as a psychologist but as soon as I got to the interview, I lost all credibility, whether the interviewer was a man or a woman. Nobody would believe I could actually do something intelligent and productive."

"I can imagine the frustration. It must have been difficult dealing with men, also."

She grimaced. "You have no idea. The men would almost line up or form a rugby scrum around me, all trying to impress me. But if I did go on a date, it wasn't long before conversation ended and the wrestling began."

Jack nodded. "I suspect that what we've been talking about, the dominance thing scared them off and they descended into trying to prove their threatened masculinity."

"Maybe that's it. And I didn't get invited out much because all the guys assumed I was owned by some super-jock or uber-male. Do you know, I didn't get to a single university dance until the graduation prom?"

"So somebody did ask you?"

She looked down at her hands. "Scott," she said. "Scott MacAdam. He was in my faculty. He kept out of my way because he didn't want to join in the scrum, but when I finally talked to him, he was the first man who actually treated me as an intelligent woman with real ideas and value. It was lovely. We planned on getting married after graduation."

"And?"

"He was killed six weeks after we graduated. We came out of a bar in Kings Cross, some thug did the fashionable one punch thing and killed him."

"Oh shit! And after that, I imagine you couldn't trust yourself to let yourself get close to another man."

"Exactly. It was either a wrestling match or I'd lose him like I lost Scott. I wouldn't risk either."

"So, again, why the police?"

"I would never have thought of it alone. I was contacted by the academy at Goulburn, they asked me to consider it. It was the first time somebody had considered me capable of something other than prancing up and down on a runway or posing in exotic clothing, and after Scott's death, the idea of helping put away the sort of thugs that did that became very attractive."

"But Melanie, you're a beautiful, healthy woman. You must have needs?"

"That one is over the line, Jack."

He nodded. "I understand. One more question about the job on hand. Why didn't you arrest Nona? She's clearly guilty of incitement to kill."

"Because we'd never get a conviction. She's obviously a few trumpets short of an orchestra and she'll probably get a commitment to a loony-bin. Meanwhile, I think I can get more information about the other killings if she's still free. I'll get her when we have more answers."

"Sounds reasonable." He looked at his watch. "It's after five. Let's call it a day and get back to it in the morning. Alex may have something for us by then."

"Let's do that." Melanie stood up, collected her handbag and left the office.

*　*　*

"What did you find, Alex?" Melanie was feeling short of energy after a poor night's sleep. The entire episode of the mental battle with Nona, the revelations about her own mental powers and the discussion about her social life had left her mind in a whirl and she was already awake when her radio came on at six.

"An interesting mix," said Alex. "As you know, the first pathology findings of the dead woman showed tiny traces of this rare poison, the Rosary Seed. There was nothing at all to connect Nona Markham to it."

"As expected," said Melanie. "If she had done as the others had done and worn the full protective clothing, she wouldn't have left a trace. Well, okay, Alex, sorry to put you through a wasted few hours."

"Actually, Sarge, you didn't."

"Oh? How's that?" Something in Alex's voice indicated excitement and Melanie began to wake up.

"So I did some more checking on other cases back through some years. And I did find a reference to Nona."

Jack and Melanie looked at each other.

"I did say the kid's bright," said Jack.

Melanie chuckled. "Alright, Alex, spill it."

"Six years ago, Nona's mother died in her bed. She wasn't that old, just late sixties, but in lousy health and the post mortem didn't show any major reason for her death. There was a reference to some discolouration in her lungs that could have been caused by suffocation but could easily have been caused by her choking, as she suffered from sleep apnoea but refused to wear a mask and use a pump. The report said that Nona was alone in the house with her mother and she was the one who called the ambulance."

"Now that is interesting," said Melanie. "Alex, how long have you been in the job?

"Just over five years, Sarge."

"Okay, that's one hurdle, five years is required. Have you taken your Senior Constable exams?"

"Next month, Sarge."

"Good. As soon as the results come through, I'll recommend your promotion and transfer to criminal investigations."

Alex simply grinned widely.

"Time to talk to the Goddess Nona again," said Melanie. "Alex, apply for a search warrant. Meanwhile, I may have a chat with my boss."

* * *

"I've been expecting this call," said Comley. His face on the computer monitor reflected anxiety. "Once Alex had raised the issue of Nona Markham, I did some investigation myself."

"That's interesting," said Melanie. "Is there something I should know?"

"There certainly is. There's a file on her, sealed many years ago."

"Sealed? That's even more interesting. Do I suspect you're about to tell me what's in there?"

"You'd be right, but I tell you, this took some heavy schmoozing with some top people to get it."

"I'm all ears, Sir."

"One of the reasons it was so hard was that Nona's father was a judge on the circuit courts, pretty high-ranking geezer, likely to be elevated to the State High Court at some time. Those people stick together and it was one of his mates that sealed the file. But both of them are dead now and we still have some influence. It seems your Nona woman is one nasty piece of work."

"Alex already found that out, Sir."

"He only got the simple stuff, the stealing, the expulsions from school and so on."

"And there's worse? Why am I not surprised?"

"Oh, there's worse alright. When she was fifteen at high school, one of her classmates, a Sarah Benson committed suicide after being hounded by several girls in the class about being a slut, having sex with several boys at the local school. Nobody at the time would say where those rumours came from, but the post mortem revealed that she was still a virgin. Some time later, two of the girls did come forward to the police and said that Nona had spread the rumour. They were in tears, because they had no reason to believe her story, they liked Sarah and couldn't believe she was a slut. But they had somehow accepted the story from Nona and played along with the hounding."

"That's pretty ugly," said Melanie, sensing disgust in her stomach.

"And now the big one," said Comley. "A few months after that nasty episode, an old woman was found in a country lane near Nona's home, she was dead from strangulation. The crime scene cops couldn't find a single clue about the killer. However, a local man walking his dog reported that he had seen a teenage girl in that area about the same time. He was curious, because he said she was wearing protective coveralls like you get for painting or car maintenance, the same things our people wear at crime scenes now. But he didn't see her again and although he was shown some pictures of girls in the area taken from school magazines, he couldn't identify her because she was also wearing a mask."

"So no evidence of any sort?"

"That's true. But I tracked down the local station officer, now retired, and he recalled the suicide case, recalled that Nona had been mentioned and went to interview her with her parents there. He said the father, the judge was furious, but the odd thing he recalled was the mother sitting saying nothing but with a smirk or a smile of some sort the whole time. It bothered him, he said, especially when he then interviewed Nona who displayed the same smirk."

"This all sounds pretty sick. Did he really think Nona had killed the old lady?"

"He said it bothered him. He asked the judge about any sort of protective gear, because at fifteen, Nona was almost as tall as her father and could have worn one of his. Judge Markham admitted he did have such an item but he was unable to find it when asked."

"That shows some amazing foresight on Nona's part, if she did that murder," said Melanie. "That was when, 1987 or so? Scene of crime officers didn't wear that sort of gear in those days."

"I agree. That woman has a very high IQ."

"And these records have been squirrelled away," said Melanie, a statement, not a question.

"Until I got a court order yesterday," said Comley. "There's no solid evidence about this, but the whole Nona history stinks like week-old cod. Melanie, be very careful interviewing her. Your last report about how she started screaming and calling herself a goddess has all the signs of a raving lunatic."

"Jack's already convinced of that, Sir," said Melanie. "And he should know."

"Indeed. He's met his fair share of those. When are you next seeing this crazy woman?"

"In a couple of hours, when I have the court order to search her house."

"Be very careful, Melanie. Take some muscle along and don't be shy about arresting her. You could almost certainly make a charge of incitement to murder stick just on the evidence of those two young ones, Roberts and Simpson."

"I agree, Sir, but I want her for the whole evil thing, all of them."

"Okay, let me know what happens."

"I will, Sir."

Melanie ended the Skype call as Alex came in, holding the court order.

Chapter 47 – The Nineteenth of November

"Why are you here again?" asked the lawyer. "My client has told you everything she knows and your persistent questioning is now obvious harassment."

Melanie studied the man standing at the open door to Nona's house. There was something different in his attitude. Gone was the arrogance and defiance. Instead, she sensed he was not comfortable with what his assignment required of him.

Was he frightened of Nona after her last outburst? she asked herself. It would not surprise her.

"As I explained, Mr Wall, we have further questions to ask your client regarding recent suspicious deaths in this area."

"What else can she possibly tell you, Sergeant? I see no reason to allow my client to be subjected further to this."

"Mr Wall, I have a warrant to search this house. We can do it with you present to watch us or we can charge you with obstructing the police in their legitimate business. Which would you prefer?"

She watched the worry play over Wall's face, the indecision and the anxiety. After a few moments, he stood aside and opened the door fully. Melanie walked in, followed by Alex and two more uniformed officers.

"Don't start immediately," she said to Alex in a soft undertone. "Give me five minutes to warn her and tell her we have the warrant, then get to it. Stay as silent as possible." He nodded and the three officers stood in the corridor as Melanie and the lawyer entered the living room. Nona was sitting in an armchair, hands folded in her lap.

"I'm sorry, Nona, I couldn't stop this," said Wall. "They have a warrant."

Nona looked up at Melanie. "Why are you doing this to me?" she asked.

"I think you know why," said Melanie and took the second armchair opposite Nona. Wall sat on the sofa between the two, looking tense and uncomfortable. "There are several statements by members of your writers' group that you personally told them to kill people," continued Melanie.

"That's just hearsay," said Wall. "Nobody would take that as proof."

"That may be," said Melanie. "But it is enough to charge you with incitement to kill and hold you until a judge can rule on it."

Nona stared at the fireplace, saying nothing.

"Nona, last time we talked, you claimed to be a goddess with the power of life and death over mortals. Will you explain that further?"

"Nona!" Wall almost shouted. "Don't say any more."

Nona seemed to sink into herself, almost becoming smaller.

"We are the Parcea, the three sisters who spin the thread of life," she said. Her voice was soft, barely heard, it almost sounded as if somebody else was talking. "My sisters are Decima and Morta and I know very well that you are Morta. I don't know where you have been for so many years and I haven't found Decima yet, but I know we will all be together again soon."

"I am not Morta," said Melanie. "Why do you believe so?"

"You have the power," said Nona. "Soon you will realise it and join me."

"Did you tell Tanya and Ollie to kill their victims? Did you also tell them to kidnap the old lady?"

"I didn't need to," said Nona. "The lives of those people were over, their thread was running out, their time had come. Tanya and Ollie knew it."

"How did they know it?" asked Melanie.

"They just knew it."

"And did Bella and Mitch Langer also know it about the two people they killed without you telling them?"

"Yes, they did." Nona's voice had become like a little girl's, her eyes were closed.

"Sergeant, you cannot arrest my client for incitement," broke in Wall. "It would simply be her word against the killers. There is no evidence that she specifically ordered the deaths."

"We shall see, Mr Wall," said Melanie without taking her eyes off Nona. "Now, Nona, when you were fifteen, did you strangle an old woman in the woods near your house?"

She heard the indrawn breath from the lawyer and Nona opened her eyes and stared at Melanie.

"The police talked to me about that and they had no reason to claim that I did."

"Actually, Nona, they did have reasons, but your father, the judge was able to get the inquiry closed."

"Sergeant, where the hell did you get that information?" Wall sounded panicked.

"We have our methods," said Melanie. "Nona, another question. Did you kill your mother?"

Nona smiled gently. "It was her time," she said. "The thread of her life had run out."

"And did you kill her?" persisted Melanie.

"The thread of her life had run out," repeated Nona.

There was a knock on the door and Alex entered. He handed Melanie two small objects.

"Found in her bathroom cupboard and her bedroom," he said.

Melanie examined the small screw-top jar. It contained two brightly-coloured red objects that looked like small gemstones. Melanie had read about these after a conversation with Doctor Mortimer.

The second item was a large ornate silver or pewter, possibly a brooch shaped like a tulip within an oval ring, about the size of a hand. Around the ring were more of the bright red gemstones but five were missing, leaving spaces where they had been.

"Nona, some time ago you denied knowing what Rosary Seeds were. Are you sticking with that denial?"

Nona said nothing.

"So can you explain why this little jar found in your bathroom appears to have two Rosary Seeds? This other ornament has several of them round the outside with gaps where five are missing. If we assume two of them are the ones in the jar, where are the other three?"

"I have no idea," said Nona. "My mother gave me that brooch, that's how it was. Three of the stones were missing, two were loose and I put those in the jar until I could get it repaired."

"When Judy Henderson was found dead in January, the postmortem found traces of the poison contained in Rosary Seeds," said Melanie. "It's a very rare drug, the seeds are almost unknown in Australia. There appears to be enough of a link between these objects here and the murder for me to consider you a suspect. Anything you wish to say?"

Neither Nona nor the lawyer said anything.

"Nona Markham, I am arresting you for the murder of Judy Henderson in January of this year and for incitement to murder of several individuals by members of your writers' group. You do not have to say anything, but anything you do say may be taken down and later used in evidence. Do you understand?"

Nona jumped to her feet.

"I am Nona, the Goddess of Life," she screamed at full volume. "It is my right to end the lives of those whose thread of life has run out. You are my sister, Morta and you must join me, we must find Decima and continue to spin the threads. I am a goddess, these ordinary mortals cannot take me, they will die if they do."

Melanie looked at Wall. His jaw had dropped and he was staring wide-eyed at Nona.

The other two officers entered the room, looking bewildered, but quickly joined Alex in subduing Nona and placing handcuffs on her.

"I'll organise a psychiatrist to examine her," said Melanie. "Mr Wall, do you want to accompany us to the station?"

The lawyer shook his head, his face white.

"Let's go," said Melanie.

Chapter 48 – The Twentieth of November, 2022

"I was able to get permission to see the complete file on Paul Johnson," said Alex. "The boss went to Defence, explained that we had a possible serial killer problem on our hands, and they were quick to let me access the files."

"Good work," said Melanie.

"Not easy to get that sort of access," said Jack. "There must have been some concerns about him already."

"There were," said Alex. "That's why he left the navy."

"Better tell us," said Melanie.

"It starts in March, 2003," said Alex. "We were busy in the Iraq war…"

March, 2003

"Jeez, I tell you, mate, we didn't face this sort of shit back in training," said Paul.

"You're right," said Casey Williams. "I know you and I did some practice dives in low viz conditions but this was grim."

"Bloody oath! When you ran into that mine-layer, you could have set off a dozen live mines."

"Tell me about it! No visibility, strong current, live mines. Talk about a nightmare."

"But we got it done. Not sure which was more fucking terrifying, our job or what those Pommy commandoes are doing, clearing out all those unexploded mortars and grenades from the town."

"Chief Petty Officer Johnson!"

"Sir!"

Paul and Casey jumped to their feet and stood at attention as Lieutenant Brad Coleman entered the battered old room that served as a recreation area of the warehouse in which the diving teams had set up camp. Coleman was younger than both of them but he had earned their respect during the severely dangerous operation to clear the mines from the sunken ship.

"Chief, gather your crew, they need us in the town to help with crowd control while the British commandos clear out more nasty ordinance."

"Sir!"

"Good man. The bus will be here in twenty minutes."

An hour later, the bus arrived in the town where the British forces were carrying out the highly dangerous business of removing live grenades and mines from a storage area.

In full combat gear, the Australians began directing the crowds of Iraqis further away from the danger zone. It was not easy, the curious local people, many of them children were not amenable to being moved, but slowly they crept further away from potential explosions.

When it happened, it was horrifying. With no warning, a young Iraqi man pulled a pistol from his clothing, screamed "Allahu Akbar!" and fired straight into Casey's face. His entire head dissolved, blood flew in all directions and blobs of bone and brain material hit Paul in his face-mask, smeared over his eyes and blinding him for a moment. When he was able to see again, a few seconds later, the killer was staring straight at him, his eyes wide in mad intensity, his gun aimed at Paul's face. He was about to pull the trigger when a bullet from one of the other Australian troops hit him in the head, causing much the same effects as before.

A small riot began, the outnumbered Australian divers surrounded by furious Iraqis and more weapons appeared.

A burst of heavy fire erupted, shooting over the mob as the British commandos pulled away from the buildings they were clearing and joined the Australians. The mob dispersed immediately and within seconds the area was empty, the silence broken only by the metallic sounds of weapons being reloaded.

"Bit of a sticky moment there, Chief," said a well-educated voice behind Paul. The speaker came nearer and was revealed as a Captain in the commandos.

Paul struggled to speak and the words came out hoarse and strained.

"He was my best friend," he said and collapsed.

* * *

"He and Casey had been friends since they were seven at school," said Alex. "They had joined the navy together, applied to diving school, graduated together and posted to Iraq at the same time."

"That's horrible," said Melanie.

"Classic conditions for PTSD," said Jack.

"And that's what happened," said Alex. "Six weeks of therapy back in Sydney, no great improvement seen and he was invalided out of the service soon after. The medical reports say he rarely spoke and appeared to have lost all empathy for other people, spending all his time in the library or on the computer reading about naval warfare."

"He was wide open to influence by a major-league dominant personality like Nona then" said Jack.

"It's a tragedy," said Melanie. "But from our point of view, while it sure points to him as the killer of the fisherman, we still don't have evidence enough to charge him."

"We need to keep looking at all of them," said Jack. "God, what a collection of damaged souls we have here. Nona must have felt she discovered buried treasure when she came across this lot."

"Excellent work, Alex," said Melanie. "Is that it?"

"No, I've got a bonus for you," said Alex. He had the expression of a small boy who had found a few dollars and bought some chocolate. The other two couldn't help smiling.

"Okay, Constable," said Melanie. "Entertain us."

"It came when I was able to look into Paul Johnson's military file," said Alex. "I'd explained to the young lady captain at the Defence Department why we needed to see the details and she got all thoughtful. She asked me what other names were in the writers' group and one of them obviously triggered something. She went to the computer, keyed in some details that obviously cleared me for something else and then walked away. It was a surprise, because the name on the screen said Colonel Jerome Greenwood."

"Greenwood?" said Melanie. "As in Gabrielle?"

"Exactly," said Alex, his smug smile broadening. "He was a specialist in jungle warfare, highly regarded and worked at Defence for a number of years. He had a good record, but there was some stuff about Gabrielle that was really interesting, going back to her childhood."

June, 1983

Ten-year-old Gabrielle Greenwood looked down at the box on the floor. It had contained a beautiful black and white cat that her parents had treasured and five new-born kittens that had mewled and squeaked in almost inaudible tones.

They were all dead now.

Gabrielle felt exhilarated as one by one she had lifted out the kittens, strangled them and then done the same with the mother. She stood up, went to her father's cabinet and found the bottles of assorted liquors. She poured a small helping of vodka and downed it in one go. Then she went to her bedroom to wait for the results.

The scream of horror came just fifteen minutes later and Gabrielle recognised her mother's tones. She smiled to herself. She knew how much her mother had loved watching the birth of the kittens and how much she loved the mother cat called Sirikit.

Her door opened with a crash and her mother stood there, tears pouring down her face.

"Did you do this?" she shouted.

"Do what, Mother?" asked Gabrielle.

"You know very well, Gabrielle. Did you kill Sirikit and her new kittens?"

"Why should I do that, Mother?" replied Gabrielle. She had learned the sweet, girlish tones from another girl at school and had discovered that it worked in a wonderful combination with her feminine appearance, curly blonde hair and perfect complexion.

"Oh my god, you are one evil bitch," said her mother. "Wait till I tell your father about this."

That did have a negative effect on Gabrielle. She absolutely worshipped her father and loved to see him in his military uniform, his tall, athletic frame standing out from the crowd. But she knew she had to kill the cat and her kittens for that reason, the animals threatened her by making her share her parents' attention and that she could not tolerate.

"Stay in your room and do not come out again," said her mother in quieter tones, her fury turning ice-cold. She slammed the door behind her and Gabrielle heard her footsteps descending the stairs.

Apart from the worries about her father's reaction, Gabrielle felt good about the morning's work.

* * *

"That was in the notes of the psychiatrist," said Alex. "Colonel Greenwood requested the help of an army colleague of his, a psychiatrist in the medical group and he spent a few hours talking to her. He concluded that she was a functioning psychopath."

"What happened after?" asked Jack. "I've met a few of these, they can be horrible problems."

"Almost classic history," said Alex. "She was expelled from two schools before she was thirteen for drinking, stealing things from other kids and all that, but her father was able to keep her out of the arm of the law with his connections. There's nothing further in the notes until she was seventeen..."

* * *

December, 1990

Gabrielle had enjoyed the party. She had become tall and pretty, long-legged and blonde and was used to the attention of the boys at school. This evening had been the best ever. One of the guys had brought in some cocaine and she had sniffed up some, having learned how to do that at a couple of other similar gatherings. The booze had flowed freely and she had consumed several Bourbon and Cokes, her favourite mix. One of the men had taken her out to the granny flat behind the main house where the party had been held and she had enjoyed some fairly violent sexual explorations, at one point managing to hurt her partner's genitals with some rough handling, something she enjoyed doing.

Her parents were away and Gabrielle had found her father's car keys and taken the car to the party, though she hadn't yet obtained her licence, but that didn't worry her. She had every faith in her ability to persuade any cop that stopped her to ignore any legal issue.

She opened the car door, started up and drove out onto the main road. The acceleration of the supercharged Nissan was exhilarating and she opened up the throttle, reaching over a hundred and forty. The curve was unexpected. She knew the road but between the alcohol and the cocaine, she hadn't been concentrating on where she was and when she reached the bend, she slammed on the brakes, skidded, spun, crossed over the road and slammed into a car parked on the side. The slide continued and she hit the telegraph pole with a sickening smash.

She sat frozen, panicking, totally without any idea of what to do next. She saw some people moving around near the car and heard the police siren approaching. Within minutes, a patrol car was alongside her, lights flashing and an ambulance arrived a moment later.

A uniform peaked hat bent over the side window. She found it would still open and the police officer stared down at her.

"Are you hurt, Miss?" he asked.

She shook her head. She tried to smile but couldn't. With some effort, the officer opened the door and one of the ambulance staff came and helped her out, leading her to the ambulance. Once seated, the police officer held a breathalyser up to her mouth.

"Blow into the tube," he ordered, then studied the result. He shook his head. "You are reading significantly over the limit," he said, then addressed the ambulance driver. "Take her to hospital, get her checked out, but she's under arrest, she'll be charged later. I'll have a female colleague meet you there."

He stood away from the ambulance and keyed his radio.

*   *   *

"Driving under the influence, driving while affected by an illegal narcotic, driving without a licence, driving without insurance, she should have faced some years of a prison sentence," said Alex.

"Don't tell me, her father pulled strings," said Melanie.

"You got it," said Alex. "The Army brass couldn't afford a scandal like that attached to one of their most senior military experts and persuaded the Public Prosecutors to hold off action. So nothing but a ban on holding a licence for five years. Of course, her poor old father lost his beloved muscle car and couldn't get insurance again for anything more exciting than a family car."

"What a case, eh?" said Jack. "I suspect she remains fearful of her father, responds to an authority figure like him and so she was another perfect candidate for Nona's special talents. She probably enjoyed killing a man."

"Almost certainly," said Melanie. "I'd like to examine her divorce records, I guess we'd see that she got nothing of value from either, perhaps because of her continual narcotics use. We saw how much she hates men when we talked to her."

"She gave me the shivers, that's a fact," said Alex. "I felt she'd love to stick a knife in my ribs."

"Meanwhile, we have Nona overnight and she'll be confronting a magistrate in three days," said Melanie. "I don't know if she'll be held over for trial or not."

"Probably released on bail," said Jack. "From what we've heard, she's almost certainly guilty as hell of inciting others to commit murder and equally guilty of the murder of an old lady with the Rosary Seed, but somehow, I don't see us having enough definitive proof for a trial where there might be sufficient doubt raised by a good barrister."

"So there's not much we can do for a few days," said Melanie. "Alex, take a couple of days off, I'm doing the same. Jack, I suspect you can start writing your paper."

"That and a few beers in the local pub," said Jack. "Are you going somewhere?"

"I need to get away," said Melanie, picked up her bag and headed out of the office.

She switched on her computer, flipped a mental coin and booked herself a flight to Adelaide. A little research and she had three or four clubs identified that looked like they would have the sort of male clientele she needed.

She packed her bag, headed down to the car park and drove down to Canberra for the flight to Adelaide. She needed a serious bout of relief from the stresses of the last few weeks.

Twenty-Fourth of November, 2022

The text from her office on her phone was short and to the point.

"Nona Markham was released on bail this morning, trial set for Monday, February 13th."

"Just about as expected," muttered Melanie. "I need a drink."

Chapter 49 – The Twenty-Sixth of November, 2022

"Nona, this is a surprise. They've let you out on bail, I assume?"

Allen Miller looked down at Nona standing two steps below him at the house front door. For the first time since she had known him, she saw some expression on his face.

"Allen, I thought we should talk and perhaps clear the air."

"Do we need to clear the air? Anyway, come in, let's see what we have to work out."

She followed him into a pleasant, spacious lounge with French windows looking out onto a neat lawn and rose bushes. He waved her into an armchair and she sat down, feeling stiff and uncomfortable. Once more she tried to read the personality behind the expressionless face and once more, she failed.

"Can I offer you a drink?" he asked.

"A brandy would be lovely, Allen, yes please."

He turned to a cabinet on one wall but not far enough so he couldn't see her, pulled out two bottles and glasses and poured some of one bottle into a small balloon glass. The other bottle provided an amber fluid into a whiskey glass.

He brought the brandy over to her and sat down across from her in the other armchair.

"Your health," he said and took a small taste of his drink. 'Virginia Gentleman's Bourbon,'" he said. "Best liquor on the planet."

She nodded and sampled her own. She knew enough about liquor to recognise this as the finest quality cognac she had ever drunk.

"Allen, we got off on the wrong foot," she said. "I know that you have realised what I am and what I can do, but I hope you understand that I would never try to control you. I know all too well that I couldn't."

"Damn right you couldn't," he said. "Others have tried, nobody has ever succeeded."

"I can believe that. Your story of the digital killing was incredible. I simply have no idea what skills that took. It was amazing."

"Hah," he said. "That was nothing. I could tell you stories that would freeze your knickers."

"What sort of things? Can you give me an example?"

"Let's just say that there are governments and corporations that would love to get their hands on me."

"Shit, Allen, that means you've managed to change identities somehow."

"Dead easy. You have no idea. But Nona, if you tried to tell the cops that or call the Immigration people, they'd laugh in your face. My record is as clean as the Queen's armpits."

She tossed her drink back in one gulp.

"Another one?" he asked.

She shook her head. "But a coffee would be nice."

He put his glass down on the side table next to his armchair and rose to go to the kitchen.

She watched him carefully, and when he was out of her view, she took a small packet from a side pocket and poured the contents into his glass.

A few moments later, he returned with a mug and a small jug of milk, placed both on the small table by her seat and returned to his own.

"So, is there anything else you need to talk about, Nona?"

"How do you think it has all gone?" she said. "We've had eleven deaths and the cops still haven't realised some of them were murders by our people."

"I'd say you've fucked up. The Langers are dead meat, they won't see daylight for thirty years, those two dumbfucks, Tanya and that muscle-bound fool Ollie will get the same. The cops aren't stupid. That woman sergeant may be a fashion plate model, but she's got a mind like a bear trap I reckon, and that shrink, he's no dimwit. They're not going to give up and they're onto you already."

"That's not true, Allen. They've got no evidence at all for the other deaths."

"That's as far as you know. They'll get to you, Nona, believe me."

She put her coffee mug down, untasted.

"I think I'll go," she said.

"Great idea. You can see yourself out." He took a gulp of his bourbon and watched as she stood up and turned to the door. The last thing she saw was him draining his glass.

As she closed the front door behind her, she smiled. Everything was as it should be.

Chapter 50 – The Second of December, 2022, 4:00am

The explosion shattered a number of windows in the area, set off car alarms up to two kilometres away and precipitated an outburst of dogs barking from further than that.

Two of the shattered windows were in the apartment that Melanie owned and she woke with a terrified yelp as glass scattered over the floor of her bedroom. Hurriedly, she threw on a dressing gown and slippers and went to the window to look out.

The scene was horrific. Several cars had been blown some distance from their parking spaces in the area reserved for tenants of the building. Many showed a great deal of damage, torn apart by the blast, some still burning.

In the middle of this was a pile of wreckage, the concrete around it burned black, not a single identifiable part of a car. It was where Melanie had parked her Gordon-Keeble the night before.

Struggling for self-control, she slipped into jeans and a sweater, shoes replaced the slippers and she ran out of the apartment, already sobbing. She barely heard the sirens of approaching emergency vehicles and could only stare at the horror in silence, tears running like rain down her cheeks.

Not really aware, she walked back to her apartment, through the people standing around in distress and fell onto the bed, tightly curled up.

"Melanie? Melanie, it's Jack."

She drifted back into awareness, realising Jack was sitting on a chair by her bed. The full shock of what had happened enveloped her again.

"It was all I had left of him," she croaked and collapsed back into a tight foetal position.

Jack took out his phone.

A long, confused nightmare kept her in a state of fear, not knowing where she was, only aware that something dreadful had happened. She woke up to realise she was in a hospital bed, alone in a single ward.

"You retreated from the world," said Jack.

She turned her head to see him sitting in an armchair in one corner.

"How long?" she asked.

"Three days."

"Have you been here the whole time?"

"No, just during the day. I went back to my hotel at night, the nurses promised to call me if you came back to the world."

"It really hit me, Jack. It was all I had left of Scott and now it's gone."

"That's what you said when I found you in your apartment."

"Can I go back there now?"

"No reason why not. The windows have been replaced, you suffered no damage but you're pretty weak. You managed to take some food in your occasional waking moments, so when the doctor checks you out, you can probably go home."

"I need to."

"I'll let you get dressed," said Jack and walked out of the ward.

Chapter 51 – The Ninth of December, 2022

"Gabrielle, Carl, I'm so glad you came."

"How could we refuse our Chairwoman's invitation?" replied Gabrielle.

"It must be important," said Carl Hitchcox and stood back to allow Gabrielle to walk through the front door as Nona held it open.

"Yes, it really is," said Nona. "Let's sit out in the back garden. I'll get some cold drinks."

The two visitors walked through the sliding doors out into the neatly-kept back garden. Several trees provided shade and two large orange-bearing bushes were laden with fruit. Gabrielle and Carl took chairs around the white metal table at one side of the lawn. A few moments later, Nona appeared with a tray containing three glasses already filled and a jug of orange juice. She selected one of the glasses for herself and let the other two take theirs.

"It's all got very nasty," said Nona. "I never expected things would turn out like this."

"But that awful woman cop arrested you, I heard," said Ollie. "What happened?"

"I had to go before a judge the next day. She said I had to have a psychiatrist examine me and if it was thought I could stay at home before the trial, I could go."

"And you did?" asked Gabrielle.

"Some stupid man talked to me for an hour, I don't know what he concluded but I was allowed to go home. I have a trial set for February."

"But Bella and Mitch have been charged with murder?" said Carl. "How did they get found out? I thought the instructions you gave us would have kept their secrets."

"They would," said Nona. She picked up her glass, stared intently at it for a moment and then drank the entire contents. "Like I said at our last meeting, they were too stupid and careless to follow orders correctly. Mitch didn't clean his vehicle properly, he should have put it through a car wash and then got underneath it to look for any hidden material."

"What did the cops find?" asked Carl.

"A tiny spot of blood under the frame of the windscreen. That alone wouldn't have done it, though it was the same blood type as the man he killed, but not big enough to get DNA. No, it was the little bit of bone underneath the car that proved it."

"Bloody hell," said Carl.

"And what gave Bella away?" asked Gabrielle.

"Again, not doing the job properly. She tried to burn the coveralls in the barbeque fire but left a couple of tiny pieces that the cops found. It wasn't enough to convict her, but somehow they found the rifle she used."

"So how did Ollie and Tanya get caught?" asked Gabrielle.

"They panicked. There was no real evidence, if they'd just shut up and kept their heads, they wouldn't have been found out."

"Are you really sure about that?" asked Carl. "That woman detective seemed very sharp. The same as her psychologist buddy. What if they've really got more clues and they haven't got round to finalising the case?"

"Well, they don't seem to have got any suspicions about either of us," said Gabrielle.

"No, you two covered everything very well," said Nona. "If they haven't brought you in for a grilling by now, they probably never will."

"And Jean's okay," said Gabrielle. "Same with Paul Johnson and Allen Miller."

"Allen has left us," said Nona. "He won't be a problem anymore."

"He's gone back to the States?" Carl looked curious. "Was he worried about being caught?"

"He just left," said Nona. "I don't know where he is."

"This is all terrible," said Carl. "We started this brilliant, exciting project and it all looked so easy, the cops were baffled, some of the things we did weren't even recognised as murders. And now almost all of us are gone, held by the cops. Four of us have been charged and if they get found guilty, they're looking at life in prison."

"It was certainly fun while it lasted," said Nona. "But now it's time to wrap up the whole thing. You two have got away with it, Jean probably has, Allen has run away, Paul seems to have avoided the cops' interest completely."

"I suppose there's only one thing left incomplete," said Gabrielle. "We were going to have one murder on the ninth of every month. Looks like we'll fall short of that."

"And publishing the book, too," said Carl. "I would have liked to have seen that come out in print."

"That's been taken care of," said Nona. "Both of those."

"But who's left to commit the last murder?" asked Carl.

"Don't worry about it," said Nona.

"What about you, Nona?" asked Gabrielle. "What's happening with you?"

"I'm out on bail. The cops know about that poisoning last January and they seem to have found out that I killed my mother, the way I told you. When they've put it all together, they'll be back for me."

"Oh Nona, that's terrible," said Gabrielle. "What can we do?"

"Nothing at all. Now go home, forget about this whole adventure."

Carl drank half his orange juice and stood up.

"Are you sure you don't want me to stay?" asked Gabrielle. "I'd really like to."

Nona shook her head.

"Better if you go."

Tears welled up in Gabrielle's eyes. She stood up, bent over Nona and kissed her on the cheek.

Then they both left.

Nona sat silently, not moving. And then the tears started running down her cheeks like tiny rivulets. She stayed like that for twenty minutes and then the first pain struck in her stomach. She gasped with the shock.

A shape appeared in front of her. With her vision already reduced, it took a moment to recognise the man approaching and taking the seat just vacated by Gabrielle.

"Hello Nona," said Allen Miller. "And how is your day?"

Her scream was muted. "You're dead," she gasped. "I killed you."

"Oh dear, Nona, do you really think I'd be so stupid as to leave you alone and out of sight long enough to poison my drink?"

She could do nothing but stare at him.

"Nona, Nona, Nona, far more capable people than you have tried to kill me. If you had looked carefully, you'd have seen a number of little cameras in the room and I saw you on the monitor in the kitchen as you dropped some of that Rosary Seed stuff into my drink. And among my many skills, I'm pretty good at the conjuring stuff. Do you know, I've even given displays to kids at birthday parties? Swapping my drink with a fresh one was no problem at all."

The pain grew and Nona groaned, pressing hard on her belly. The pain spread through her torso and her breathing became difficult.

"Oh, if only I'd known it was this bad," she moaned as her vision became blurred.

"So now it's my special treat to watch you die, Nona," said Miller.

Nona was no longer able to see the man before her, the orange bushes and the flowers in the beds round the lawn. The sky had turned dark. A massive spasm shook her whole body, forcing her out of her chair onto the grass and she convulsed.

The horror went on for another twenty minutes.

And then she died.

* * *

"Who called you in?" asked Doctor Mortimer. He bent over the body of the woman on the grass and took swabs from her mouth.

"A woman," said Melanie. "I think it was Gabrielle, but she was crying so hard, I couldn't be sure."

"My professional guess, based on what we've seen before is that it's that Rosary Seed stuff again," said Doctor Mortimer. "I'll know more when I get her on the slab and can do a tox report. Meanwhile, will you bag those three glasses?"

"We'll check fingerprints," said Melanie. "Then you'll get them back to see if that stuff was in any of them."

"It will be informative to discover who the other two visitors were," said the doctor. "I worry she might have poisoned all three, not just herself."

"The fourth and fifth Rosary Seeds," said Melanie.

"What?" asked the doctor.

"When we interviewed her last," said Melanie, "Alex found an ornate brooch with those seeds around the rim. There were five missing. We found two in a little jar, we think that one of the ones from the brooch was used to kill Judy Henderson last January. I reckon she may have used the fourth one to kill Allen Miller, if that's what's happened, though we haven't found his body yet, and the last one for herself and I hope only herself. We'd retained the pills and that brooch but she must have kept the last one somewhere else to use for just this event if it became necessary."

"Or it could be one of the visitors poisoning her," said Alex.

"Out of revenge?" suggested Mortimer.

"Or perhaps trying to hide the connection between themselves and the other deaths. We may have our suspicions about some of those deaths but still not enough real evidence to bring charges."

"We should probably check the remaining members of the group," said Alex. "See who's still alive."

"Yes, you do that, Alex. I'll go with the doctor and see the postmortem," said Melanie. "Are you done here, Doc?"

He nodded and Melanie waved to the two coroner's men to take the body away.

Chapter 52 – The Tenth of December, 2022

"It's almost all wrapped up," said Melanie. "We've got the Langers being prosecuted, the same with Tanya and Ollie. Allen Miller will soon be sent back to the USA and Nona seems to have offed herself with the same Rosary Seed poison she used before."

"Which leaves us Gabrielle, Jean, Paul Johnson and Carl Hitchcox," said Jack. "Lots of indicators to their guilt but not enough yet to charge them and convict them. Did you find anything in those glasses at Nona's place?"

"Pretty well what we expected," said Melanie. "One glass had Nona's fingerprints and that also showed traces of the Rosary Seed. The other two had Hitchcox's prints and Gabrielle's, also Nona's. So it looks like our first thought was right, Nona committed suicide, timed to die after the other two had left."

"And those two were still fit and healthy when I called on them," said Alex. "They seemed genuinely horrified to hear that Nona was dead, Gabrielle especially was shattered."

"I wonder if that's related to those sex toys we found in Nona's place," said Jack. "They were typical of lesbian activity, so perhaps she and Gabrielle were having a sexual relationship."

"Did you read that in her at all?" asked Melanie. "I didn't sense any sexual interest in me at all."

"That's because she was terrified of you," said Jack. "And she saw you as a sister Goddess, not another available woman. No, I think those things were just another tool of domination that she could use if the situation required it."

"Damn, but I hate the idea of loose ends in this."

"I can imagine," said Jack. "But you've solved seven murders and a kidnapping, you two, all in a few months. That's a shit load of promotional brownie points for you."

"But we just know those other four are guilty as hell," said Alex. "It's not going to be good enough to know we got some of the mob while they're getting away with it because there isn't conclusive evidence."

A knock on the door interrupted the discussion. A police constable came in, carrying a large brown envelope and a note. He handed them to Melanie.

"The note's from D.I. Comley, Sarge" he said. "The package came in a few moments ago, hand delivered."

"Who delivered them?"

"A kid, about twelve," said the constable. "He said some bloke had given him five bucks to deliver them here."

"Suspicious," said Jack.

"Thanks," said Melanie and nodded at the constable who left.

Melanie unfolded the note and read it carefully.

"Something bad?" asked Jack.

"Immigration arrived at Allen Miller's house this morning. There was no answer, they broke in and found the house empty. He'd gone. There was an empty whiskey glass on the table, they said it had contained bourbon."

"Poisoned?" said Alex.

"On a side table by the other armchair was an empty brandy glass and an untouched mug of coffee. There were fingerprints on both, they're sending them over for us to check and the lab will see if there's a trace of the poison in the glass."

"Nona," said Jack, a statement with complete conviction.

"Bet your life," said Melanie. "And like I said, I bet that's where the last missing Rosary Seed ended up in Miller's whiskey. But without a body, we have no idea what happened."

"I don't get it," said Alex. "What reason could she have? And why would she be so careless about leaving her fingerprints? And if he's dead, who removed the body? It's almost as if she wanted to be found out. This whole situation is bizarre."

"She must have done it after she got out on bail," said Jack. "Miller could have been dead for a few days."

"The authorities aren't going to have a pleasant time telling the FBI that their biggest criminal has disappeared," said Jack. "They might be pleased that he's dead, but I'm sure they'd rather have handled him themselves."

"Without a doubt," said Alex. "I hope we find the body soon and close out that particular chapter."

Melanie tore open the envelope and extracted a thick file of papers. They seemed to be computer printouts. Melanie read the title of the first few pages.

"I think Santa Clause has come early," she said. "This looks like all the stories of the killings written by the members of the group. The first couple I've seen are dated and signed. Can I give each of you some of these, just check that all the stories are here?"

"Where the hell did that come from?" asked Alex, taking a number of pages.

"Hand delivered," said Melanie. "Jack, will you take some?"

Only ten minutes were needed to confirm that there was a printed story of each of the murders, all signed and dated by the authors.

"And... holy shit," said Alex. "An extra bonus! Here are the minutes of each meeting from January through to June, signed by Caroline Collins, the secretary. She was killed in July, wasn't she?"

"That's correct," said Melanie. "Read us a bit, would you?"

"This is the report of the minutes of the January meeting," said Alex. "This will blow your mind, I kid you not."

"Minutes of the meeting of January 14th, 2022. After welcoming the members to the new year session, Nona Markham changed the program. Instead of running a workshop on ways of hiding all possible clues when committing a murder, Nona read a short story of the murder of an old woman by an exotic poison known as 'Rosary Seed.'

"But as one member pointed out, it appeared to echo a news report that an old lady of the name used in Nona's story had been found dead of a heart attack. Nona astonished us all by telling us that she had been the killer, and we spent the next hour listening to her description of how it felt, how she had prevented any clue to her presence at the scene and the exhilaration she felt at knowing the police had accepted the death as natural causes. All the members of the group admitted to having had fantasies of killing somebody and getting away with it. They all committed to keeping the secret of this death. Then Carl Hitchcox announced that he would like to try something and would present a short story at the February meeting. The group agreed to await his story and keep the details secret."

"And here's Carl's story," said Jack, pulling out some pages from the stack he had. "And it's a detailed description of how he obtained steel cable, strung it up and watched as it drove a car over the edge of the cliff."

The room was silent for several moments.

"Christ alive!" said Jack.

"We've got them," said Melanie.

* * *

"Paul Johnson, I am arresting you for the murder of William Grant on the ninth of April. You do not have to say anything but anything you do say will be taken down and may be used in evidence against you. Do you understand?"

* * *

"Carl Hitchcox, I am arresting you for the murder of Christine Fairfax on the ninth of February. You do not have to say anything but anything you do say will be taken down and may be used in evidence against you. Do you understand?"

* * *

"Jean Worrall, I am arresting you for the murder of Anders Jensen on the ninth of June...."

* * *

Alex pounded on the door of Gabrielle's house.

"Gabrielle Greenwood? This is the police. Open up."

There was no response. Alex looked back at Melanie who nodded at the two constables standing with her. One of them took his weighted hammer and swung it at the keyhole of the front door which smashed open. A small splinter of wood flew off into the hallway as the door swung against the wall. The three constables entered, calling "Police!" in loud tones. As they checked each room, they shouted "Clear" and moved on. It took only a few moments before one of them returned to where Melanie was standing by the front door.

"Sergeant," he said and stood back to let her enter the lounge room.

Gabrielle's body was lying on the carpet, face up. One look at the discoloured face and the bruises on the neck was enough to indicate the cause of death.

Melanie took her phone from her pocket.

* * *

Melanie sat down in front of her computer, intent on writing the reports of the last few days. Police procedures had to be followed. She opened her notebook and started typing.

This lasted less than a minute.

She sat back in dismay as the screen became jumbled, words scrambled, flashes of colour erupting like fireworks.

"What the hell...?" she muttered, her first thought being to call technical support. Then the screen cleared.

"Hello Melanie," said Allen Miller. "Surprised to see me?"

She was silent for a moment, her mind racing.

"Where are you?" she asked.

Miller laughed. "Why, so you could call the Immigration Department to come and get me? That didn't work too well last time, Sergeant."

"So why this call, Miller?"

"Just for my own entertainment, I suppose, but I can clear up a few loose ends for you."

"Such as?"

"I killed Gabrielle, if you hadn't already worked that one out. I really couldn't stand that sour-faced blonde dyke. And Nona had tried to kill me with that Rosary Seed stuff, but much cleverer people have tried that trick on me and failed miserably. I had her under observation as she dropped the stuff in my drink while I was in the kitchen, switched glasses when I came back and she left, grinning all over her silly face, thinking I'd be dead soon. You know what I enjoyed most about that?"

"You're obviously about to tell me."

"As she sat in her garden, having drunk her own poison and waiting to die, I walked in on her. As you can imagine, she was a tad surprised to see me."

Melanie said nothing.

"And I told her how I'd watched her on a monitor in my kitchen as she dropped the poison in my drink and then we sat for twenty minutes while she went through hell and finally shuffled off her mortal coil. It was real fun."

"And now what, Miller?"

He smiled pleasantly.

"Allen Miller's dead, Sergeant. I wiped every single reference to him from the government files. I never immigrated here, I never paid taxes here, never had a driving licence, nothing. I never existed. I'm somebody else now."

She tried to keep her face expressionless, shaken by the degree of skill he must have to achieve what he just claimed.

"Did you send me the copies of the stories?"

"Of course. I realised you didn't have enough serious proof of the crimes of that insane bunch in the writers' group, so I thought I'd help you along a bit. No, don't thank me, I was glad to do it. So you've got them all now. I imagine your promotion to Inspector won't take long. In fact, I could help that along a lot if you'd like. Adding some significant recommendations to your file would be simple."

"Please don't. I'll make my own way."

"No problems. Oh, of course, you probably would like to know, I blew up your car."

"Of course you did. Why?

He shrugged his shoulders. "I dunno, maybe envy? That was much too nice a vehicle for a pretty young girl. And anyway, what's a gorgeous chick like you doing as a cop?"

"Not your business, Miller. Now, is there anything else you want to say?"

"Just that you really annoyed me. Here's this gorgeous doll, could have made it big on screen or the runway and you never wore anything but pantsuits. I could tell you had nice tits but I wanted to see your legs. I bet they're great. Given time, I could have got you into the sack and I could tell you miss that."

"Fuck off, Miller," she snapped and turned the monitor off.

It took an hour to recover her composure.

Chapter 53 – March, 2023

Melanie strolled along the High Street feeling at peace with the world. The case was resolved, every one of the killers was either dead or in prison. The only exception was Allen Miller and she could still not prevent a small shiver of rage about him every time he broke into her mind.

Still, she thought, *we have his DNA. At some stage, he's going to make a mistake again.*

She forced her mind off the topic. The insurance had come through for her car and although she still felt grief at the last connection she had with Scott, the thought of a huge sum of money reaching her bank account was a great comfort and she was enjoying doing the research into the vehicles available and wondering about how exotic her next car would be.

She reached the bookshop and from habit, glanced in the window and stopped.

"What the fuck?" she exclaimed out loud, causing two elderly women behind her to burst out laughing.

Laid out on a circular display stand was a large number of books, all the same. The title was *'The Ninth of the Month Murders.'* The author was shown as Allen Miller. At the top of the display was a colourful notice announcing the book as 'The New Best-Seller Hitting the World.'

Having trouble breathing, Melanie stared for a couple of minutes, feeling a small sickness in the pit of her stomach before forcing herself to enter the book shop.

There was another display stand against one wall, all showing the same book. She picked one up, turned it over and felt the sickness increase. The blurb said,

> *'A series of murders is occurring in a small country town, though some of them are at first believed to be accidents or suicide. The beautiful lady Detective Sergeant Melissa Clarke is totally baffled. Who is committing these murders, why is there not a single clue to the killer and how are they so brilliantly disguised that they are not even recognised as such for many months?'*

Feeling her hands trembling, Melanie took the book to the cash desk and gave her credit card to the young woman behind the counter who smiled as she put the book into a paper bag.

"We can't keep this one on the shelves," she said. I've never seen a book sell like this, not even the *'Harry Potter'* series."

"When did it come out?" asked Melanie.

"Beginning of February and we've sold thousands."

"Where do you get them from?"

"It's published by a company in Brisbane, they're called Grisham. The books appeared in their catalogue and we were told that there would be a lot of advertising and publicity for them, so the boss ordered a hundred and they'd gone by the end of the day. It just grew from there."

Feeling sweat in her hands, Melanie put the book in her bag and headed home. Pouring a stiff drink, she sat down, took out the book and examined it. Slowly checking each chapter, she realised every one of them was the story she had received in the big envelope. Each murder was described and in between each chapter was a fictional episode of how the police were baffled and couldn't even identify some of them as murders at all.

Almost as bad was the description of herself. She was obvious. Miller had described her in flowery terms as *'drop-dead gorgeous with an exquisite body partially hidden under a pants suit.'* Jack was described as *'an ancient, retired psychologist who badly needed a refresher course,'* and Alex got a brief mention as *'a shallow young man, barely out of high school, with almost no experience of the real world.'*

Stifling her anger, she went to the initial pages and found the publisher's name. As the clerk had told her, Grisham was in Brisbane. Melanie stood up, went to her computer and soon found them and their phone number.

"Good morning," she said as the call was answered. "I am Detective Sergeant Melanie Carter of the New South Wales Police, Homicide Division. I need to talk to whoever is responsible for publishing this book, *'The Ninth of the Month Murders.'*"

"That will be our Dan Smethwick," said the voice at the other end. "Putting you through."

Melanie waited a moment, forcing self-control.

"This is Dan Smethwick," said a deep bass voice. "I understand you are a Detective Sergeant with the police in New South Wales. What is your interest in this book?"

"I'll come to that in a moment, but the first thing is that the book is not fiction, despite the claim at the front and your company may be in deep trouble for revealing information that was never made public."

"What?" The bass voice rose a notch.

"So let's leave that for now," said Melanie. "First, how did you come by this manuscript?"

"It was sent to our self-publishing operation. The author submitted it with a cover, he had acquired an ISBN, he had all the necessary details and we printed it for him. We do hundreds of these, it's the most popular way of publishing one's own book."

"And the book goes on a catalogue of some sort and that goes to book sellers?"

"Book sellers all over the world, Sergeant. They order copies, we pay the author royalties."

Melanie felt a surge of interest.

"You pay those royalties directly to a bank account? Can you give me those detail and those of the author?"

"One moment. Let me bring up the computer records."

There was a tense silence for a moment.

"Ah yes, now I can clear this up for you, Sergeant. The author made special arrangements that had us all interested. He doesn't receive any payments himself. Our instructions are to pay them to three different charities, the Animal Protection Society, the Cancer Council and a Children's Hospital in Sydney."

"What contact details do you have for the author?"

"I have an address in Queanbeyan, but Mr Miller instructed us not to send any material there. Having the royalties paid to third parties as they are, we have no need to communicate with him."

"Why do you think this has become such a best seller? What's the appeal?"

"Sergeant, let me be honest. I think the book is terrible. The stories are amateurish and the police department is painted in a ridiculously negative way. But the answer is simple. Mr Miller paid a very large sum to a public relations firm in Sydney to get the book advertised in many media, all over the world."

"Can you give me those details?"

"Yes, we needed to work with them as they advised us that large numbers would be sold and we should prepare our printing capabilities. But we have companies in the UK and the USA, so they did much of the work also. The company is Dalgetty, you can find their website easily."

"Thank you, Mr Smethwick. Let me fill you in a little. All those killings actually took place, they were committed by a group of amateur writers who had somehow been corrupted by an extraordinary woman who is now dead. I'm the detective sergeant who led the investigation, the psychologist was once the best criminal profiler the police had ever had and the young constable is one of the brightest assets we have, he has just been promoted and transferred to the detective force."

"Holy shit!" said Smethwick. "I can see the problem. Will you start defamation proceedings or anything else?"

"I'll leave that to my superiors. Given the destination of the royalties, it may be an option to leave things alone. But somebody may get back to you. Meanwhile, give me that address you have for the author."

* * *

"Jack, it's bloody obscene. That book is selling millions all over the world."

"So I see. I saw copies in my local village up here and bought one. It's pretty crappy." His image on the monitor displayed the book for a second as he held it up.

"The whole story is weird. I talked to the publisher in Brisbane and he was horrified to learn it was not fiction. But the interesting thing is that the royalties are all going to several charities."

"Of course they are," said Jack. "No way would he provide any identification. It's not as if he needs the money."

"I sent Alex to check the address they gave me and of course it was false."

"How about the bank?"

"They have records showing that Allen Miller once had an account there, but it was closed down last

November, the money was sent to yet another charity, no forwarding details, nothing."

"Melanie, he's laughing at us. He's displaying his brilliance. The money is irrelevant. But how did that pile of dreck become a global best seller?"

"He paid a public relations firm a massive amount to do that. I talked to them, they said they received a quarter million bucks as a direct transfer for their fees and four million for advertising and the instructions were just to make it a best seller to make Harry Potter look small."

"They sure did a good job," said Jack. "What are you going to do about it?"

"Nothing. People on a higher pay grade than me have said that people will believe it's all fiction and the money is going to good causes. They said just leave it and the book will die out eventually."

"Probably wise. Melanie, do the same. Forget it, you did an amazing job and the promotions board will look fondly on you when promotions time comes round. I expect you to be Commissioner before you retire. And remember, you still have his DNA. It's quite probable he'll slip up again and you'll get him."

She laughed. "Okay Jack, get back to the alpaca and grandchildren you're raising up there."

* * *

Ten minutes later, her computer buzzed, indicating a Skype call.

"I'm glad you had that little chat with Jack," said Allen Miller. "You all made a good decision to leave the book alone."

Melanie said nothing, suppressing the anger.

"Anyway, Melanie, I wanted to tell you how sorry I am that I destroyed that beautiful car. I hadn't realised the emotional connection you had."

Melanie stayed silent.

"It took some searching, but I think you'll like what I've done. This is the last time we'll talk, so I hope you'll remember me more kindly."

He smiled and the image faded.

She heard a truck draw up outside her front door and there was the sound of rattling of metal parts. Curious, she went to the door just as the bell rang.

"Miss Melanie Carter?" A large man holding a clip board almost hid the light.

"Yes."

"Delivery for you. Sign here, please."

"Delivery of what?" She tried to look beyond the man, could only see the front of a large vehicle.

"Would you sign, Miss?"

Irritated but curious, she took the clipboard, signed her name where indicated and the man handed over an envelope containing several sheets of paper and something hard and metallic.

"I think you'll like it," he said and moved away.

Melanie walked out of the door and stared.

The Gordon-Keeble looked perfect. It was in deep blue, the same as her previous one. Breathing hard, she opened the envelope. The registration papers showed her as the owner, the insurance covered her for a full year, a complete maintenance log was included and the metallic object was the key.

"This I don't believe," she muttered as the delivery truck pulled away. Her policewoman's instincts made her bend down and study the underside of the vehicle. Seeing no obvious bomb, she opened the bonnet and found nothing that shouldn't be there.

She opened the driver's side door and eased herself into the seat. The inside was immaculate. Despite the more than fifty years age of the car, it looked new. She inserted the key in the ignition and started the engine, holding her breath but nothing happened other than the familiar soft purr of the massive engine.

"Allen Miller, who and what the hell are you?" she said aloud and put the car in gear. After a quick test drive round the block, she returned home. She still had to pack her bag for a flight to Melbourne that she had booked the day before.